MRS. JEFFRIES
SPEAKS HER MIND

Berkley Prime Crime titles by Emily Brightwell

THE INSPECTOR AND MRS. JEFFRIES
MRS. JEFFRIES DUSTS FOR CLUES
THE GHOST AND MRS. JEFFRIES
MRS. JEFFRIES TAKES STOCK
MRS. JEFFRIES ON THE BALL
MRS. JEFFRIES ON THE TRAIL
MRS. JEFFRIES PLAYS THE COOK
MRS. JEFFRIES AND THE MISSING ALIBI
MRS. JEFFRIES STANDS CORRECTED
MRS. JEFFRIES TAKES THE STAGE
MRS. JEFFRIES QUESTIONS THE ANSWER
MRS. JEFFRIES REVEALS HER ART
MRS. JEFFRIES TAKES THE CAKE
MRS. JEFFRIES ROCKS THE BOAT
MRS. JEFFRIES WEEDS THE PLOT
MRS. JEFFRIES PINCHES THE POST
MRS. JEFFRIES PLEADS HER CASE
MRS. JEFFRIES SWEEPS THE CHIMNEY
MRS. JEFFRIES STALKS THE HUNTER
MRS. JEFFRIES AND THE SILENT KNIGHT
MRS. JEFFRIES APPEALS THE VERDICT
MRS. JEFFRIES AND THE BEST LAID PLANS
MRS. JEFFRIES AND THE FEAST OF ST. STEPHEN
MRS. JEFFRIES HOLDS THE TRUMP
MRS. JEFFRIES IN THE NICK OF TIME
MRS. JEFFRIES AND THE YULETIDE WEDDINGS
MRS. JEFFRIES SPEAKS HER MIND

Anthology

MRS. JEFFRIES LEARNS THE TRADE

MRS. JEFFRIES
SPEAKS HER MIND

EMILY BRIGHTWELL

BERKLEY PRIME CRIME, NEW YORK

THE BERKLEY PUBLISHING GROUP
Published by the Penguin Group
Penguin Group (USA) Inc.
375 Hudson Street, New York, New York 10014, USA
Penguin Group (Canada), 90 Eglinton Avenue East, Suite 700, Toronto, Ontario M4P 2Y3, Canada
(a division of Pearson Penguin Canada Inc.)
Penguin Books Ltd., 80 Strand, London WC2R 0RL, England
Penguin Group Ireland, 25 St. Stephen's Green, Dublin 2, Ireland (a division of Penguin Books Ltd.)
Penguin Group (Australia), 250 Camberwell Road, Camberwell, Victoria 3124, Australia
(a division of Pearson Australia Group Pty. Ltd.)
Penguin Books India Pvt. Ltd., 11 Community Centre, Panchsheel Park, New Delhi—110 017, India
Penguin Group (NZ), 67 Apollo Drive, Rosedale, North Shore 0632, New Zealand
(a division of Pearson New Zealand Ltd.)
Penguin Books (South Africa) (Pty.) Ltd., 24 Sturdee Avenue, Rosebank, Johannesburg 2196,
South Africa

Penguin Books Ltd., Registered Offices: 80 Strand, London WC2R 0RL, England

This is a work of fiction. Names, characters, places, and incidents either are the product of the author's imagination or are used fictitiously, and any resemblance to actual persons, living or dead, business establishments, events, or locales is entirely coincidental. The publisher does not have any control over and does not assume any responsibility for author or third-party websites or their content.

MRS. JEFFRIES SPEAKS HER MIND

A Berkley Prime Crime Book / published by arrangement with the author

ISBN-13: 978-1-61664-603-5

BERKLEY® PRIME CRIME
Berkley Prime Crime Books are published by The Berkley Publishing Group,
a division of Penguin Group (USA) Inc.,
375 Hudson Street, New York, New York 10014.
BERKLEY® PRIME CRIME and the PRIME CRIME logo are trademarks of Penguin Group
(USA) Inc.

PRINTED IN THE UNITED STATES OF AMERICA

*This book is dedicated to
the Reverend Dr. Paul Tellström
and the delightful Mr. Carl Whidden,
two wonderful people who have
enriched my life greatly.*

CHAPTER 1

Olive Kettering looked over her shoulder as she hurried toward the staircase. She didn't see anyone in the long, gloomy hallway, but that didn't mean no one was there. It was broad daylight, almost nine o'clock in the morning, and she should have been safe, but she knew she wasn't. They'd been waiting for this, for her to be alone in the house. From behind her, she heard a heavy banging noise, like someone thumping along the upper corridor. She'd been a fool to let all the servants take the day off; that's what came of being a good Christian soul— her own generosity would be her undoing. She ought to have made at least one of them stay here today; all of them hadn't needed to go to Cook's funeral. It wasn't as if most of them had even liked the woman.

Rain slashed at the panes of the tall window at the end of the corridor, masking any telltale sounds of her pursuers, but she knew they were gaining on her. She could feel them. Just as she reached the top of the stairs, she heard a door open behind her.

Olive knew she had to get out of the house. She hitched up her brown wool skirt, grabbed the banister, and charged down the stairs toward the first-floor landing.

From behind her, she could hear footsteps pounding over the thick hall rug as they came after her. They weren't even trying to be discreet now. There was no need; she was all alone. She picked up her pace, her hands skimming along the smooth wood as she rushed down the staircase, flew across the landing, and continued on toward the foyer. Oh, God, if she could just get outside, just get to the street, maybe she could find someone to help her.

When she reached the bottom, she didn't waste time looking around to see if they were close. She simply ran toward the huge double front door. She skidded on the black and white tiles, found her footing, and flung herself forward.

The footsteps were on the stairs now, thumping down them like a horde of devils uncaring of how much noise they made. Her hands reached for the brass doorknob and, for a split second, she couldn't remember which way to turn the wretched thing—the housekeeper always opened the door—but, finally, she gave it a mighty twist and the lock clicked. She pulled it open and rushed outside.

Overhead, the portico protected her from an immediate soaking, but the wind had blown water onto the gray marble slabs of the terrace floor. Her only hope was to get to the street. Even in a storm, there would be people. There were always plenty of people in this part of London.

Olive turned her head sharply as she heard a thud coming from behind her. The door was half opened, but she couldn't see anything. But she knew they were coming. Choking back a scream, she started across the terrace toward the steps and safety. Her foot slipped on a patch of water, and she almost went down, but she managed to right herself and keep on going. Behind her, the front door creaked open and this time she didn't bother to look over her shoulder; she knew they were there. A gust of wind blew a newspaper across her face just as she reached the top step; she screamed and lost her footing. Rather than risk falling backward into the arms of the hell that was chasing her, she twisted her body to her left, causing her to crash into a thorny bush. Thunder crashed overhead as she flailed her arms to regain her feet. Unable to see because of the newspaper across her face, she tossed her head from side to side trying to dislodge it, but the rain held it firmly against her skin. Sobbing, she finally managed to scrape it away just as lightning flashed, blinding her because she was staring straight up into it. Terrified, she heaved herself up and, in her panic, turned toward the side of the house rather than the street.

Tears mingled with the pouring rain and streamed down her cheeks as she ran around the corner. She tried to say the Twenty-third Psalm but found that it took all her concentration to keep going.

Trees and shrubs dominated the garden on the side of the house. Olive dodged around a yew tree and had just turned and started back toward the street when she heard them closing the distance. "Help me, Lord," she muttered, "help me." She found the strength to go on and raced around the corner to the back. A sob escaped her as the carriage house came into view. Thank God, Bernadine was home. She skidded on the mud but kept her feet and then stumbled over the protruding root of a huge old oak and went down hard. She pulled herself up on her hands and knees.

Olive raised her head and sobbed in relief as a figure stepped out and into view. Thank God, she thought, thank God. Relieved that she was going to be rescued, she tried to give a warning. "They're behind me." She lifted her hand to be helped up as the person approached. "We've got to get—"

"There's no one behind you, you stupid woman," a harsh voice said.

Olive's mouth opened in shock and her eyes widened as she saw the gun pointed directly at her head. Directly above her was a flash of lightning, but when the thunder crashed a few seconds later, Olive didn't hear it. She was already dead.

"I must say, holding my tongue was becoming more and more difficult," Mrs. Jeffries said to the others gathered around the kitchen table. Hepzibah Jeffries, the housekeeper to Inspector Gerald Witherspoon of the Metropolitan Police Force, was a woman of late middle age. Her auburn hair was threaded with gray, there were freckles sprinkled over her nose, and her mouth was generally set in a cheerful smile, but she wasn't smiling today. She looked positively grim as she recounted her latest encounter with the new vicar of St. John's Church.

"There's no law that says we 'ave to go to church," Wiggins, the footman, exclaimed. He was a handsome young man with brown hair and round, apple cheeks.

"In my last household, they made all the servants go to church every Sunday, whether we wanted to or not," Phyllis muttered. "But I suppose in my case it wouldn't matter, as I don't live in like the rest of you do." Phyllis Thomlinson was a plump girl of nineteen with dark blonde hair, brown eyes, porcelain skin, and a face as round as a pie tin. She'd worked in the household since Christmas and she was still a bit shy about saying too much in front of the others.

"It doesn't matter whether you live in or not, no one here is forced to go to church. That's not the custom in this household," Mrs. Goodge, the cook, declared. She was elderly and white haired, but her mind and her opinions were both still sharp. "The inspector believes in letting people make up their own minds about such things. A person's religion is their own business and employers should have no say in the matter. Isn't that right, Mrs. Jeffries?"

Mrs. Jeffries ducked her head to hide a smile. When this household had first come together, the cook would have been the first to say that a servant should be made to go to church and that the master of the household always knew best. But, like the rest of them, Mrs. Goodge's attitudes about society had changed greatly in the past few years. Having worked for some of the richest and most aristocratic families in all of England, Mrs. Goodge had appeared to be a hidebound old snob when she'd come to work for Inspector Gerald Witherspoon. Yet the first chink in her armor had already been made before she'd even walked in the door. Her previous employers had sacked her without so much as a by-your-leave just because she'd gotten old. When Mrs. Jeffries had first interviewed her, Mrs. Goodge had mouthed a number of platitudes about what was right and proper in the world, but the housekeeper had seen that despite her stuffy manner, behind her wire-rimmed spectacles her eyes had been haunted with fear. She was old and she'd no place to go. She'd learned firsthand how cruel life could be when one was at the mercy of the whims of the rich. In the years that had passed, their investigations into Inspector Witherspoon's murders had completed the task of changing the cook's attitudes. "Yes, that's precisely what I told Reverend Cheney," she replied.

"I thought you said you held your tongue," Betsy, the pretty blonde maid, said as she reached for the teapot.

"I did. I wanted to say far more than I actually said." The housekeeper laughed. "Believe me, the urge to speak my mind was very strong, but I was very polite—when what I wanted to tell him was to mind his own business."

Everyone laughed.

"Reverend Cheney isn't at all like the other one, is 'e?" Wiggins commented. "Reverend Glassell didn't give a toss if we went to church or not. I liked 'im."

"I liked him, too." Betsy glanced at her husband, Smythe. "And I'm glad it was him and not Reverend Cheney that married us. Did Miss Euphemia Witherspoon ever make you lot go to church?"

Smythe was the coachman. He and Betsy were newlyweds, having only just tied the knot at Christmas. He grinned broadly. "You've got to be joking. I don't recall her ever setting foot in a church. As long as we did our work, she left us alone."

Smythe's history with the household of Upper Edmonton Gardens was the longest of all of them. Years earlier, he'd come to the Witherspoon house as a young

coachman for the inspector's aunt, Euphemia Witherspoon. She'd paid a good wage and treated her servants
decently. He'd worked hard and saved his money until
he had enough for passage to Australia. He wanted to
seek his fortune and he'd gotten lucky. He'd made a
fortune mining opals in the outback, used that as seed
money for other investments, and, years later, come
back to England a very wealthy man. He'd only stopped
in to pay his respects to his old employer. But Euphemia
Witherspoon was sick, lying in squalor, and dying. The
only one of her servants trying to take care of her had
been a very young Wiggins, who kept vigil by her bed-
side and did the best he could.

Smythe had immediately taken charge. He'd sent the
lad for a doctor, fired the lazy servants, and set about
putting the house in order so the poor woman could
have a bit of comfort.

But though she hung on for a number of weeks, even
the best medical care couldn't save her. Before she
died, Euphemia made Smythe swear he'd stay on in the
household for a few weeks to see her only relative, her
nephew, Inspector Gerald Witherspoon, safely settled in
the house. The inspector had been raised in very modest circumstances, and now that she was leaving him a
huge house as well as a fortune, she didn't want anyone
taking advantage of him as they'd taken advantage of
her. Smythe had agreed.

That was when his life had really gotten complicated.
Inspector Witherspoon had moved into the house, Mrs.
Jeffries had come along to be the housekeeper, she'd
hired Mrs. Goodge as the cook, and then his beloved
Betsy had collapsed on their doorstep. They had nursed
her back to health and she stayed on as the maid. Just

when he'd decided the new staff wasn't the sort to take advantage of anyone, Mrs. Jeffries had encouraged the inspector to try his hand at solving those horrible Kensington High Street murders and sent the rest of them out to snoop about for clues. Not that they had any idea what they were doing, at least not at first, but they'd soon figured it out and each and every one of them had found investigating murder to their liking. So, without telling any of them how rich he was, Smythe had stayed on for a bit more, just to see how the case turned out. But then Inspector Witherspoon had "solved" the case, gotten transferred from the Records Room at Scotland Yard to the Ladbroke Road Police Station, and, almost immediately, had another case to work on.

By then it was too late. Smythe was involved, half in love with Betsy, and despite the fifteen-year age difference between them she'd let him know she had feelings for him. So he'd stayed and now he thanked his lucky stars he'd made the right choice. He and Betsy were happily married, the household had helped solved dozens of murders, and they'd become a "family." Naturally, he'd told Betsy about his wealth before they wed. He didn't believe in keeping secrets from his wife. Mrs. Jeffries had sussed out that he had plenty as well, but he felt a bit guilty that he'd never found the best moment to tell Mrs. Goodge and Wiggins. The time never seemed right and now it was a bit awkward.

"She once sent me over to St. John's with some money for the poor box," Wiggins added. "But she didn't say I had to stay for the service, so I didn't."

Phyllis got to her feet and gave them all a sunny smile. "Church or not, this is the best place I've ever worked. When I worked for the Lowery household we only got a half day off once a week and then only after we'd cleared up the lunch table and done the washing up. Here, I've got the whole day to myself. I suppose I'd best go; I only stopped by to get my umbrella and I've spent an hour with you having tea." She giggled. "I'd never have done that at my old place. But you're all so nice."

Mrs. Jeffries stifled a surge of guilt. Phyllis hadn't been with them very long. She'd been hired a few weeks before Christmas and didn't take part in their investigations. But the position was only supposed to be temporary, the housekeeper told herself, and they had kept Phyllis on well past Betsy and Smythe's wedding. She'd not had the heart to let the girl go, she'd needed the position so badly. "You work very hard and you deserve your day out."

Phyllis' smile faltered. "But, please excuse me, I don't mean to seem ungrateful, but the rest of you don't seem to have as much time off as I do. I love working here—I don't want to lose my position because you think I'm lazy . . ."

"We have plenty of time off," Mrs. Goodge said quickly. "You just don't notice because . . . because . . ."

"Because you're always so busy," Mrs. Jeffries finished. "Now, don't worry yourself about your position. Go along now or you'll miss your train. I'm sure your family can't wait to see you. We'll see you tomorrow morning."

Phyllis laughed, grabbed her overcoat from the coat tree and her umbrella from the stand, and disappeared down the back hall.

"What on earth are we going to do?" The cook shook

her head. "We've been lucky so far; the inspector hasn't had a homicide case since Christmas."

"We managed during that one," Wiggins pointed out. "But I know what you mean, it's hard always watchin' what we say. I'm afraid I'm goin' to slip up and mention one of our cases. I like Phyllis. She's a right nice girl and she's so grateful to 'ave a job."

Mrs. Jeffries shrugged. "I like her, too, and she certainly tries very hard. Are you suggesting we tell her the truth?" She looked at Wiggins as she spoke.

He sighed heavily. "I don't know. Sometimes it seems like half of London knows what we're up to when we're on the hunt, so there's a part of me that thinks what difference would it make if we told her."

"We shouldn't say anything," Betsy said quickly. "It'll only make her feel bad because she won't be able to help. So I think we ought to just go along as we are. Like Wiggins said, we managed during the last case. She's not even here when we have our meetings."

When she'd hired Phyllis, Mrs. Jeffries had deliberately given her a short day. She didn't start work until after their normal morning meeting time and she left before they had their afternoon meeting.

"I thought she was only here because of the weddin' and us bein' so tied up on our last case," Smythe said curiously. "I like the girl, but is she goin' to be here all the time?"

He had a reason for asking, but he didn't want to share it with the others just yet. After their wedding, he and Betsy had decided to "live out" rather than stay in the house. He'd bought a building close by and had the best flat done up for the two of them. He knew his beloved would never give up their investigations, but he also knew that with his wealth, at some point it wouldn't be right for the two of them to keep working as servants. He donated all his salary to a variety of charities that helped the poor, and he suspected that, considering Betsy's reaction when he'd handed her the household accounts and told her to spend what she liked, she'd probably follow suit and donate her wages as well. He'd not realized he'd feel so guilty taking wages when there were so many unemployed in London. Blast a Spaniard, what a silly mess!

Just then, there was a pounding on the front door. Mrs. Jeffries started to get up, but Wiggins beat her to it. "I'll get it, Mrs. Jeffries," he offered as he hurried toward the stairs.

The footman took the steps two at a time, raced up the hall, and threw open the front door. A uniformed constable stood there. Alarmed, Wiggins frowned. "Is the inspector alright?"

The constable smiled reassuringly. "He's fine. He's been called out on a case, though, and he wanted me to stop by and let the household know."

Wiggins knew what to do. Inspector Witherspoon wouldn't have sent a constable around with a message this early in the day unless he had been called out on something important, like a murder. "Would you like to come inside for a cup of tea, Constable? It's an awful day out and right cold."

The constable glanced up, frowned anxiously, and then looked back at Wiggins. "That's a lovely offer but I don't think this lull in the storm is going to last and I'm on my way home. I worked the night shift." He started to go back down the stairs.

"Wait, did our inspector say when he'd be home?"

Wiggins knew he had to get some facts out of the fellow.

He stopped. "He didn't say, but it's murder so I expect he'll be late for dinner."

"Cor blimey." Wiggins shook his head. "Some poor person got done in."

"The victim was a Miss Olive Kettering and she's either rich or important, because within two minutes of us getting the call from the constables on patrol, Inspector Witherspoon was notified that he had to take the case."

Wiggins grinned. "That happens to our inspector a lot. I hope he didn't have to go too far." He looked past the constable's shoulder as more rain began to fall. The constable noticed it as well and began edging down the stairs toward the street.

"He didn't go far, just to Brook Green. The victim lived on Fox Lane."

"Thank you, Constable, I'll let the housekeeper know he'll be late." Wiggins smiled gratefully. Now that he had a street location and a name, he knew he and Smythe could suss out the rest on their own.

"Right, then, I'd best be off." The constable nodded and left.

Wiggins closed the door, ran down the hall, and flew down the back stairs, taking them two at a time. As he raced into the kitchen, he yelled, "The inspector's been called out on a murder and won't be home till late. We've finally got us another case."

Olive Kettering lived in a huge six-story white stone house set well back from the street. A garden filled with bushes, flower beds, hedges, and trees was behind a black iron fence. The house was at the end of the road, separated from the row of elegant town houses that were the nearest neighbors by a copse of pine trees on one side. On the far side was the green itself.

Inspector Gerald Witherspoon stood beside the front gate and pulled his coat tighter as he glanced at the sky. "We're in luck, the rain has stopped." He was a middle-aged man with thinning brown hair, a mustache, and a pale, bony face. "Is the body at the back of the house?" he asked.

Constable Barnes, a savvy old copper with a full head of iron gray hair under his helmet, a ruddy complexion, and a sharp gaze that took in every little detail, said, "Yes, sir." He pushed open the gate and stepped through. He and the inspector had worked together on dozens of cases so he knew exactly what to do.

Two police constables standing beneath the portico by the front door started toward them as they advanced up the paved stone walkway.

"Good day, sir," the first one said, nodding respectfully. "She's just this way." He veered off and began moving toward the corner of the huge mansion. "We've not touched the body nor disturbed the scene."

"But we did put up tarpaulins to preserve any evidence," the second constable added. "Your methods have become quite well-known."

Witherspoon nodded modestly in acknowledgment of the compliment even though he was very embarrassed. He couldn't quite recall when he'd come up with "his methods," but then again, he must have done so because everyone except him seemed to know all about them. "Well, preserving the crime scene isn't really unique to me," he murmured. "The Metropolitan Police have done it for quite some time now."

Witherspoon stopped as they rounded the corner. The truth was, he was quite squeamish about bodies and he needed a moment to steel himself for the task at hand.

"Are you alright, sir?" one of the constables asked.

"The inspector likes to have a good look at the area before he examines the body," Barnes said quickly.

Witherspoon smiled gratefully and took a deep breath. "I'm ready now."

"The body is over there, sir." Barnes pointed to a spot beneath a gray tarpaulin that had been stretched between four poles, forming a cover. A man in plain clothes crouched over the body and two other police constables, both very young, stood next to the corpse. Witherspoon guessed the man in plain clothes was the police surgeon.

Barnes turned his attention to the constables. "Go back to the front and keep watch. Let me know who comes along."

"Yes, sir," they said in unison. They went back to the front of the house.

As soon as they were out of earshot, Witherspoon asked, "Do we know how the victim was murdered?"

"The first report said she was shot," Barnes said as they approached the body. "But we'll know more once we hear what the police surgeon's got to say."

"They generally don't like to say anything at all until they've done the postmortem," Witherspoon muttered.

Barnes chuckled and nodded at the two policemen standing guard over the body. One was tall and lanky, with a blonde mustache, and the other was short, stocky, and clean shaven.

The man in plain clothes rose to his feet. Witherspoon recognized him, it was Dr. Amalfi. "Hello, Doctor." He extended his hand and they shook. "It's good to see you again."

"I was hoping they'd give you this one." Amalfi smiled in pleasure at being recognized and remembered. He'd only worked a couple of the inspector's previous cases. "It's going to be quite ugly. It's an out-and-out murder. This poor woman has been shot in the head."

"It couldn't have been an accident?" Witherspoon asked hopefully.

"I'm afraid not." Amalfi pointed to the victim. "You can see where the bullet went into her forehead. Accidental shootings are rarely so precise."

"Can you hazard a guess as to how long she's been dead?" Barnes asked.

Amalfi hesitated. "Rigor hasn't set in yet, so I think it's probably less than an hour, but then again, that's only a guess on my part. I'll know more after the post-mortem." He stepped away from the body. "I'm aware of your methods, Inspector, so I've placed her back into the position she was in when I arrived."

"We didn't touch her, either," the clean-shaven constable added, "except to ascertain that Miss Kettering was dead."

"Thank you," the inspector said. He glanced down at the dead woman and then realized her body wasn't terribly mutilated, there was merely a small hole directly in the center of her forehead. He swallowed heavily and knelt down beside her. He knew his duty. He examined her closely. She was a woman of late middle age, slender, with pale skin, deep-set eyes, and dark hair pulled back in a severe knot at the nape of her neck. She was dressed in a high-necked brown wool dress with an overskirt of brown and black stripes. "Her clothes are soaking wet, but that doesn't necessarily mean she's been out here for very long."

"It's been raining heavily all morning," Barnes added. He knelt down on the other side of the victim. "It's let up for the moment, but I think we've another bout on the way."

She lay on her back, her eyes staring straight up toward the sky. There were no rings on her fingers, no earrings, no jewelry of any kind. On her feet were high-topped black leather shoes with short, stubby heels. He glanced up at the short, stocky constable. "You referred to her as Miss Kettering. Did you know her?"

"Only because I used to walk this beat, sir," he replied. "She used to stop me to complain about the street vendors. She said they made too much noise. Well, they do hawk their wares, but they have a right to make a living, just like anyone else. She got quite cross when I told her there wasn't anything we could do about them, that unless they were breaking a law, we couldn't arrest them."

"Is she the owner of this property?" Barnes asked.

"Yes, sir," the other constable replied.

"Who found her?" Barnes continued.

"Mrs. Fox, she's a tenant on the property. She lives in a flat over the carriage house in the back. She was quite upset so we sent her back to her house to wait for you."

Barnes scanned the area under the tarpaulin. "Has anyone found a coat or an umbrella?"

"Not as yet, sir," the tall constable with the mustache replied.

"That's odd." Barnes frowned. "Why would anyone in their right mind come out in the middle of a storm?"

"Perhaps she tried to run away from her killer," Witherspoon speculated. He glanced toward the house. "Have you spoken to any of the servants?"

"There aren't any, sir," the constable with the mustache replied. "Mrs. Fox said they are all at a funeral this morning. Apparently Miss Kettering's cook died and she gave them the morning off to attend the service."

Witherspoon looked up. "Did Mrs. Fox say why she hadn't gone to the funeral as well?"

"I asked her that very question, sir"—he beamed proudly—"and she told me she stayed home because she's not been well and she didn't want to go out in this weather."

The inspector nodded and got to his feet. "Have any other witnesses come forward?" He knew it was a faint hope, but it was important to ask. Perhaps one day, he'd actually get a case where someone saw the murder and the murderer.

"Not as yet, sir," he replied. "But we've followed procedure and we've got men out taking statements from around the neighborhood. Unfortunately, there aren't any close neighbors and with the weather being so awful, I doubt there was anyone outside."

"And Faroe Road was flooding this morning." The stocky one stepped forward and pointed to the street that was perpendicular to Fox Lane. "So no one would have been out and about there, either. But we've got men searching the grounds just in case the killer left us some evidence."

"Good work." The inspector glanced at Barnes. "Let's go and interview Mrs. Fox. Perhaps she can tell us a bit more."

Barnes got up. "Yes, sir." He turned to Dr. Amalfi. "We're through here, Doctor. You can take her away. Have one of the lads at the front send off for the mortuary van."

Amalfi nodded and started toward the front of the house. "I'm planning on doing the postmortem right away. I'll send my report to you as soon as I've finished," he called as he disappeared around the corner.

"Come and get us immediately when the servants return," Barnes instructed the two constables as he and Witherspoon headed toward the carriage house.

"That's got to be it." Smythe pointed to a cluster of constables standing at the end of Fox Lane. They milled about in front of the wrought-iron gates leading to a huge white mansion set well back from the street. "Blast a Spaniard," he continued. "There aren't any near neighbors so we'll not be using any stairwells to 'ide in."

"What about those trees over there?" Wiggins nodded his chin toward a copse of trees on the side of the house. "We could cut around the far side of the green to get a closer look."

Smythe shook his head. "That won't work. The inspector's probably got men searchin' the grounds as we speak and we might get caught."

Wiggins held his breath as one of the constables by the gate looked toward them. He exhaled in relief when he didn't recognize the man. That was one of the problems they faced—too many of the inspector's subordinates knew who they were.

"We passed a pub on Faroe Street." Smythe jerked his chin back the way they'd just come. "Let's see if news of the murder has traveled that far."

Quietly, so as not to draw any attention to themselves, they turned and began to retreat. A few moments later, they stepped inside the doors of the Nag's Head Pub.

The room was full. The customers were mainly work-ingmen and -women. They stood at the bar, some with coats over their servant garb, along with shopkeepers who'd popped in to hear the latest gossip and clerks with their bowlers lying atop the counter. A fire burned in the hearth next to the bar, there were people at the few tables scattered about the room, and the benches along the walls were full as well. A buzz of excitement, over and above normal pub chatter, filled the room.

Smythe grinned at Wiggins. "We're in luck, they've heard of the murder."

Just then, two men wearing greengrocer's smocks moved away from the counter and toward the door. Smythe and Wiggins quickly took their place.

"What'll you have?" the barman asked.

"Two pints, please," Smythe replied. He glanced to his left and caught the gaze of a lone, gaunt-looking man lifting a glass of gin to his lips. He tried a friendly smile but the fellow just knocked back his drink and turned his head. No gossip to be had there.

Wiggins eased closer to the two women standing next to him and cocked his head toward their conversation.

"I'm not surprised someone finally did her in," the older of the ladies said. She was a portly woman wearing a long gray coat and a black knitted cap. "Considering the way she treated poor Elsa, God rest her soul, she's not one that anyone will be shedding any tears over."

The barman slid a pint under Wiggins' nose and he absently nodded his thanks. He made eye contact with Smythe and gave a small shake of his head toward the ladies.

"She wasn't a nice person," the younger lady, a tall redhead, replied. "But she didn't deserve to be hacked up in her own garden."

"She weren't hacked up, she were shot," a workman in a flat cap said from the other side of the women.

"Was someone killed?" Wiggins asked innocently.

The two women and the man looked at him. He smiled shyly. "Sorry, I couldn't 'elp overhearin'."

"The woman that owns that big house across the way got herself shot," the man said. "Her name's Olive Kettering and she's a spinster lady."

"Did they catch who did it?" Smythe leaned forward over the bar.

"I doubt it; she were only killed this mornin'," the redhead said. "So they're not likely to know much, now, are they?"

"Cor blimey, that's terrible. The poor lady," Wiggins added.

"Poor lady my foot," the older one put in. "I'm not one for speakin' ill of the dead, but Olive Kettering was a mean-spirited old cow and I don't much care who hears me say it. She was so miserable to her servants she wouldn't even let them take a few hours off to go to the doctor and now look what's happened. Elsa Grant is dead."

"Someone else is dead?" Wiggins exclaimed.

"Yes, but she wasn't murdered." The man reached for his glass. "Elsa Grant was the cook at the Kettering house. She died and her funeral is today."

"We don't know that she wasn't done in." The red-head glared at the workman.

"She died of natural causes," he protested. "She had something wrong with her stomach. God knows she'd been complainin' about it for months."

"He's right," the older woman added. "She'd been feelin' poorly for months. Dr. Hilton thinks she probably had the cancer, leastways that's what he told my Ned when he was there putting in those fancy new lamps in the surgery."

"Yes, but she didn't get to see Dr. Hilton until it was too late, did she?" the redhead argued. "So he don't know what it was that killed her. It might have been something simple that he could have cured if she'd been allowed to go see him. But Olive Kettering wouldn't give her time off, would she?"

"Elsa had an afternoon out, just like everyone else in the household," the man pointed out. "She's the one who didn't want to waste her time going to a doctor until it was too late."

"But the Kettering woman wouldn't let her go then, would she?" the redhead snapped. "She knew how sick Elsa was and she wouldn't let her off to see a doctor and didn't call one to the house until it was too late. Seems to me Olive Kettering got exactly what she deserved."

The flat over the carriage house was large, airy, and spacious. Witherspoon had noticed the small but modern kitchen they'd passed as Mrs. Fox had led them down the short corridor to the drawing room. It was quite an impressive room, with tall windows draped with blue and cream silk curtains and a polished wooden floor laid out in an intricate diamond pattern. The walls were painted a pale rose cream and topped with carved white crown moldings. A cut-glass chandelier hung from the ceiling and all the French Regency furniture filling the room was upholstered in a dark sapphire and rose striped fabric.

Bernadine Fox stared at her two visitors. They were sitting in front of the fireplace; she was on the center of the sofa and Witherspoon was on her right. Barnes had taken a straight-backed chair by the hearth. She was a small, slender, rather attractive middle-aged woman with blue eyes and streaks of gray in her dark brown hair. She wore a gray skirt and a high-necked white blouse with an onyx and gold pin at her neck. "I wouldn't have even seen her if I hadn't glanced out the window." She bit her lip and looked away.

Witherspoon nodded sympathetically. "It must have been a terrible shock for you."

She sniffed, pulled a white handkerchief out of her sleeve, and dabbed at her eyes. "It certainly was. One doesn't expect to see one's neighbor lying in the garden."

Barnes looked up from his little brown notebook. "What time was this, Mrs. Fox?"

"It was just past ten o'clock," she replied.

"You looked at the clock?"

"Yes"—she pointed at the grandfather clock standing by the door—"and I noted the time. I was wondering if Olive—Miss Kettering—was going to come over for a cup of coffee." She sighed.

"Was it Miss Kettering's habit to come over each morning?" the inspector asked.

"It wasn't a habit, but she did occasionally come by and we'd have our morning coffee together. I was all alone here, as I'd let my maid go to a funeral, and I knew she was alone as well."

"They all went to Elsa Grant's funeral, is that correct?" Barnes asked.

She nodded. "Yes, that's right. She was Miss Kettering's cook. Her death was sad, but certainly not unexpected. She'd been ill on and off for some time."

"This flat is beautiful." Witherspoon glanced around the room as he spoke. "Did Miss Kettering let it furnished?"

"Certainly not," she replied. "The furnishings and the fixtures are all mine. It was nothing but bare walls when I rented the place."

Witherspoon nodded. "Do you live here alone?"

"Yes. I moved in when my husband passed away." Her eyes narrowed slightly. "I have a maid, but she doesn't live in, and before you ask, I pay the maid's wages, not Miss Kettering."

"How long have you lived here?" Barnes asked.

"Five years, but what does that have to do with Olive's death?"

The constable smiled slightly. "It's just routine, ma'am," he assured her.

"Can you tell us everything that happened this morning?" Witherspoon asked softly.

"There isn't much to tell." She shrugged. "I went to the window to see if the rain had let up—I knew Olive wouldn't venture out if it was still storming. When I looked out, I saw her lying on the ground. I grabbed my cloak and rushed out. At that point, I didn't know she'd been shot." Her voice trailed off and she closed her eyes.

"Please go on," the inspector prompted. "I know

this is difficult, but the more we know, the faster we can catch the person who did this to her."

She nodded. "Yes, of course. As I said, I rushed out and when I reached her, I saw straightaway that she'd been shot. For a moment, I simply stood there, blinking my eyes, sure that I was seeing things. Then I realized I had to fetch the police."

"Had the rain completely stopped by then?" Barnes asked.

"I think so." She frowned slightly. "Oh, to be honest, I don't remember. I don't remember much of anything except running toward Faroe Road. I had my cloak over my head so I don't . . . actually, I think the rain had stopped. Yes, yes, it had. I remember now. When I got there, I saw the constable up the road so I screamed and waved my arms. He came straightaway and when I told him what I'd seen, that someone had been shot, he blew his whistle and summoned more help. Then we came back here."

Witherspoon eased back against the cushions. "What time are the servants due back from the funeral?"

"I'm not sure. Cook's funeral was in Kent and I gave my maid the day off. Her family lives in that region so I said she needn't come back until tomorrow. But I should think Olive's staff would be back soon. The train service is quite good, and even if they stayed for the reception, I'm sure Olive expected them back by the early afternoon. She wasn't one to take care of herself for long periods of time. Truth to tell, I was surprised that Olive—Miss Kettering—gave all of them the morning off at the same time."

"Surely she didn't begrudge them paying their respects to their colleague," Witherspoon exclaimed.

"She doesn't sound as if she treated her staff very well at all."

"By her standards she treated them very well." Mrs. Fox smiled. "By theirs, I'm sure they felt very hard done by. I'm sure she complained bitterly about being left on her own, but in the end, she did let them go."

"Then exactly why were you surprised, ma'am?" Barnes gazed at her curiously.

"She didn't like being alone in the house," Mrs. Fox replied. "For some reason, it made her nervous. Recently, there had also been some friction between Miss Kettering and her servants."

Witherspoon sat up straighter. "What kind of friction?"

Mrs. Fox looked down at her hands and then lifted her eyes to meet the inspector's. "They blamed her for Elsa Grant's death. I overheard the downstairs maid telling the gardener that all of them blamed her and that most of them were going to start looking for new positions."

The inspector's heart sank. Ye gods, surely there wasn't going to be another murder. "Exactly how did the cook die?"

"From natural causes, I assure you." Mrs. Fox waved her hand dismissively. "Mrs. Grant died from a stomach ailment. She'd had it for months."

"Then why did the servants think Miss Kettering was to blame for the woman's death?" Barnes asked reasonably.

Mrs. Fox shrugged. "None of them like Miss Kettering, she has very exacting standards."

"Lots of servants don't like their masters, but they rarely accuse them of murder," the constable pointed out.

"As I said, Miss Kettering has very exacting standards; she works her servants quite hard," she replied. "The staff seemed to think that the cook took a turn for the worse a few days ago. Miss Kettering insisted the cook finish preparing dinner instead of going to the doctor. They seem to believe that if Mrs. Grant had seen the physician, she'd still be alive today."

"Even for a woman with exacting standards, not allowing a sick woman to see her doctor is fairly harsh," Witherspoon muttered.

"But she'd no idea that cook was as ill as she turned out to be. The woman was always complaining about her health," Mrs. Fox said defensively. "How was she to know that this time, Mrs. Grant was genuinely ill? Olive had an important dinner party planned for that night and, frankly, if I'd been in her place, I'd have done the very same thing. Her actions were totally blameless and she certainly wasn't responsible for anyone dying."

"An important dinner party," Witherspoon echoed. He'd found that if he repeated words back to people, they frequently said more.

"She was hosting a dinner for Reverend Richards and she'd invited a number of influential people. Of course she needed a superb meal that evening." She sniffed and dabbed at her eyes again.

"Did Miss Kettering have any enemies?" Barnes asked. "Had she had any trouble with anyone lately?"

Mrs. Fox thought for a moment before answering. "I wouldn't say that she had enemies, but there were a good number of people who weren't fond of her."

"Other than her servants," Witherspoon clarified.

"Yes. To begin with, there's her cousin, Dorian Kettering. There's been no love lost between the two of them lately. Pity, really. They used to be quite close."

"What happened between them?" The inspector glanced out the window and saw that the rain had started again.

"Religion, Inspector. Dorian's a true seeker after knowledge and, though he's nowhere near as wealthy as Olive was, he has enough money that he can spend his time in study and travel. He's just come back from a study tour that took him to the Holy Land and the United States. Apparently, the experience convinced him that God is love. Olive also had a spiritual awakening of sorts, but hers convinced her of the complete opposite." She shook her head. "Needless to say, after Dorian returned home, the two of them had some loud and rather vicious arguments."

"Does Miss Kettering have any other relatives in London?" Witherspoon asked.

"She has a niece here as well, but the two of them haven't spoken in several years." She smiled sadly. "Olive had a difficult time with relatives. She simply couldn't stop herself from constantly interfering in their lives."

CHAPTER 2

It was half past three by the time Smythe and Wiggins arrived back at Upper Edmonton Gardens. After leaving the pub, they'd debated staying in the area and trying to learn a few more details of the crime, but decided against that course of action. They knew the others were waiting for them and it wouldn't have been fair. They'd also noticed the number of constables in the area seemed to have tripled, thereby increasing the odds of being spotted by someone who'd recognize them.

Betsy rose to her feet as they came into the kitchen. "Did you find out anything? Do we really have a murder?"

Fred, the household's mongrel dog, who'd been sleeping peacefully on the rug by the cooker, leapt up and raced toward the two men.

"We've got a murder, alright." Smythe dropped a kiss on his wife's nose.

"Did you eat while you were out?" Mrs. Goodge moved toward the cooker.

"We didn't have time." Wiggins licked his lips. "And I'm hungry enough to eat a 'orse." He stopped long enough to pet the dog. "'Ello, boy, did you miss me while I was gone?"

"That's what I thought. We've saved your lunch. It's still nice and hot." Mrs. Goodge grabbed a pot holder and yanked down the door of the warming oven. "You can tell us everything while you eat. Sit down and I'll serve up."

Mrs. Jeffries, who'd been rearranging the shelves in the first-floor cupboard, came rushing into the room. "I thought I heard the two of you." She grinned. "We've a case, don't we?"

"We do. And it's goin' to be a 'ard one, too." Wiggins hung up his coat and scarf, and with Fred dogging his heels he went to the table and sat down just as Mrs. Goodge put his plate in front of him. "Ta, Mrs. Goodge."

"They're all hard," the cook muttered as she slid Smythe's lunch into his spot. "That's what makes them interesting."

"Go ahead and eat," Mrs. Jeffries instructed as she slipped into her chair. "I've sent a message to Luty and Hatchet, and if they're home, I expect they'll be here any moment."

Luty Belle Crookshank and her butler, Hatchet, were friend of theirs. They'd gotten involved in one of the inspector's earlier cases and had insisted on being included on all of them.

"And I went over to Ruth's. She'll be here as soon

as she can get away from her luncheon engagement," Betsy added.

Lady Cannonberry, or Ruth, as the household called her when they were alone with her, was their neighbor across the communal gardens. She was a widow and a very special friend of the inspector's. She had also gotten involved in their cases and, like Luty and Hatchet, she now insisted on helping.

For the next few minutes, the room was silent save for the clink of cutlery as both men tucked into their beef stew. Betsy got up and went to the back door to see if Ruth was coming across the garden, and every time a vehicle came up the street, Mrs. Goodge headed toward the window, hoping to see the Crookshank carriage pulling up in front of the house.

Betsy returned from the back hall and shook her head. "No sign of Ruth yet."

"And Luty and Hatchet are taking their sweet time," the cook groused as she watched another carriage pass without stopping.

Smythe frowned and put down his fork. "They might not be able to come. For all we know, Luty and Hatchet aren't even home and Ruth might be stuck with one of those old sticks that won't take a hint and leave. Maybe we should go ahead and start without them. It's gettin' a bit late."

Mrs. Jeffries glanced over her shoulder toward the back hall. "Let's give them a bit more time. If they're not here in five minutes, we'll go ahead and start."

Fred got to his feet just as they heard a knock on the back door and a second later, before any of them could move, the sound of the door opening. "Yoo-hoo," Luty's voice echoed through the house. "We're here and we're comin' in."

"Looks like they got the message after all." Smythe grinned broadly.

"Come on in." Mrs. Jeffries stood up. "We've been waiting for you."

Betsy, who'd been hovering behind Smythe's chair, grabbed the teakettle and went to the sink to fill it with water.

Fred's tail wagged in greeting as Luty and Ruth came into the kitchen. Hatchet followed behind. The dog rushed over to welcome his friends.

"Howdy, Fred." Luty didn't have to bend very far to pet the animal. She was a tiny gray-haired American woman who looked as if a gust of wind could blow her away. She favored brightly colored clothes and extravagant jewelry. Today she was dressed in a vivid red cloak and a huge bonnet decorated with feathers and trailing yards of crimson veiling. A pearl broach bigger than an ostrich egg was pinned on her chest. Luty was rich, eccentric, and devoted to both her adopted country and her homeland. She socialized with aristocrats and played poker with half of Parliament. Her wealth had opened the doors to dozens of connections in the financial world. Hatchet, her tall, dignified, white-haired butler, had resources of his own.

"We're not too late, are we?" Luty asked anxiously as she gave Fred one last pat on the head and peered anxiously at Smythe. "Ya ain't started telling what you know, have ya?" She shrugged out of her cloak.

"For goodness' sake, madam." Hatchet grabbed the garment before it landed on Fred's head and started for the coat tree. "I'm certain they'll tell us all the pertinent details even if we've missed something." He wore a black greatcoat and an old-fashioned top hat. He hung those up next to the cloak.

"I'm so sorry it took me such a long time to get here," Ruth said as she slipped into the seat next to Wiggins. "But I had a very difficult time getting rid of my guest." She was an attractive, middle-aged woman with blue eyes and blonde hair. A widow, she frequently got called out of town to nurse her late husband's vast number of elderly relatives, all of whom appeared to believe they were at death's door. Though she'd been married to a peer of the realm, she was the daughter of a clergyman, and she took the admonition to love her neighbor quite seriously. Consequently, she had become a staunch advocate for women's rights, didn't approve of the British class system, and felt it was high time the poor and the meek inherited the Earth.

"Don't apologize, Ruth. You weren't to know we'd get a case, and we've not started," Mrs. Jeffries reassured her.

"But we can now that everyone's 'ere." Smythe pushed his plate away. "Finding the murder house was dead easy, if you'll pardon the expression. It's the only house on Fox Lane."

"It's a monster of a place," Wiggins added. "I think it's been there a long time and the city has built up around it. The grounds are huge and there's even a carriage house round the back."

Smythe nodded in agreement. "The victim's name was Olive Kettering and she was shot to death in her back garden earlier this morning."

"Before, during, or after the storm?" Hatchet asked.

"We think it was still raining, but we don't know for

certain," Wiggins answered. "But she was rich, that's for certain. The property isn't just big, it's nicely done up. The building looks freshly painted and there's not so much as a chip on the stonework, leastways not that I could see. There's got to be at least one full-time gardener for the grounds."

"Kettering . . . Kettering," Mrs. Jeffries repeated. "That name sounds familiar. I wonder if she was connected to the Kettering Brewery."

"One and the same," Smythe replied. "According to what we 'eard at the pub, that's where her money come from."

"You were in the pub?" Betsy stared at her husband. "All this time?"

"We couldn't hide anywhere close to the house," he protested. "She was killed in broad daylight and, rain or not, there were police everywhere and the house sits far enough away from the nearest neighbor that we couldn't find a stairwell or a doorway to use as a hiding place."

Betsy snorted delicately as the kettle whistled. She got up to make the tea.

"But our time wasn't wasted at the pub," Smythe said defensively. "We found out plenty about the victim."

The drawing room of the Kettering house was dark, formal, and very cold. The wallpaper was an embossed gold Celtic ring pattern against a deep hunter green background that should have been elegant but wasn't. The cavernous room was made even gloomier by tightly drawn green damask curtains that blocked out what little light there was from the dreary, overcast day. The fringed runners on the cabinets and tabletops were of the same dark fabric as the drapes, and the settee, love seat, ottoman, and chairs were all upholstered in a dark gray green material that blended with the gray slate floor but looked neither attractive nor comfortable.

Yet the inspector could tell the furnishings hadn't been cheap. He wondered how any room could have such a miserably oppressive air. Even the fire in the hearth at the far end of the room did nothing to cheer the place up. His gaze moved up from the carved oak of the mantel to the painting above it. It certainly wasn't anything he'd allow in his house. He thought it must be a portrait of hell, as it showed people being cast off a cliff while all manner of terrible things were done to them. One person was covered in boils, another had his mouth held open by demons while molten liquid was poured down his throat, while another was having his flesh burned off by flames that appeared out of nowhere. He suppressed a shudder and turned his attention back to Maura McAllister, Olive Kettering's housekeeper.

She was a short, black-haired woman who appeared to be in her early forties. She sat in the overstuffed chair across from where he sat on the sofa and stared blindly at the floor.

"This must have been a horrible shock for you, Mrs. McAllister," Witherspoon said softly.

She took a deep breath, slowly exhaled, and lifted her gaze to meet his. "I'll not lie and say I was fond of the woman," she replied. "Miss Kettering wasn't an easy person to work for, but she certainly didn't deserve to be murdered."

"How long have you worked for Miss Kettering?"

"Fifteen years," she replied.

"And you're the housekeeper," he prompted. He wanted to get her talking freely. He'd found that people frequently gave away more than they intended once one could just get them chatting.

"That's correct."

"I understand you're in charge of the household, that you've no butler," he continued.

"There used to be a butler here." Her plump face creased in a slight smile. "We had one until last year, then Miss Kettering decided that it wasn't right having unmarried men about the place so she let him go."

"Was the butler upset at being discharged?" Witherspoon asked eagerly.

She gave a negative shake of her head. "No, he was getting ready to retire so he didn't much care. But the gardener was upset at being forced to live out. She made him go as well. Mind you, Miss Kettering did give him a raise in his wages so he could pay for his room."

Witherspoon's eyebrows rose. "How upset was the fellow?"

"Not enough to kill her, if that's what you're asking," she replied. "Danny Taylor wouldn't hurt a fly. One can get upset without doing violence."

"Where does Danny Taylor live?"

"He's got a room at Mrs. Chalmer's lodging house at the end of Faroe Road. But he couldn't have done it as he was with us today at Cook's funeral."

"What time did you and the other servants leave the house this morning?" he asked.

"At eight o'clock, just after the breakfast was cleared away. Cook's family home was in Kent, not that she's any family left these days, but nonetheless, that's where she wanted to be buried. So we went to the station and caught the eight thirty-two to Maidstone. We barely made it to the church as the service started at nine thirty." She closed her eyes and shook her head. "But we didn't dare complain because it was difficult enough getting her to agree to let all of us go to the funeral."

"So Miss Kettering was alone here in the house starting at eight this morning?" The inspector wanted to get some sense of a time line. He'd found time lines very useful in many of his other cases.

She nodded vigorously. "That's right, but even though she'd given us permission to go, she made it clear she wasn't happy about the situation. I'm sure all the other staff will be saying the same to your constable, so I'm not speaking ill of the dead."

"Of course you're not," Witherspoon said soothingly. Constable Barnes was in the dining room, interviewing the other servants. "What was the reason for her attitude?" He wanted to know whether the dead woman had been afraid of being alone in the house or if she'd been upset that she didn't have people here to serve her needs. He knew what Bernadine Fox had told him, but he wanted to hear what the housekeeper had to say. On his previous cases, he'd felt sure it helped to get more than one point of view about the victim.

Mrs. McAllister pursed her lips in thought. "A few months ago, I'd have said it was because we weren't here to fetch and carry for her. But recently I noticed there was a change in her demeanor. I think she was apprehensive about being left alone in the house."

"Had she had companions living with her previously?" he asked. "I mean, people other than her servants?" He knew that many wealthy women had paid, impoverished gentlewomen as companions.

"Oh no, she's lived on her own for the past fifteen years," she replied. "So she's used to being by herself except for the servants. And it's not the house, either; she's familiar with the moans and groans of the old place. But lately, she'd become very nervous. She was always looking over her shoulder and asking one or the other of us if we'd heard noises in the night."

"Have you?"

"No, none of us have heard anything."

Witherspoon nodded. "Did she describe the sort of noises she'd heard?"

"She said she heard people walking about the grounds and the house at night," Mrs. McAllister said slowly. "But none of us ever heard anything. Yet now that she's been murdered, maybe she was telling the truth. Maybe she did hear someone outside her bedroom window the other night."

"What night was this?" Witherspoon sat up straighter.

"Two nights ago," she replied. Her eyes filled with tears. "But that wasn't the first time she'd claimed she heard someone about the place. Oh dear, I feel so awful. None of us believed her. We all thought she was just getting fanciful. It happens sometimes to people as they get older." She broke off and clasped her hands together. "And last week we did find wet footprints in the hall-way outside her bedroom. But at the time, I thought they were caused by one of the servants forgetting to clean their shoes when they came in from the outside and not wanting to own up to it. Miss Kettering was real particular about everyone wiping their feet before coming into the house."

"So she's been worried about someone being on her property for some time now?" he pressed.

"Yes, but as we couldn't ever find anyone about the

place nor did we ever hear anything," the woman cried, "we thought she was just imagining things." She dabbed at her cheeks with the back of her hand. "None of us took her seriously and now she's been murdered."

"I'm sure you did the best you could at the time," he said. "Now, please go on. What sort of things did the staff think she was imagining?"

"She'd come in to breakfast and claim that someone had been on the balcony outside her door during the night." Mrs. McAllister dabbed at her cheeks. "But my room is just above hers and I'm a light sleeper, so if there really had been someone there, I'd have heard them as well. But I never heard anything. I was never awakened."

"Was that the only time she complained of hearing things?" he asked.

"No, sometimes in the evenings, when she was in the drawing room, she'd ring for me and say that she heard someone walking in the room above her, her morning room. I'd always go check, but there was never anyone there."

"Did Miss Kettering have any enemies?" He always felt foolish asking this question. The woman had been murdered so there was obviously someone who hated her.

The housekeeper sighed again. "That's hard to say. It's not that she had what I would call 'enemies.' It's more like for the last few years, she'd gone from being mildly annoying to downright mean."

"Could you explain that, please?"

"Well, she's always been an exacting employer, but she wasn't rigid in her attitudes. I mean, she wouldn't get furious and stop speaking to someone because they disagreed with her about their religious beliefs." She paused. "But that changed about a year ago. She suddenly became very religious, but not in a nice sort of way."

Witherspoon frowned in confusion. He wasn't particularly religious himself, but he did believe in God and go to church occasionally. "I'm sorry, I don't believe I understand. Could you be a bit more specific?"

"It's hard to explain, Inspector." She sighed. "But you know how some people when they get religious become very kind and very concerned that the less fortunate have enough to eat and a roof over their heads? That didn't happen to Miss Kettering. When she started going to the Society of the Humble Servant, which, by the way, isn't a proper church at all but meets in the front room of Reverend Richards' house, Miss Kettering became less kind and less concerned about the fate of the poor. She certainly didn't become any more humble, either." She crossed her arms over her chest. "And furthermore, it was about then that she started acting as if the staff was doing terrible things behind her back. She started watching us like we were a bunch of thieves."

"Thieves?" he repeated. "Were things missing from the house?"

"A few," she replied. "But it wasn't the servants that were stealing from her, it was those odd people from that religious society. But she wouldn't believe that; she always accused us when something went missing. But why would any of us steal from her? We needed our jobs. If we didn't, we'd certainly not have stayed here."

"What kind of objects were taken?" he asked.

"Little things mostly." She pointed to a nearby table. "There used to be a silver bowl that sat there. It held some pretty-colored stones that Miss Kettering's father had found in India. That was the first thing that went missing and it was right after she'd allowed the society to begin meeting here."

"And you know for certain it was stolen, not simply moved somewhere else." He glanced around the room. Gracious, this house was so large, if someone moved an object, it might take years before it turned up.

"Of course, Inspector." She gave a delicate, derisive snort. "I'm not a fool. The stones were scattered about on the tabletop. The thief had dumped them out to be able to slip the bowl into their pocket."

"Did you notify the police?"

"No, that's how I knew it wasn't any of the servants who were doing the stealing from her. Dulcie, the downstairs maid, noticed the bowl was missing when she came in to clean the next morning. When I told Miss Kettering, her first reaction was that one of us had taken it." Her eyes narrowed in remembered anger. "She actually wanted to search all our rooms. I couldn't believe it. I told her if she was going to distrust her servants so, then she ought to notify the police so the search could be done properly. Then I pointed out that none of the servants had been in here after her church meeting had ended and that perhaps one of those visitors had taken the wretched thing. I reminded her that just prior to everyone arriving, I'd been in this room making sure everything was ready for her guests and I'd not noticed the bowl being gone."

"And as you were in here to ascertain that all was in order, I'm sure you'd have noticed if it was missing," he mused. "Was that the only thing that has gone missing?"

"Oh no, we've lost quite a number of things. A

Dresden figurine of a shepherdess was taken out of the morning room, a cherrywood box with a carved ivory top is missing from the library, and over there"— she pointed to the mantel—"used to be two tall silver candlesticks. But they're gone as well. What's more, it's always after the Society of the Humble Servant has met here that something is missing."

In the dining room, Constable Barnes was interviewing the scullery maid, Susan Edwards. "When did your cook actually die?" he asked.

"Friday morning," she replied. She was a fair-haired girl who looked to be in her late teens. Her skin was pale, her eyes brown, and she was thin as a rail. "Mrs. Grant took a turn for the worse during the night and died that morning. Miss Kettering had finally sent for the doctor, but by then it was too late."

"That's unfortunate, but we've heard that the cook had been ill for some time, is that correct?" He wanted to verify the information they'd heard from Bernadine Fox.

"That's right." Susan tucked a strand of hair that had slipped out from beneath her cap back behind her ear. "I overheard the doctor telling Mrs. McAllister that he thought she might have had the cancer."

"And was there a great deal of resentment over the fact that Miss Kettering delayed calling in a doctor?" He wanted to find out how angry the staff was at their mistress. He didn't think any of them would have been furious enough to kill, but such acts weren't unknown.

"If you're askin' if we was angry about her lettin' Cook lay there and die, then the answer is yes." Susan cocked her head to one side and crossed her arms over her chest. "We were all at Cook's funeral, so even though we didn't like Miss Kettering very much, none of us coulda killed the woman. If you don't believe me, you can ask anyone who was at the funeral. The whole village turned out, and Cook hadn't lived there in years."

"What's the name of the village?"

"Leston," she replied. "Mind you, they thought it mean that Miss Kettering couldn't be bothered to pay her respects."

Barnes nodded thoughtfully. "Why didn't Miss Kettering go to the service? I understand Elsa Grant had been the cook here for ten years."

"Mrs. McAllister asked her if she was coming—I know because I was standing in the back stairwell and I heard her as clear as a bell—but Miss Kettering just said she couldn't, that she was too busy." Susan snorted and uncrossed her arms. "Too busy, can you believe that! She didn't have anything to do today."

"Perhaps Miss Kettering didn't want to go out in the storm," he suggested. "Or perhaps she was expecting a friend to come for a visit." He had no idea why the victim had decided to stay in today, but his years of experience had taught him that a good way of learning more was to toss out a bit of idle speculation.

"She's not got any friends," Susan exclaimed. "None of her relatives like her enough to visit. Mrs. Fox is civil because they've known each other for years, and those people from the Society of the Humble only butter her up because she gives them money. Besides, I know the real reason she didn't want to go to the funeral."

"And what would that be?"

Susan smiled grimly. "She was scared to leave the house!"

* * *

"We've a name and an address, that's enough to get started," Betsy declared as she got to her feet. "There's enough time for me to get to Brook Green and ask a few questions."

Betsy was very talented at getting information about both victims and suspects out of the local merchants. She was also determined to prove to the others and herself that just because she and Smythe had married and didn't live in the house, it would make no difference in her ability to contribute to their cases!

"Be careful, Betsy, the news of the woman's death might not have spread to the locals as yet," Mrs. Jeffries warned.

"And it looks like it might be goin' to rain some more." Smythe had gotten to his feet as well and was staring at the window over the sink. "Are you sure you want to go?"

"I'm sure." She went to the coat tree. "I've got a good cloak and a big umbrella, so I'll be fine."

Smythe was right on her heels. He grabbed her cloak and draped it over her shoulders. "Right, then, mind you're back in time for supper. If you find out anything, maybe we can 'ave a short meetin' before the inspector gets home."

Mrs. Jeffries stared at Betsy. "You'll have to hurry; it's already past four and it'll take you a good half hour to get to Brook Green." She suspected that the maid's determination to start the case immediately had less to do with justice and more to do with her state of mind. Betsy seemed to be trying to prove something, either to herself or to them. Mrs. Jeffries wasn't sure which it was, but she'd recently realized that Betsy hadn't quite adjusted to the recent changes in her circumstances. She loved her husband and her new home but she hadn't warmed up very well to Phyllis coming into the household. Mrs. Jeffries had noticed that though Betsy was always polite to the girl, she'd rebuffed her efforts to become friends. That wasn't like Betsy; she was generally the first to offer the hand of friendship. Oh well, she was sure it would sort itself out eventually.

"We can get her there in fifteen minutes in the carriage," Luty interjected as she got up. "We'd best be goin'. I've got to git ready to go out tonight. Maybe I'll have a bit to contribute tomorrow at our mornin' meeting. I'm goin' to Lord and Lady Palmer's tonight." She giggled. "And I know that someone there will have heard about the Kettering murder."

"Really, madam." Hatchet gave her a sour look. "You must be careful tonight, we can't let anyone realize we've found out about the poor woman's murder . . ."

"You always think I don't have a brain in my head," Luty interrupted with a glare at her butler. "Of course I'll be discreet. I'm the very soul of discretion."

Hatchet raised an eyebrow but said nothing. He got up and went to the coat tree for their outer garments. "We'll be here at our usual time tomorrow." He glanced at Mrs. Jeffries as he returned to the table and draped Luty's cloak over her shoulders.

"You might want to come a few minutes earlier," Betsy said as she stepped away from her husband. "Just in case Phyllis takes it into her head to come early. I've noticed that she's getting here before nine."

"I told her she could come early and have a bit of breakfast," Mrs. Jeffries said.

"They're a bit stingy with food at her cousin's house,"

Mrs. Goodge added. "Which I think is downright sin-ful, considerin' what they're chargin' her for lodgin' with them."

"Oh, I see." Betsy forced a smile. "I didn't know that. No one's mentioned it before. Well, then, that's alright. I just hope it doesn't interfere with our morning meeting."

"Come along, madam, Miss Betsy." Hatchet ushered them toward the back hall. "We must get moving if we're to have anything useful to report tomorrow morning."

"Mind you get back here on time," Smythe called to his wife as the three of them disappeared. He grabbed his coat and put it on. "I might as well see if I can find out anything else. There was another pub in the neigh-borhood. Maybe lightning will strike twice and I'll find out something else."

"Do you want me to come, too?" Wiggins asked.

Smythe shook his head and started for the back door. "No, I'll go on my own. Sometimes it's easier to get peo-ple to talk when there's only one of you." He could also pass a bit of silver about more easily if he was by himself. Money did wonders in getting tongues to loosen up.

"If everyone else is goin' out, I'm goin', too," Wig-gins declared as he leapt up, raced to the coat tree, and grabbed his jacket. "I've time to get there and have a go at findin' a servant and still get back 'ere by suppertime."

Fred followed after Wiggins, his tail wagging hope-fully. "We don't have time for walkies now, old boy," Wiggins told him as he slipped on his coat. "But I'll take you out as soon as I come back. You can come to the door with us." He grinned at the women as he and the dog hurried to catch up with Smythe.

As they went past, Samson, Mrs. Goodge's fat orange tabby cat, stared disdainfully at the two of them from his perch on the top of a stool. The staff had rescued the cat in the aftermath of one of their earlier cases. He was mean-spirited and nasty to everyone except the cook. She, on the other hand, couldn't understand why the entire household disliked her beloved pet, but then again, he'd never taken a chunk out of her arm or scratched her fingers.

"I must go as well," Ruth said. "I've a dinner party at Lord Cahill's to attend and I'll very carefully see if any of them have heard of Olive Kettering or her murder."

"That would be very helpful." Mrs. Jeffries knew all of them would be discreet, but still, she was worried. It was so early in the investigation that she was afraid someone would mention to the inspector that on the very day of the murder, strangers had been asking questions about the victim. That situation, of course, could lead to some very awkward moments.

Gerald Witherspoon had no idea that much of his success was due to the fact that he had a great deal of help on his cases. With the aid of Constable Barnes, who'd soon figured out that the household was snooping about on their own and finding out some very useful bits of information, they made sure their inspector learned everything they'd found out about the victims and the suspects in any given case.

Witherspoon had been in charge of the Records Room when Mrs. Jeffries had become his housekeeper, and in the passing years, he'd become the most successful homicide detective in the history of the Metropolitan Police Force. His household and their friends were determined to keep him in the dark about this little fact. Truth to tell, in recent years, the inspector had become very proficient on his own. Still, he'd never

learn near as much without their assistance, and, furthermore, helping the cause of justice was important to
all of them.

It gave their lives meaning on a level that none of
them could explain very well, but which they felt deep
inside. But of course, keeping the inspector in the dark
about them was only one of their current difficulties.
Mrs. Jeffries had seen the other brewing since Betsy
and Smythe had come back from their wedding trip and
moved into their own flat.

As soon as the kitchen was quiet, the cook sighed.
"Did you see that? We've got a problem and I'm not
talking about our case."

"I know." Mrs. Jeffries helped herself to another cup
of tea. "Betsy could barely make herself be civil when
Phyllis' name came up. I don't know why she doesn't
like her; the girl tries so very hard to please. And
frankly, it's not like Betsy to be so aloof."

"I don't think Betsy will let herself feel kindly toward
Phyllis," Mrs. Goodge replied.

"But the question is why." Mrs. Jeffries shook her
head. "I simply can't understand it. Phyllis goes out of
her way to be friendly and Betsy is simply polite."

"It's all the changes in her life," the cook said wisely.
"They're good changes mainly, but all change is hard."

"Do you think she's frightened that Phyllis is going
to take her place?"

Mrs. Goodge shrugged. "Probably. But she'll have
to get over that. She'll just have to trust in us, that we'd
never push her aside."

Betsy climbed down from the carriage and stepped out
onto the pavement. She waved at Luty and Hatchet.

"Mind you be careful," Luty called to her as the carriage pulled away. "It's getting dark."

She nodded and then turned and started up the street toward the row of shops just ahead. I knew this was going to happen, she told herself. She knew the minute she and Smythe left the house that everything would be different and now it was happening. That girl was worming her way into the household and before long, she and Smythe would be out in the cold.

Betsy dodged around an elderly matron carrying a shopping basket. She knew she was being unreasonable, that the household would never push them aside, that the bonds they'd forged these past few years wouldn't get frayed just because she and her husband lived around the corner. But fear wasn't reasonable and the truth was, she was just afraid.

When she reached the corner, she stopped and took a deep breath. She'd worry about Phyllis later; right now she had work to do. Important work that would prove to everyone that she was valuable, that she had worth. Betsy gasped when she realized what she'd been thinking. What on earth was wrong with her? She was acting like a silly fool. She sighed, brought her thoughts under control, and took her bearings.

On the opposite side of the road was a greengrocer's, a chemist's, an ironmonger's, and a draper's. She glanced at the shops on this side of the street. There was a grocer's, a fishmonger's, a tobacconist's, and a men's haberdashery. Betsy had always had decent luck at greengrocers' so she waited for a break in the traffic and then crossed the street.

She paused outside the stall and saw that the clerk was a young man. He was helping an elderly woman.

Betsy grinned to herself. Young lads like this fellow were usually eager to talk. She knew she had to be careful, that the knowledge of the murder might not have spread to the high street as yet, but there was a part of her that was desperate to prove she was still useful, that moving out of the house at Upper Edmonton Gardens hadn't rendered her completely incapable. She gave herself a shake as she realized where her thoughts were going again and stepped into the open stall.

The elderly customer left and Betsy took the spot she'd just vacated.

"May I help you?" the clerk asked.

Betsy gave him a shy smile. "Yes, thank you, may I have some of those carrots, please? About a pound should do it."

He nodded respectfully, reached into the bin, and pulled out a huge handful of vegetables. He kept glancing at Betsy as he put them on the scales. "This is a pound, ma'am," he commented. "Will this do you?"

Betsy blinked and drew a sharp breath. He'd called her "ma'am." It wasn't the first time she'd been addressed in that manner, but it was the first time it had happened when she was on a case and giving a young man her best sweet-young-girl shy smile.

"Are you alright, ma'am?" The clerk stared at her anxiously.

"Of course I'm alright," she snapped.

"I'm sorry, I didn't mean any disrespect, it's just that I thought I heard you make a sound . . ." He blushed furiously and looked away.

Betsy realized she must have gasped aloud in surprise and now she felt like a fool. "Please, it's my fault. I did make a funny sound." She forced herself to smile.

"I'm sorry. It's just that I'm dreadfully upset." In for a penny, in for a pound, she thought as she made an instant decision to put her bad behavior to good use. "But I'd no right to be rude to you. You see, I heard a rumor that someone I know has just died. As a matter of fact, she lives quite close to here. I wonder if you've heard of her, it's a Miss Olive Kettering."

He drew back in surprise. "You're a friend of hers? I'm sorry, ma'am, but I'm afraid the rumor is true."

"Oh no." Betsy's hand flew to her mouth. She wished she could cry easily or at least tear up a bit but her eyes were as dry as a piece of old newspaper. It wasn't fair; only a few minutes ago she'd been ready to bawl like a baby and now, when a few tears might come in handy, she couldn't do it.

He stared at her sympathetically. "I'm sorry, ma'am. This is a hard way to find out such terrible news. Was Miss Kettering a close friend?"

"She wasn't really a friend," Betsy admitted. "But I did know her. How on earth did she die? The last time I saw her, she was the picture of health."

"Oh dear, this is most unpleasant, but you'll know soon enough. Miss Kettering was murdered this morning. I know it for a fact, as Tommy—he's the lad that delivers for us—brought us in a huge order from the Kettering house and he said it was for the reception after the funeral." He dropped his voice to a whisper. "The police are there now. They're questioning everyone."

"That's awful. Poor Miss Kettering. Do you have any idea how she died? How she was murdered?"

"She was shot in the head," he replied. "That's what Tommy said."

"But who on earth would want to kill her?" Betsy

exclaimed. She was groping in the dark here, hoping to hit something.

His sympathetic expression vanished and he stared at her warily. "Are you sure you know Olive Kettering? Because frankly, she was not a very nice person. From what I've heard, they're lots about that would love to see her six feet under."

"This is Mr. Dorian Kettering," Mrs. McAllister said as she led the tall, slender man into the drawing room. "He's Miss Kettering's cousin. I haven't told him anything."

Dorian Kettering stared at the two of them in confusion. He had strong, prominent cheekbones, brown eyes, and a wide, full mouth. He stepped forward and extended his hand. "How do you do, sir?"

"I'll leave the two of you alone, then." Mrs. McAllister nodded respectfully, then turned and left, closing the drawing room door behind her.

"Excuse me, sir, but who exactly are you and why are there policemen everywhere?" Kettering blurted out.

"I'm Inspector Gerald Witherspoon and I'm afraid I've some very bad news. Your cousin was murdered this morning."

Kettering sucked in his breath as the blood drained out of his face. "Oh, my Lord, murdered? But how can that be? Who would kill Olive?"

"Why don't you sit down, sir?" Witherspoon gestured toward the settee. He didn't necessarily think that going pale was a sign of complete innocence. Murderers were often quite good actors.

"Why would anyone want to harm Olive?" He sat

down and put his head in his hands. "May God have mercy on her soul."

"Are you a clergyman, sir?" Witherspoon asked.

Kettering looked up. "No, I studied divinity at the University of Edinburgh but I'm not a clergyman. I'm merely a student of different religious traditions."

"Do you have an occupation, sir?"

He shook his head. "I'm most fortunate, sir, in that I've a small yearly income that allows me to indulge my passion. I've recently come back from America. There has been the most interesting religious revival movement in that country. I met with some of the most amazing people, a Mr. Washington Gladden, he's a pastor of the First Congregational Church in Cleveland, Ohio, and he's forging new ideas about Christianity, it's about love for thy neighbor and putting the words of the Lord into actions . . . oh dear me, I'm blabbering on and my poor cousin is dead. Forgive me, sir, I don't know what has come over me. I don't usually behave in such a manner. I'm sure you've questions you must ask."

"That's quite alright, sir," he replied. "Sometimes shock makes us behave in odd ways. I understand that you and a niece were Miss Kettering's only close family? Is that correct?"

"Yes, my niece and I are the only ones left. Poor Patricia, she'll be most upset."

"And where does your niece live?" He glanced out the window to see if it had started to rain again.

"Patricia—er, Mrs. Cameron—lives here in London, in Clapham. I'll need to go see her right away. I don't want her getting the grim news from the papers. She and Olive haven't seen or spoken to one another since Patricia's marriage three years ago. Olive didn't approve, you see. But they were once very close."

Witherspoon turned to stare at him. "Miss Kettering hadn't spoken to her niece in three years?"

Dorian grimaced slightly, as though he were embarrassed. "Don't think badly of her, Inspector. My cousin had some very strong notions about right and wrong, but she wasn't a bad person. She didn't approve of Patricia's choice of a husband, but that's not an unheard-of situation in many families."

"Why did you come to see your cousin this afternoon?" he asked. "Did you have an appointment? Was she expecting you?"

"No, I came by to try to talk some sense into her, but she didn't know I was coming. We've been at odds recently and that was weighing heavily upon my heart, Inspector."

"You and Miss Kettering had some difficulties with one another?"

"You could say that," he replied.

"Let me make certain I understand you correctly. Olive Kettering hasn't any family except for you and her niece, Mrs. Cameron, and she was at odds with both of you?"

Dorian nodded slowly. "I'm afraid that's right. Oh, we've some other distant relations, but there's been no contact with that branch of the family in years. But as I said, my cousin had very strong notions about right and wrong and apparently, she thinks both Patricia and I are in the wrong."

"And what did you hope to accomplish by coming to see her today?" he pressed.

Kettering smiled sadly. "I'd hoped she would open

her heart a bit, but in truth, I didn't think I'd have much success. Now that the Reverend Samuel Richards has his greedy little hooks into her, I doubt that the Second Coming could have made her open her heart and look favorably upon her own family."

CHAPTER 3

"You look dreadfully tired, sir," Mrs. Jeffries said as she reached for the inspector's bowler hat. It was after seven o'clock and he did look exhausted. His face was pale, there were dark circles under his eyes, and rain was dripping off his mustache.

"I'm fine," he declared as he unbuttoned his heavy overcoat. "It's just been a long day." He slipped off the garment and hung it on the peg under his hat. "I take it the constable came by with the message?"

"Yes, sir," she replied. "He said you'd got a murder at Brook Green and that you'd be late home. Mrs. Goodge has a nice supper in the oven; shall I bring it up now or would you like to have a glass of sherry and relax before your meal?"

"A sherry sounds lovely." He headed toward the drawing room. Mrs. Jeffries hurried after him. He sank down in his big overstuffed chair and she went past him to the cabinet on the other side of the room. She pulled out a bottle of Harvey's Bristol Cream and two small crystal glasses. Mrs. Jeffries knew he expected her to pour one for herself. They'd been through this ritual many, many times. She handed the inspector his glass and sat down on the settee close to his chair. "Was it a dreadful murder, sir?"

"No more than usual." He took a sip. "The deliberate taking of a human life is always a terrible thing. The victim was a woman of late middle age named Olive Kettering. She was wealthy and lived alone except for her servants. Sad, really; from what I learned today, she lived her life in such a manner that I don't think there will be many to truly mourn her."

"How was she killed?" she asked. She knew very well, but it was important to ask the right questions.

"She was shot in the forehead. She was out in her garden, which is a bit odd considering the murder occurred this morning during that awful storm. She wasn't wearing a coat or a hat nor had she taken an umbrella out with her. When the first constable arrived on the scene, he found her front door partially open, as if she'd just rushed out of her house for no apparent reason."

Mrs. Jeffries wanted to ask how big the bullet hole had been but she knew she couldn't. She'd save that question for their friend Dr. Bosworth. "As you often say when you're on a case, sir, there's always a reason for everything. No sensible person runs outside in the middle of a downpour. I'm sure you'll eventually find out what led her to dash outside like that." He had actually once said those very words to her, so she was quite happy to repeat them to him.

The inspector often lost faith in himself and she'd

come to the conclusion over their many cases that it was best to bolster his confidence in his detecting abilities right from the very start.

"Thank you for reminding me, Mrs. Jeffries." Witherspoon smiled gratefully. "Yes, I'm sure we'll figure it out eventually. It's going to be a strange case, I can feel it. Most people make certain they keep on the right side of their rich relatives, but from what I learned today, Olive Kettering only has two close relations and she'd managed to become estranged from both of them."

"That does sound odd, sir," she agreed. "Did you find out why?"

"Apparently, her quarrel with her cousin was over religious differences and with the other one, a niece, she didn't approve of the fellow the girl married. Still, one can quarrel with relatives without disinheriting them." He paused, took another sip, and then continued speaking.

Mrs. Jeffries listened carefully, occasionally asking a question or nodding in agreement as he gave her all the details of his day. By the time he went into the dining room to eat his supper, she was fairly certain she knew everything that he did. But just to be on the safe side, she'd have a short chat with Constable Barnes tomorrow morning when he came to fetch the inspector.

Mrs. Goodge handed Constable Barnes a mug of hot tea. "Ta," he replied as he sat down at the table. He'd come a half hour early to have a quick word with the household. Soon after he'd been assigned to the inspector, Barnes had realized that Witherspoon was getting help on all his cases. But being a sensible sort of man, instead of taking offense, he'd kept his eyes and ears open until he'd figured out that it was the inspector's own household that was lending a hand. Gradually, once they'd learned to trust one another, he'd let Mrs. Jeffries know he understood what they were doing and that he approved.

The truth of the matter was that he'd accomplished more in the service of justice in the last few years than ever before. That was important to the constable, very important, and it didn't hurt that Inspector Witherspoon's string of solved cases had made him a legend. He worked with the man, so everyone else on the force considered him a bit of a legend as well. That wasn't why he did it, of course, but he'd not be human if he didn't admit that his vanity enjoyed the whispers of admiration when he walked through a local police station or Scotland Yard.

Mrs. Jeffries took her seat. In the early morning, the kitchen was quiet, save for the ticking of the clock and the faint noises from the street as Londoners woke up for the day. "You had quite a full day yesterday."

Barnes grinned. "That we did, Mrs. Jeffries. We've another odd murder on our hands. The victim was found lying in her back garden with a bullet in her forehead, but you already know all that, don't you? Let me give you the details I found out from the servants. To begin with, they didn't much like her."

"Did they dislike her enough to murder her?" Mrs. Jeffries asked. Barnes was no fool; his opinion of the household could go a long way in eliminating suspects.

He shook his head. "It's possible, but I don't think it's likely. She was hard on them, but she wasn't cruel and I finally got the housemaid to admit that she did pay top wages. But what is interesting is that they blamed her for the death of the cook."

"The inspector mentioned there was a bit of resentment over the woman's death," Mrs. Jeffries murmured.

"It was a bit more than resentment," Barnes declared. "The gardener was so furious, he'd already started looking for a new position, and from what I saw of those grounds, he'll get one, too. He's a fine gardener. The scullery maid and the downstairs maid were also trying to find new posts."

"But the inspector told Mrs. Jeffries the cook died of natural causes," Mrs. Goodge protested. "So why were they so angry? Did they suspect she'd killed the woman?"

"No, that was never mentioned," Barnes replied. "They were upset because Miss Kettering made it clear she thought the cook was malingering to get out of her duties. Apparently, the woman would become ill, take to her bed for a day or two, and then just as quickly recover. When she had this final bout of illness, Miss Kettering didn't let them call the doctor until it was too late."

"So they blamed her," Mrs. Jeffries mused. "But if they're trying to find new positions, why would one of them kill her? Furthermore, they were all at a funeral in Kent when the murder was committed."

"As far as we know, that's true." Barnes took another swig from his mug. "But we've no real confirmation of the actual time of death, and if the servants were in a conspiracy to kill her, they could have done it before they left that day."

"But that would have been very risky for them," Mrs. Jeffries pointed out. "The inspector said that Mrs. Fox saw the body when she glanced out her window at ten o'clock. If the servants were in a conspiracy and killed her, they'd have had to put the body out before they caught the train to Kent, and if they'd done that, they could have easily been spotted by Mrs. Fox."

"I agree, I don't think they did it, either, but it's always good to talk through the possibilities," he replied. "Besides, after taking their statements yesterday, I got the impression that the staff wasn't just angry at the woman, they were a bit frightened of her as well."

"Frightened?" the cook repeated. "Why?"

"All of them claimed she'd been acting strange lately. She claimed to hear people walking about at night or standing on her balcony. She'd wake the household up at all hours of the night and make them search the house, and I think they were getting fed up with that."

"They never saw anyone when they went to look," the cook muttered. "I once worked in a household where the mistress started getting fanciful. It *was* very frightening. You never knew what she would do or say next. One minute, she'd be right as rain, and the next, she'd be accusing all of us of spying on her or trying to push her down the staircase. I don't blame the staff for wanting to leave if that was the way of it."

"That's not the only reason most of them had started looking for new positions," Barnes said. "I'm sure the inspector has told you that, recently, small but valuable items were going missing from the house and she'd started accusing her servants of theft."

"No one likes being called a thief," Mrs. Goodge

murmured, "and once a servant gets painted with that brush, new positions are almost impossible to find."

"True." He glanced at the carriage clock on the pine sideboard. "But don't feel too sorry for them, they got a bit of their own back. The scullery maid told me that Miss Kettering had been sent some very expensive drinking chocolate from Holland. It came in a fancy tin and Miss Kettering gave strict instructions that it was only to be used for her nightly cocoa." He grinned broadly. "But Susan Edwards told me she saw the cook switch the fancy cocoa in the tin for ordinary English drinking chocolate and that Miss Kettering never knew the difference."

Mrs. Goodge laughed heartily. The other two looked at her, their expressions curious. "Oh dear, I know I shouldn't carry on so, but the truth is, I once did the very same thing," she admitted. "At my last household, the mistress of the house had started getting nastier and nastier to me. Nothing I did was right and she found fault with every meal I cooked. A few weeks before I left, they were sent some expensive Darjeeling tea from India. I was so annoyed that I switched it with some old stuff I'd found in the dry larder. I used to laugh myself silly when I'd hear that woman going on and on to her friends about the exquisite tea she was serving. Oh, it was wonderful; I'd sneak upstairs and peek into the drawing room when she had guests and watch them try to choke that stale stuff down. I know it was a terrible thing to do, but honestly, I'm not in the least sorry."

Barnes, who'd began to chuckle as she told the story, said, "I don't blame you, Mrs. Goodge. Anyone who finds fault with your cooking deserves to drink stale

tea. But there's more I need to tell you. I had a quick
word with the lads that searched the grounds and did
the house-to-house in the neighborhood."

"They found something." Mrs. Jeffries leaned forward eagerly.

"Not so much what they found, as what they didn't
find. Namely, the gun. So that means the killer took it
with him," he said. "But it's also possible that he—or
she—tossed it in the river. Unfortunately, there aren't
any close neighbors so no one saw anything suspicious.
But we're going to continue asking about the neighborhood. You never know what might turn up."

"Was the Kettering house searched?" Mrs. Goodge
asked.

Barnes frowned. "It was, but it's such a huge place
and I don't think the lads were as thorough as they
ought to have been. They were in and out in an hour. I'm
going to suggest to the inspector that we have another
look round."

"I'll go first," Mrs. Jeffries declared as they took their
places around the table for their morning meeting. For
once, everyone was a bit early. "I want to share everything I've found out from the inspector and Constable
Barnes."

"I found out a few bits myself," Luty, grinning mis-
chievously, added, "and I can tell by the way Hatchet's
been preenin' this mornin' that he's stumbled onto
something, too."

"I do not preen and I certainly didn't 'stumble' onto
information." He gave her a sour look.

"Does that mean you ain't found out anything?"

"The point of my comment was to deny that I stumble

onto useful items." He stuck his nose in the air. "I have a number of excellent sources which I cultivate in an intelligent and logical manner. Stumble, indeed."

"If we've all got something to share, we'd better be quick about it. It's already a quarter past eight and Phyllis might take it into her head to come even earlier than usual," Betsy said.

"She'll not be here this early." Mrs. Jeffries gave her a reproachful look and then turned her attention back to the others. She told them everything she'd learned from Witherspoon and Constable Barnes.

"Cor blimey, sounds like there's lots of people that won't be cryin' at Miss Kettering's funeral," Wiggins observed when she'd finished. "Fancy accusin' her servants of stealin', especially when she'd a houseful of those people from that Society of the Humble Shepherd."

"Servant," Mrs. Goodge corrected. "It's the Society of the Humble Servant."

"Just because people claim to have religion," he continued with a nod toward the cook, "that don't mean they're not above stickin' a pretty trinket in their pocket."

"Apparently that is precisely what Miss Kettering's housekeeper pointed out to her mistress," Mrs. Jeffries remarked. "Yet it didn't seem to have a great deal of influence on Miss Kettering's attitude toward her staff."

"Yes, but she didn't sack them, did she?" Mrs. Goodge snorted. "And believe me, if she'd really thought her servants were to blame for the thefts, she'd have given them the boot faster than Samson can gulp down a dish of cream. Olive Kettering didn't want to

believe her friends would steal, when it's so much easier to blame some poor servant. Stupid woman, she's
lucky the whole lot of them didn't up and leave." She'd
worked in houses where the staff had taken the blame
for the misdeeds of family or friends. She understood
and hated the unfairness of it all.

Mrs. Jeffries glanced at the clock. Despite her admonition to Betsy, they had better move along or Phyllis
might come walking in the back door. "Who'd like to
go next?"

"I will," Ruth said eagerly. "I went to a dinner party
at Lord Cahill's town house last night and the only topic
of conversation was the murder. What's more, Isabella
March mentioned that the inspector and I were friends,
so everyone at the table talked to me about the crime.
It was amazing. I didn't even have to ask any questions.
No one mentioned anything about the murder per se,
but I heard all sorts of gossip about Olive Kettering and
the Kettering family. She was very rich and the money
came from the Kettering Brewery."

"Does she still own it?" Hatchet asked. "My sources
thought the family might have sold out years ago."

"They did." Ruth nodded her thanks as Mrs. Goodge
handed her a cup of tea. "Her parents sold the brewery twenty-five years ago for a huge amount of money.
Olive was their only child and when they died, she got
it all. What's more, she took control of her finances and
apparently she's quite a good businesswoman. Everyone
seemed to think she doubled the wealth she inherited,
which wasn't insubstantial to begin with."

"Now that she's dead, who gets the goods?" Wiggins
asked cheerfully.

Ruth laughed. "Everyone at the dinner party seemed

to think she'd leave it to her family, except for Lady Cahill. She claimed she'd heard that Miss Kettering was estranged from her relations and that she'd cut all of them out of the estate. But no one at the party really knew for certain." She leaned back in her chair. "That's all I found out."

"I'll go next," Luty offered. "I know we're on the clock. My source told me pretty much the same as Ruth has reported, except that I also found out that she's definitely disinherited her niece, Patricia Cameron. The girl married a man Olive felt was beneath the family and the two women haven't spoken to one another in three years. So I don't think Mrs. Cameron will be inheriting from her late aunt."

Patricia Kettering Cameron lived on the top floor of a six-story building in Notting Hill. She was a tall, slender woman with red hair piled high on her head, fair skin, high cheekbones, a full mouth, and bright blue eyes. She was very lovely.

She motioned for Witherspoon and Barnes to come inside. "Please keep your voices down; my husband is sleeping. He hasn't been well lately."

Witherspoon nodded his assent and they stepped inside.

She closed the door quietly and motioned for them to follow her. They went down the short hall past a closed door and into a room that appeared to function as a drawing room and a dining room combined. A round table with two high-backed straight chairs was at the far end, and directly behind that was a tiny kitchen with a cooker and water pump. The walls were covered with green and beige striped wallpaper, beige curtains hung limply at the windows, and a faded Oriental carpet covered the floor. The only bright spots in the dismal flat were the paintings. A beautiful portrait of Patricia Cameron held pride of place in the center of the wall, flanked on each side by smaller but equally lovely paintings of London street life. Witherspoon was no art expert but even he could see that these works were outstanding.

"Please sit down." She waved at a brown settee next to the windows. "But I'd appreciate it if you'd keep your voices very low. I know why you've come. It's about Aunt Olive's murder."

The two men sat down where she'd indicated. "I take it you've spoken with Mr. Dorian Kettering," the inspector said.

She nodded, but she said nothing.

"When was the last time you saw your aunt?" he asked.

"The day before yesterday." She sank down on the love seat opposite them. "We had a horrible argument. I called her all sorts of ugly names and now she's dead."

Witherspoon glanced at Barnes. None of the servants had mentioned Patricia Cameron's visit.

"What time did you arrive at your aunt's that day?" Barnes asked.

"I didn't go to the house." Her eyes filled with tears. "I didn't want to give her the opportunity to have poor Mrs. McAllister claim she wasn't at home. That's what she usually did when I tried to see her."

"Where did you see your aunt?" the inspector asked softly.

She yanked a white handkerchief out of her pocket and dabbed at her eyes. "On Brook Green. She walks there every morning after she has her breakfast. I waited behind a tree until she started up the path and then I joined her." She smiled bitterly. "She wasn't happy to see me, but she was civil."

"Mrs. Cameron, I understand this must be very difficult for you. But could you tell me why you and your aunt were at odds?" Witherspoon asked. Previous experience had taught him that when a rich victim was alienated from her closest family, it was important to find out why and not just accept what one was told. Dorian Kettering had already given one explanation for the reason the two women were estranged, but he wanted to hear what she had to say on the matter.

She gave a harsh, ugly laugh and then clapped her hand over her mouth as the sound echoed loudly in the quiet room. She glanced at the closed door in the hallway and then turned back to the two policemen. "Oh dear, I don't want to wake Angus. The usual reason, Inspector. My aunt didn't approve of the man I chose to marry. Though I've never really understood her objection—Angus' family is far older and more illustrious than ours. Cousin Dorian told me that years ago our two families were friends."

"So why did you go to see your aunt?" Barnes inquired. "Were you hoping to reconcile?"

"I went to beg her for money," she admitted. "My husband is very ill. It's his lungs, you see. His doctor says that the only way he'll get well is if we get him to a warm, dry climate. I wanted to take him to Spain." She dabbed at her eyes again. "He's an artist and he's always wanted to go there. The light is supposed to be wonderful for painters."

"I take it your aunt refused to help you," Wither-spoon said. "Otherwise you'd not have had an argument with her."

She sighed and closed her eyes. "It was stupid of me to go to her in the first place."

"How long were you and your aunt together?" the inspector asked.

"Less than ten minutes," she replied. "She told me I'd made my bed and now I must lie in it."

Barnes stopped writing in his notebook. "Did your aunt threaten to disinherit you?"

"You mean when I last saw her? Of course not; she'd already cut me out of the will." She smiled sardonically. "Aunt Olive told me if I married over her objections then I could expect nothing from her. I imagine she was on her way to see her solicitor the moment Angus and I said our vows. She wasn't the sort of person to make idle threats. If she said she was going to do something, she did it."

Witherspoon frowned slightly. He'd gotten the impression from Dorian Kettering that he thought he was out of the will as well. If Olive Kettering had cut both of her relatives out of the estate, then who on earth was going to inherit? He made a mental note to go along and see the Kettering solicitor as soon as possible. "You admitted that you said all sorts of ugly things to your aunt. I take it you were upset with her?"

"Upset," she repeated. She stared at him as though he were a half-wit. "I wasn't upset, Inspector, I was furi-ous. For God's sake, I was desperate. My husband might be dying and Aunt Olive refused to help. Anyone would be enraged. It's not as if she were poor. But I wasn't the only one losing my temper. She had a few choice words for me as well."

"So you were only interested in reconciling with her because you needed financial help," Barnes suggested. "Is that what made her so angry?"

"That's not true," she snapped. "Our family is rather small, Constable, and despite her domineering ways, she was my aunt and I loved her. I tried to see her as soon as Angus and I returned from our wedding trip. But she wouldn't let me into the house, and even with that, I've tried to see her on a number of other occasions, but she never, ever let me in—"

Witherspoon interrupted. "Please don't be upset, Mrs. Cameron, these are questions we must ask."

"That wasn't a question." She glared at Barnes. "That was a nasty attack on my character. I wonder how you'd feel if someone you loved was at death's door and there was a hard-hearted old shrew that could help, but wouldn't."

"I shouldn't like it at all," he replied. "And I certainly never meant to upset you, Mrs. Cameron." Though of course he knew perfectly well what he was doing and really didn't care if she was offended. He'd made his comment to get her riled up and further loosen her tongue. It had worked, too.

"Is that what you said to Miss Kettering?" Witherspoon interjected quickly. "That she was a hard-hearted old shrew?"

"That wasn't all. I also told her she'd no right to call herself a Christian and that if she thought God approved of the way she treated other people, she was sadly mistaken." She sighed as the last of the anger drained away.

"That really made her furious. This, of course, was precisely why I said it. I'm so sorry now. She's dead and we'll never have another chance to heal the breach between us."

"Where were you yesterday morning?" Witherspoon asked.

She crossed her arms over her chest. "My husband is ill, Inspector; I was here taking care of him."

"So you were in all day yesterday?" he pressed.

Her brows drew together as she realized the implication of his question. "Surely you don't think I had anything to do with her death, do you?"

He smiled faintly. It always amazed him that people were surprised by a few simple questions. Gracious, how did they think the police solved crimes? "Mrs. Cameron, we're only trying to find out who murdered your aunt, we're not accusing you of anything."

"It certainly sounds as if you are," she retorted. "But I suppose you're only doing your job. As a matter of fact, when the rain let up a bit, I went to the chemist's to buy a sleeping powder for Angus. He'd not slept very well."

"What time did you leave here?" Barnes shifted slightly to get more comfortable. The seat was hard as a rock.

"I didn't look at the clock, Constable, but as I said, it was after the rain had stopped."

"But it rained on and off all day," he pointed out.

"Oh, for goodness' sake, it was probably around half past nine," she replied irritably. "But that's the best I can do. Now, if you've quite finished—"

The inspector cut her off. "We've only a couple more questions, Mrs. Cameron. Do you know of anyone who had a reason to want to harm your aunt?"

"Aunt Olive wasn't a very nice person," she said. "But I don't know of anyone who would want her dead."

"What about Mr. Dorian Kettering?" Barnes pressed. "How did he get along with her? Were they on good terms?"

"Cousin Dorian is a wonderful man who wouldn't hurt a fly. Aunt Olive and he had their differences, but they weren't estranged."

"We've heard she didn't approve of his religious beliefs," Witherspoon commented.

"I wouldn't know about that," she said. "As I said, Inspector, I've only seen my aunt once in three years, and Cousin Dorian certainly wouldn't discuss any arguments the two of them might have had with me. But I do know that Aunt Olive was very set in her ways, and I should have remembered that before I asked her for help. I don't know why I imagined she'd change her tune; I suppose it was desperation that made me think she might have softened. But she hadn't; if anything, she'd become even more enraged about life."

"Enraged about life," Witherspoon repeated curiously. "What do you mean?"

"She hates life." Patricia Cameron smiled bitterly. "I used to wonder why someone like her, someone who had everything—money, position, and good health— could end up so miserable. Well, she's finally got her wish; she's finally free of this vale of tears. That's what she used to call life, Inspector, a vale of tears."

The woman smiled at Wiggins as she reached for her glass of gin. He'd gone back to Fox Lane and Fortune had smiled on him, because he got there just as Lila Perkins had slipped out the front gate of the murder house.

He'd noticed the furtive way she'd glanced over her shoulder as she'd hurried down the walkway, and she'd opened the wrought-iron front gate slowly so it wouldn't squeak. She'd kept looking over her shoulder all the way to Faroe Road, and as he'd been following her, he'd had to do some fancy dodging to keep her from spotting him. He'd seen her enter the pub and he'd waited a few minutes before going in himself. He wanted to give her time to get through her first drink.

He'd been hesitant about striking up a conversation but he needn't have worried, all it had taken was him stepping up next to her at the bar and pulling out a handful of coins. She'd been the one to start chatting. From a distance, he'd thought she was quite young, but up close, he'd seen she was well into her thirties. She was one of Olive Kettering's servants.

"It's very nice of you to buy me a drink." Lila sighed and tossed back her gin. "I must tell you, I'm grateful. It's been a miserable couple of days where I work."

"It's nice of you to keep me company. I've been in London for two days now and you're the first person to give me the time of day." Wiggins was dressed in his best jacket and shirt so he'd told her he'd come to the city looking for work. He'd learned that if people thought you were a simple country lad, they weren't as apt to guard their tongue. "The least I can do is buy you a drink. I've a bit of coin as I've got a job, but it's not to start for two days so I'm on me own. Now, what's made your household so miserable?"

She stared at him speculatively and then looked pointedly down at her now empty glass. He immediately signaled the barman for another one. "Ta, that's right nice of ya. Well, it started a few days back when

Cook got ill—mind you, she'd been feelin' poorly off and on for some weeks, but we thought she was over the worst of it. But then she up and died and there was all a to-do because everyone in the household wanted to go to her funeral and the mistress raised a bit of a fuss."

"You mean she didn't want you to go?" he exclaimed.

"But that wasn't the worst of it—" She broke off and nodded her thanks as the barman slipped another glass in front of her.

Wiggins dug out more coins from his pocket and paid him. "What could be worse than a death in the 'ousehold?"

"Comin' home from Cook's funeral and findin' out the mistress has been murdered," she said dryly. "That's what's worse. The police were there all yesterday afternoon and they're back today. That's why I was able to slip away; they wanted everyone out from under their feet while they searched the house again. Mind you, I don't know what they expect to find." She raised her glass and tossed back the drink.

"Cor blimey, that must 'ave been a terrible shock for you," he said sympathetically. He saw her look at the barman again. Wiggins warred with his conscience. He'd already bought her two drinks and she'd had one before he arrived. If he bought her another one he could probably loosen her tongue even more. But on the other hand, he knew what drink could do to a person and he didn't want to contribute to her downfall. Still, murder had been done and who was he to pass judgment on how other people, especially someone of her age, chose to live their lives? "Would you like another?" He waved the barman over and pointed to her empty glass.

"That's very kind of you." She grinned broadly. "I don't usually drink like this, but as I said, it's been a very tryin' time at our household and we've no idea what's goin' to happen to us. No one has told us how much longer we'll be kept on or even if we'll be kept on at all."

"That's terrible." He shook his head in sympathy. "I know what it's like to wonder if you're going to 'ave a job come tomorrow. Do you know who might have killed your mistress? Was it like them Ripper murders?"

"'Course I don't. Mind you, if I was the police, I'd take a look at that Reverend Samuel Richards— leastways, that's what he calls himself, but he's no more a reverend than I am the Queen's ruddy cousin." She snorted and then quickly smiled as another drink appeared.

"What's wrong with him?" Wiggins pressed.

"He's a confidence trickster, that's what's wrong with him," she replied. "Any fool can see that, but Miss Kettering thought the sun rose and set on the fellow."

"You mean he's not a real vicar?"

"'Course not!" She laughed. "He runs something called the Society of the Humble, but it's not a proper church. But she didn't care about that; she only cared that he told her what she wanted to hear."

"She was a religious woman, then?" he asked.

"Only if your religion calls for everyone and their brother to burn in hell." She grinned. "She was always goin' on about how people were goin' to hell, how they were evil and the devil was just waiting to get his hands on their souls. That's why she left St. Matthew's. The vicar there wasn't nasty enough for the likes of her."

Wiggins noticed her glass was empty again. He nodded at the barman and then turned his attention back to his companion. "What does that mean?"

She smiled in delight as another drink appeared on the counter. "Ta." She grabbed the glass and hoisted it to her mouth, drained it, and slapped it back on the counter. "It means that Reverend Clark talked too much about love and compassion and not enough about sin and misery."

"She stopped goin' to church because the vicar was too kind?" Wiggins said in surprise. He wasn't sure if he was learning anything useful, but he thought he might as well continue.

"She didn't stop right away," Lila said. "It was only after she met Rizshards that she stopped going to St. Matthew's. He's an oily one, he is. He's goin' to be right upset when he finds out she's dead. He shought he had her right in the palm of his haannd."

Wiggins realized he'd bought the woman one drink too many. Cor blimey, now she was slurring her words. "Do you need to go back to work today?" he asked anxiously. He didn't like the idea of her chopping vegetables in her current condition. "I don't want you to get into trouble because you've been . . . uh, keepin' me company."

"'Course I gotta go back to work, but I don't have much to do." She giggled. "Bein' as the cook is dead, we're having a cold supper, and with the police underfoot Mrs. McAllister doesn't have time to keep track of the likes of us. Besides, she's gone up to the attic with Mrs. Fox to get the crepe. Mrs. Fox wants the house draped in black before the funeral reception. I think it's right cheeky of her to come in and take over; she's not family, she's only a tenant. But Mrs. McAllister is deferring to her and doin' what she says."

Relieved, he nodded. "What did you mean when you said that the preacher had your late mistress right where he wanted her?"

"Whadda ya think I meant? Miss Kettering was giving him money." Lila hiccuped. "Lots of it. Oh, she pretended it was for that society of his, but from what my cousin Emma told me, he spent more of it on himself than he did buyin' Bibles. Emma says that Richards has a cupboard full of expensive suits and he keeps cash in a strongbox under his bed."

"And how does Emma know all of this?" Wiggins asked.

Lila waved her arms so widely that he had to duck to avoid getting clouted on the chin. "Because she bloomin' well works for him," she cried. "Emma lives there and sees it with her own eyes. That's how she knows what's what. She's their maid and if she weren't desperate for the job, she'd be out of that house faster than a running hound. But like the rest of us, she's no choice but to stay there. Mind you, I feel a bit bad because I'm the one that told her about the position there."

"She doesn't like working there?" Wiggins asked halfheartedly. He was beginning to wonder how reliable this information might be. Lila was fairly soused.

"She hates it and she'd not be there if it weren't for me. It's my fault she's stuck there," she said. "A few months ago I overheard Richards tellin' Miss Kettering that they was lookin' for a general maid. Emma was out of work so I told her about the position and she got the job."

"Sounds to me like you were just tryin' to do her a favor," Wiggins said.

"Some favor," she snorted. "Poor Emma, she does the work of three people and that wife of his is a right old tartar. She sits in that wheelchair of hers and orders Emma about like she's the Queen of Sheba."

"His wife is crippled?"

Lila snorted again. "She pretends to be, but Emma told me the woman's faking her illness. Emma thinks it's so they can get more money out of people. Every Sunday morning, the reverend wheels her into their meeting so everyone can get a good look at 'em. But she's no more crippled than I am."

"And Emma knows this for a fact, does she?"

"She does." Her eyes narrowed angrily and Wiggins realized she wasn't as far gone as he thought she was.

"I mean, how does she know?" He deliberately made his tone more conversational as he asked the question.

"Because Emma's seen her walking about the place late at night," she replied. "Mrs. Richards didn't know anyone was up, but Emma had crept downstairs to get a glass of water and she saw the woman plain as day walking about on her own two legs. What's more, last week when the Richardses were having a fierce argument, Emma saw the woman leap out of her chair and box the good reverend's ears."

Barnes closed his notebook and tucked it into his jacket pocket as the inspector rose to his feet and smiled at Patricia Cameron. "We appreciate your cooperation, Mrs. Cameron," he began.

"Patty, who is out there with you?" The voice was weak and the accent Scots.

The two policemen turned to see a man standing in the open doorway of the room across from the kitchen.

He was a tall, very slender man wearing a maroon dressing gown over his nightclothes. His black hair was mussed, his face unshaven and pale, and there were dark circles around his deep-set brown eyes.

Patricia quickly got to her feet and rushed across the room. "Darling, I'm so sorry. We didn't mean to wake you. But what are you doing out of bed? You know what the doctor said, you must rest."

"You didn't wake me and I'm tired of resting." He didn't take his gaze off the two policemen. "What are they doing here?"

Witherspoon crossed the room and extended his hand. "I'm Inspector Gerald Witherspoon and this is Constable Barnes."

"I'm Angus Cameron," he replied. They shook hands and he nodded politely at Barnes. "Waking up to find two policemen in my drawing room is a bit of a surprise. Why are you here?"

"Oh, darling, please go back to bed," his wife pleaded. She put her hand on his arm. "It doesn't matter why they are here. Let me take care of this. You know what the doctor said. You're not to have any excitement."

"Hush, Patty, I'm fine." He kept his gaze on Witherspoon. "Inspector, my wife exaggerates. I assure you, sir, I'm not going to keel over dead regardless of why you're here. Please tell me what's wrong."

"I'm afraid we've come on a most unhappy errand. Unfortunately, your wife's aunt, Olive Kettering, was murdered yesterday."

He said nothing for a moment, he simply stared at them. Then he grinned broadly. "Well, well, so the old witch finally drove someone too far."

Patricia Cameron jerked her hand away from him

like it was on fire and drew in a deep breath. "Angus, that's a terrible thing to say. I know you don't mean it." She looked at Witherspoon. "You mustn't pay any attention to him. He's been taking a lot of medicine and doesn't mean what he says."

"They're not fools, darling." Angus laughed and looked at his wife. "They can see for themselves that I have my wits about me and that I mean every word. I'm sorry; I know she was your family. But she's done everything possible to destroy us."

"Don't say that—nothing could ever destroy us." Her eyes filled with tears. "But even if that were true, Aunt Olive could be hard as nails, but she didn't deserve to be murdered."

"Someone thought she did." He moved to the love seat and sat down on the spot his wife had just vacated and looked back at Witherspoon. "How was she killed?"

"She was shot yesterday morning in her back garden."

Angus turned his head and stared at Patricia. "You knew, didn't you? That's why your cousin came to see you yesterday. You should have told me."

"I didn't want you upset," she protested. "You were sleeping and the doctor said you needed your rest. Besides, you've made it quite clear you loathed her."

"Why shouldn't I hate her? She's done nothing but bring misery and pain to both of us. Look at how she treated you when you went to ask her for help."

She gasped and he laughed softly. "You didn't think I knew you'd gone to see her, did you?"

"How did you find out? I slipped out when you were asleep," she said.

"I woke up and found you gone. I got up to make

myself some tea and happened to look out the window just as you came home. I could see by your face that you were upset. Darling, there's only one person in the world who could have made you look like that. Olive Kettering." His expression hardened. "So don't expect me to cry any crocodile tears now that someone has done the world a favor and dispatched the woman to her final resting place."

CHAPTER 4

—❦—

Mrs. Goodge slid the plate of chocolate biscuits in front of her visitor and sat down. "Help yourself, Doris. As I recall, you always did have a bit of a sweet tooth." She'd dug deep into her list of former work colleagues to find Doris Atherton. They'd worked together years earlier at Lord Rotherhide's London house. Doris had been the scullery maid.

"You've got a good memory." Doris reached for a biscuit. "These look good. Let's see if your baking is as good as it used to be." She popped the treat into her mouth.

"It's an American recipe." Mrs. Goodge watched her visitor closely, hoping to see a look of pleasure on her homely face. Even as a young girl, Doris had never been a beauty; she had buckteeth, bad skin, and very thin blonde hair. But she'd had a quick mind, a sweet disposition, and, most importantly, a good heart. Mrs. Goodge hoped the years had treated her kindly.

"Mmm." Doris sighed happily. "These are wonderful. If you don't mind, I'll help myself to another. I must say, I was rather surprised to get your note. How on earth did you find me?"

"Ida Leahcock told me where you lived and I wanted to see you. I think more and more about the past these days. I always admired you so very much."

Doris gasped in delight. "What a nice thing to say. I never even realized you knew my name. You were so much above the rest of us in the kitchen."

Mrs. Goodge cringed inwardly. She was lying through her teeth. She'd only contacted Doris because she'd found out that she once worked for Dorian Kettering. Add to that, she was suddenly deeply ashamed of the way she'd once thought she must treat those "below" her. But back in those days, it had never occurred to her to question the way things were, that in rich households, the cook, the housekeeper, and the butler were to keep to themselves and to keep the rest of the servants very much in their place. But she wasn't the same person she'd been back then; her own experience of being sacked by her last employer and tossed out onto the street for being "too old" had shown her that the current system was just plain wrong. This household's murder investigations had also taught her that when it came to right and wrong, there were many shades of gray.

The rich, the aristocratic, and the powerful were capable of heinous crimes, and the poor, the humble, and the meek were capable of heroism and self-sacrifice. "I'm so sorry you felt that way," she admitted honestly. "But back then being friendly was frowned upon. But I noticed how smart and observant you were and I always wondered what had happened to you. Imagine my surprise when Ida told me that you worked your way up to being a housekeeper. I was ever so pleased for you." Oddly enough, it was the truth; she'd been delighted when she'd found out that the former scullery maid had done so well in life.

Doris shrugged modestly. "I never had the skills to be a cook, so after I left Lord Rotherhide's, I switched from being a kitchen maid to a housemaid and worked my way up from there. But I've left service for good now. My last employer went off to America and as I'd saved my wages for years, I had enough to settle in my own little place and live comfortably enough."

"How very clever of you." Mrs. Goodge saw Samson slip into the room and head for the rug next to the cooker. That particular spot was Fred's favorite, but luckily he wasn't there at the moment. "You must have been quite relieved when your employer went off like that and gave you a good reason to retire and take it easy."

"Not really." Doris sighed heavily. "Wouldn't you know it, the last one was the best employer I ever had. He was easy to please, paid more than a decent wage, and never interfered in the running of the household. Mr. Kettering was a right prince of a man. It's worked out fine for me, but at the time, I almost cried when he said he was going off."

"Oh dear, that's hard luck. Why did he go away? Did he emigrate?"

Doris rolled her eyes. "No, he went to America to study religion, of all the silly things. He didn't go to a university or anything like that; he left because he kept going on and on about some sort of 'religious revival movement' and he wanted to see what it was all about."

"Isn't it just the way. It's always the good ones that we end up losing." Mrs. Goodge chuckled. She saw Fred trot into the room and amble over to where Samson was sitting in front of the cooker. The two animals stared at one another and Mrs. Goodge silently prayed she wouldn't have to pull them apart if they decided to go at it. Doris was getting ready to talk and she didn't want her distracted by a fight between the two household pets. On the other hand, Mrs. Goodge wasn't going to let her beloved cat be bullied. The fur along Samson's back stood up and he got to his feet. Fred bared his teeth but didn't growl. Just as she was sure she'd have to intervene, Samson hissed, flicked his tail in Fred's face, and trotted off. The dog narrowed his eyes and immediately curled up in the very spot that the cat had just vacated.

"That's always the way it is," Doris agreed. "If he'd not left, I'd still be working for him, he was that decent a master."

"I know just what you mean." Mrs. Goodge poured another cup of tea for herself. "That's why I like working for the inspector; he treats us decently and never loses his temper, no matter how pressed he is on a case."

"Oh, Mr. Kettering could lose his temper," Doris said. "But never at us. He only got angry at that cousin of his, Olive Kettering."

"Olive Kettering," she repeated. "Now where have I heard that name before?"

"Maybe your inspector mentioned her name or perhaps you read about her in the newspapers." Doris leaned forward eagerly. "She was just murdered."

"Oh, my goodness." Mrs. Goodge pretended surprise.

"You're absolutely right. I believe the inspector did say something about it when he came home yesterday."

Doris' eyes widened. "Is he the one trying to solve her murder? Did he get that case?"

"Actually," she admitted, smiling hesitantly, "I don't really know. He usually mentions that sort of thing to Mrs. Jeffries, our housekeeper, but she's not the sort of person to pass along any tidbits she hears. She's a bit of a snob, if you know what I mean." She silently begged the housekeeper's pardon for telling such a bold-faced lie, but in the interests of justice, one had to bend the truth as one saw fit.

"I know exactly what you mean." Doris shook her head in agreement. "Just between us, I made it a point to be very friendly to the staff that worked under me. If I heard good gossip, I shared it with all of them. Now, back to Olive Kettering; frankly, I'm not surprised someone ended up killing her. She could drive a saint to drinking." She broke off and giggled. "That's what she did with Mr. Kettering. The only time he ever drank to excess was after she'd been to dinner, and the only time he ever raised his voice was when they were at the table together."

"They argued often?"

"Every time she came to supper. Mind you, when I first started working for him, their arguments were the kind that most families have—you know the sort I mean, they'd pick at each other but they seemed to genuinely enjoy one another's company. So it wasn't too bad. But that all changed about six months before Mr. Kettering went abroad. They started having terrible disagreements, and every time she came to the house, it seemed to get worse and worse. It was very nerve-wracking for the staff."

Mrs. Goodge pretended to be shocked. "What on earth did they fight about?"

"All manner of things." Doris took a sip of her tea. "Suddenly nothing he did seemed to please the woman. She nagged him about the way he lived his life, going on and on about how a man of his station had a duty to marry a suitable woman." She snorted. "This was ridiculous, really, because he was well into his fifties by then. And then she'd start in on him because of his religious beliefs."

"His religion." Mrs. Goodge clucked her tongue. "But surely that was his business."

"That's what he thought." Doris nodded quickly in agreement. "But Miss Kettering had joined some sort of strange religious group and she tried to get him to join as well. He went to one of their meetings and that only made matters worse. He told her she was being had by a charlatan and she ought to go back to a proper church. He said if she didn't like the Church of England there was the Church of Scotland or the Methodists, but she wouldn't hear of it. She said those churches were too soft on sinners and she'd not set foot in one of them. Those last few months before he went off were terrible. Every week she'd come to dinner and she'd start in on the poor man before the maid served the first course. By the time they got to the meat dish, they'd be going at it like fishwives."

"Why did he keep inviting her to his home if all they did was quarrel?"

"I used to wonder the same thing myself," she replied. "Neither of them had much family, you see, so even though they argued a lot, they were actually very fond of each other. Mind you, it didn't help matters any when their niece up and married a man that Miss Kettering didn't approve of and she cut the girl out of her life. He thought that was criminal and didn't mince any words when they talked about it. He told Miss Kettering that she wasn't being a very good Christian and that God was going to have some very harsh words for her when she finally faced him. Needless to say, that didn't set well with her. The last time she was over, she stormed out of the house in the middle of the meal and he was so furious, he didn't even see that she got safely into a hansom. That wasn't like him at all; first and foremost, Mr. Kettering is a gentleman."

"Did the niece marry beneath her? Was that why Miss Kettering cut her off?"

Doris shook her head. "That was what everyone thought, but that wasn't the reason. I overheard Mr. Kettering telling Mrs. Williams that the Camerons were a fine old family. The niece married a man named Angus Cameron. His branch had lost all their money, but he was well educated and certainly an acceptable husband. Olive Kettering disowned the girl because of his profession. He's an artist."

"What's wrong with that?" Mrs. Goodge frowned. "Artists are often poor, but it's a respectable calling." She wondered who Mrs. Williams might be.

"Not respectable enough for Miss Kettering," Doris replied. "But then again, I don't think anyone could measure up to her standards."

"Was this Mrs. Williams a friend of Miss Kettering?" She watched Doris closely as she asked the question. She didn't want to make her suspicious. But her companion simply reached for another biscuit.

"Oh no, Mrs. Williams is Mr. Kettering's friend. As far as I know she and Miss Kettering never even met."

*   *   *

"'The Society of the Humble Servant,'" Constable Barnes read from the small sign in the front window of the four-story brown brick town house on a small street off Goldhawk Road. "'All are welcome. Meetings Sundays at nine a.m. and Tuesdays at six p.m.'" He glanced at Witherspoon. "Odd sort of neighborhood for something like this, wouldn't you say, sir?"

"I would." The inspector frowned. "It's not an exclusive or luxurious neighborhood, but it's not poor, either. The houses are quite large and all of them along this street have good-sized front gardens. Usually one finds these sorts of strange religious societies in much more working-class districts."

"We're being watched, sir." Barnes flicked his gaze rapidly up and then back to the inspector. He grinned. "The curtains on the top floor just moved."

"Then perhaps we'd better go inside." Witherspoon stepped through the wooden gate and went up the walkway. Just as he reached the short flight of wide steps the front door opened, revealing a tall, dark-haired man wearing a black suit and a clerical collar.

"I'm the Reverend Samuel Richards," he said. "I've been expecting you. Please come inside." He stepped back and held the door open.

"Thank you, sir," the inspector said. "I'm Inspector Gerald Witherspoon and this is Constable Barnes."

The two policemen stepped inside the wide foyer, which was empty except for a coat tree and a plain brown umbrella stand. Directly ahead, there was a staircase and a long hallway. Richards moved to a set of double doors. "Let's go into the drawing room; we might as well be comfortable."

Witherspoon stopped inside the doorway. The room was massive. The top half of the walls was painted in a dull golden color and the lower half was paneled in a dark wood. Long muslin curtains in gold and green stripes hung from the windows and the wooden floor was bare of rugs or carpets. At the far end, a pale yellow upholstered settee and matching love seat were grouped in front of a fireplace, over which was a picture of the crucified Christ. At this end of the room, six rows of wooden straight-backed chairs were lined up facing forward toward a wooden podium and a piano. Books, probably hymnals, were on each chair. A white banner proclaiming "The Wages of Sin Is Death" in huge black letters was draped on the wall behind the podium.

Witherspoon didn't consider himself to be an overly devout person, but occasionally, after a particularly heinous case, he'd found his local parish church to be a most comforting place. The stained-glass windows, the polished stone floors, and the singing of the hymns had soothed his soul and reminded him of all the good in the world. But this was the most depressing place he'd ever seen. He couldn't imagine anyone getting spiritual comfort in this place.

"We use that area for our meetings," Richards explained, pointing toward the podium as he led them toward the other end of the room. "Please sit down and make yourselves comfortable." He swept his hand toward the settee. "Would you like tea?"

"No, thank you." The inspector unbuttoned his coat before taking a seat. The room was depressing and chilly. Barnes settled down at the other end of the settee. Richards sat down on the love seat.

"Then if I can't offer you my hospitality, let's get this over with." Richards sighed heavily.

"You know why we're here, sir," Witherspoon commented.

Richards closed his eyes for a moment. "Yes, we heard the horrible news. I still can't quite believe it. Poor Miss Kettering. She must have been utterly terrified. It's dreadful that an innocent woman isn't even safe in her own home. Our world has much to answer for when intruders can go about murdering at their will."

"What makes you think she was killed by an intruder?" Barnes pulled his notebook out of his pocket.

Richards drew back in surprise. "Who else would have killed her? Obviously it was some maniac. Olive Kettering was a most genteel lady; she certainly didn't consort with people who commit murder."

"She was killed in the middle of the morning, in the middle of a dreadful storm," Witherspoon said. "Most lunatics who commit this sort of crime do it at night when no one can see them. We think Miss Kettering knew her killer, that it was someone who felt comfortable coming onto her property."

Richards stared at the two policemen wordlessly for a moment, and then his expression turned to horror as he realized what the inspector had just said. "She knew her killer? Oh, my gracious, that's awful. You're saying that in the last moments of Miss Kettering's life, she wasn't just murdered, she was betrayed."

"Yes, sir," Witherspoon replied. Though he didn't really see that it made all that much difference. Betrayed or not, the poor woman was still dead. "That's precisely what we're saying."

"How long have you known Miss Kettering?" Barnes asked.

Richards seemed to get a hold of himself; his expression cleared and he leaned back against the cushions, crossing his arms over his chest. "I'm not sure of the exact date, but I think I first met her about two and a half years ago."

"How did you meet her?" Witherspoon asked. "Did she come here for one of your meetings?"

"That's correct," Richards replied. "She first came to us on a Sunday evening. After the meeting, she introduced herself and began coming quite regularly. In the past two years, she's become one of our most ardent supporters."

"Your meetings are religious in nature?" the inspector asked.

"Oh yes, that's one of the reasons Miss Kettering kept coming back." He smiled proudly. "We don't have formal services, of course, but we have lively discussions on the nature of good and evil, we read our Bible passages, and then we do communal prayer. We're a humble group, sir, just as our name implies. We let the spirit lead us."

"And you're an ordained clergyman?" Barnes asked.

"Of course. I completed my education at Borden Theological Seminary in Edmonton."

"Canada?"

"Yes, I was born there but I grew up both here and in Canada. My mother was English."

"When was the last time you saw Miss Kettering?" Witherspoon shifted position on the settee.

"Two days ago; I had dinner with her." He smiled sadly. "She was interested in funding some missionary work and wanted my opinion as to the best way to go about such an activity."

"I understand you had meetings at her house as well as here. Is that correct?"

He looked surprised by the question. "Yes, that's true."

"Yet you seem to have very good facilities here." Witherspoon looked pointedly toward the rows of straight-backed chairs on the other side of the room. He might find the place dismal and horrid, but it was clean and spacious.

"We do, but Miss Kettering wanted to open her home to us." He frowned slightly. "Actually, she insisted on having our meetings there."

"Do you know why?"

He hesitated. "One doesn't like to pass judgment, but in the past few months, she became increasingly anxious about leaving her home. She insisted we have the Tuesday meetings at her house. She didn't mind coming to the Sunday morning meetings, but she had developed an aversion to going out at night. She was convinced that something terrible was going to happen to her. She was terrified about going out—she was frightened of something evil; and apparently she was right to be concerned. The poor woman is dead."

"Did you ask her what—or, more importantly, who—had frightened her?" Witherspoon held his breath, hoping against hope that the woman had actually uttered a name. That would certainly make catching her killer much easier.

Richards shook his head. "She had no idea who was trying to hurt her, but she was convinced she was in danger. I'm ashamed to admit that I didn't take her seriously.

Honestly, the things that she complained about, they all seemed so silly. But I should have listened; I should have understood that she knew something evil was intent on harming her. Her death is on my conscience, Inspector, may God forgive me."

Witherspoon nodded sympathetically. "Silly in what way?"

"She claimed that there were people in the house, that they walked about at night and played tricks on her. I spoke to her servants myself, Inspector, and none of them heard or saw anything. But she must have known something was wrong, she must have sensed it, because someone murdered her."

"Someone murdered her because they hated her," a woman's voice said from the open doorway.

Barnes and Witherspoon turned.

She smiled at them. Her hair was black, parted in the middle and then swept up on her head in a wide topknot; her skin porcelain; her features perfect; and her eyes a startling shade of blue. She was, without doubt, the most beautiful woman that Witherspoon had ever seen. She wore a high-necked blue dress with a gray shawl around her shoulders. She was in a wheelchair.

The men got to their feet.

"Olga, you're supposed to be resting." Richards hurried across the room to her. "You know what the doctor said."

"Don't be absurd," she retorted. "There's no point in resting when one is wide awake. These policemen are here about *her*, aren't they?"

"We're investigating the death of Miss Olive Kettering," Witherspoon said, finally finding his tongue. "I take it you're acquainted with the lady?"

"Of course I am. I just said she was murdered because she was hated," she replied. "I would hardly make such a statement if I didn't know the woman. I'm Olga Richards, the reverend's wife."

"And who do you think might have hated Miss Kettering?" Barnes asked curiously.

She smiled maliciously. "Well, me for one. I loathed her."

Luty walked over to the mahogany sideboard and pulled the cork out of the bottle of fine old brandy she'd had sent up from the wine cellar. "You'll have another, won't you?" She smiled at her guest.

Edmund Slater grinned broadly. "I really shouldn't—after all, it's the middle of the afternoon—but it's so delicious, how can I resist?"

Luty glanced at the closed door of the drawing room and hoped that none of the servants would come snooping around. She'd worked hard to get Edmund here and she didn't want to be interrupted while she plied him with liquor and got him talking. She picked up the bottle and moved back toward her guest.

Slater was a financier and had been after some of Luty's investment business for years. That was how she'd managed to get him here today, by dropping a hint that she might have some business for him. More importantly, the tall, balding fellow was an awful gossip who knew everything there was to know about everyone who mattered in the City. He was also a heavy drinker.

"You shouldn't." She poured brandy into his glass and set the bottle down on the table. "Brandy this good is to be enjoyed at any time of the day."

He nodded in agreement and took a sip. "My Lord, this is wonderful," he said in a hushed voice.

Luty sat down in the wing-back chair opposite him and decided to make her move. "I'll bet you're wonderin' why I asked you to come by today. The truth of the matter is I'm thinkin' of investin' in a brewery and, bein' as you have some expertise in that kind of business, I was hoping you might be able to handle the business end of it if I decide to go ahead."

He blinked in surprise and sat up straighter. Luty tried not to smile at his reaction. Slater was no more an expert about the brewery business than the man in the moon, but she knew for a fact that he was acquainted with Olive Kettering. "Well, I do know a bit about that industry," he sputtered. "Are you thinking of acquiring shares in a brewery?"

"That was my idea." Luty leaned back. "And I thought of you because someone told me you handled the Kettering Brewery . . ."

"Oh dear." His long face fell in disappointment. "You've been misinformed. That's a completely private company; they don't sell shares at all."

"Are you sure?" she persisted.

"Positive," he replied. "The Kettering Brewery was and still is completely private. It was once owned by the Kettering family but they sold it years ago. I am well acquainted with the Kettering family."

"Maybe that's why everyone assumed you had something to do with their old business." Luty sighed heavily. "That's too bad. I had a hankerin' to buy me a brewery. During good times or bad, people will always want to liquor up."

"True," he agreed. "Pity, really, about the Ketterings. Even with all their wealth, they don't have much luck in life. You know that Olive Kettering—she was the heiress who inherited most of the money when the brewery was sold—was just murdered."

"You knew her?" Luty looked suitably impressed.

"I've met her a few times," he replied. "But I actually knew her cousin, Dorian Kettering, much better. We were at school together. He's a very nice sort of chap, very kindhearted."

"Kindhearted?" Luty picked up her own glass of brandy and took a small sip. She didn't like the taste but she wanted to keep Slater talking.

"Bit of a softie, really; the other boys used to tease him mercilessly but he took it well." Slater smiled in remembrance. "He was the sort of person who was always feeding stray cats and making certain the staff got their Christmas boxes."

Luty was disappointed but didn't let it show on her face. "So you haven't seen him since you were in school?"

"Oh no, we've stayed in touch. As a matter of fact, Dorian always comes to me when he needs a commercial or a business recommendation. I suggested he ask my brother-in-law to be the solicitor when his cousin, Miss Olive, the one who was just murdered, bought the Fox house on Brook Green."

That got her attention. She sat up. "The Fox house?" she repeated.

"That's right, the house that Olive Kettering owns was once owned by the Fox family of Hampshire," he replied. "At one time, there was a rumor that Dorian and one of the daughters in the family were to be engaged. But nothing ever came of it and Dorian never married."

"Was there a particular reason for your dislike of Miss Kettering?" Witherspoon asked.

"Olga, don't be ridiculous. You didn't hate Olive Kettering," Richards snapped.

He glared at his wife. But it had no effect on her; she merely laughed at his discomfort. "This isn't amusing; these men are policemen and they're investigating the woman's murder."

"I know why they're here." Her smile disappeared. "I intend to be completely truthful."

"You need to go upstairs and lie down." He put his hand on the back of her chair but she yanked the wheels and moved away from him. He started after her.

Witherspoon dashed across the room, managing to get between the irate husband and his spouse. Barnes was close at his heels.

Richards stopped in his tracks, an expression of shocked surprise on his face. "Really, Inspector, there's no need for you to leap about in such a manner—"

The inspector interrupted. "I'd like to hear what Mrs. Richards has to say," he said. His tone was calm but firm.

Richard stared at him for a long moment, gave a shrug, and went back to his seat. "My wife has a very odd sense of humor, Inspector. You really mustn't take everything she says seriously. She barely knew Olive Kettering."

"I certainly didn't know her as well as you did," Olga Richards shot back. "But then, you knew her very well indeed." She turned her attention to Witherspoon. "What do you want to know?"

"Why did you hate Olive Kettering?"

She looked amused. "Because she was a terrible person, Inspector. She was small-minded, mean-spirited, and petty. On top of that, she was trying to steal my husband."

"Olga!" Richards yelled. "Don't say such nonsense. Olive was a decent, Christian woman. You've no right to cast such aspersions on her character, especially as she's not here to defend herself."

"But you'll defend her, won't you?" she cried.

Barnes glanced at the inspector, who gave a barely perceptible shrug, indicating they might learn more by keeping silent and letting the Richards argument continue than by interrupting with a question.

Richards got up again and came toward them, stepping around the two policemen and heading toward his wife. "She was a member of my flock and always spoke highly of you. As I recall, she was very good to you, always sending over clothes and making sure you went to the doctor."

Witherspoon and Barnes moved closer to the wheelchair. The inspector didn't think Richards would get violent with his wife, but he knew it was a possibility. Some of his previous cases had proven that angry spouses could cause a substantial amount of damage to one another.

"Olive Kettering wasn't doing me any favors," she snarled. "She gave me the castoffs that she didn't want anymore and sent that quack of a medical man around so she could see how close I was to dying. She was in love with you and wanted me out of the way."

Richards balled his hands into fists. The two policemen moved to stand directly between Mrs. Richards and her husband. But their precautions weren't needed, as the good reverend took a deep breath, exhaled, and then smiled at his wife. "Olga, you know that isn't true. Miss Kettering was a good friend to both of us and I know that deep in your heart, you're very sad she's dead."

Amused, she laughed and then turned her attention to the inspector. "It's obvious I didn't like the woman, so I imagine you have some questions for me."

Witherspoon blinked in surprise. "Er, uh . . ."

"Where were you yesterday morning?" Barnes, who'd been a copper long enough to know when such a storm had passed, moved back to the settee, sat down, and picked up his notebook. He was more cynical than the inspector and didn't take her being in a wheelchair at face value. He'd once arrested a thief who strapped his calf to his thigh, pretending to be crippled, and then used his crutches to cosh innocent people over the head and steal their purses.

"I was here, Constable." She turned her head and addressed him directly.

"Can anyone verify you were here?" Witherspoon asked.

"Don't be ridiculous, Inspector." Richards frowned impatiently. "My wife shouldn't need to answer for her whereabouts. She's hardly capable of leaving the house, making her way across town, and committing murder."

"What about you, sir?" The inspector cocked his head to one side. "Where were you yesterday morning?"

"I was in my study working on a sermon," he replied. "I went in directly after breakfast and I didn't come out until Mrs. Malfrey called me for lunch."

"Mrs. Malfrey is your cook?" Barnes queried.

"And she's our housekeeper as well," Olga Richards

interjected. "We can't afford one of each. But we do have a maid. Considering the size of this house, it's not really enough staff, but as I said, it's all my husband can afford."

Barnes looked up from his notebook. "Can she verify that both of you were here that morning?"

"I don't know what time Olive Kettering was killed, but Mrs. Malfrey was late that day because of the storm. She didn't get here until almost noon." Olga Richards laughed. "Neither of us can prove we were here when she was killed."

"We're getting a late start this afternoon," Mrs. Jeffries warned as she took her place at the head of the table. "So we'd best get right to it."

"What about Phyllis?" Betsy tried to keep her voice casual. "Is she still here?"

"She left ten minutes ago." Mrs. Goodge poured herself a cup of tea. "And I gave her an errand to run before she comes tomorrow morning, so we'll have plenty of time for our morning meeting."

Betsy looked away. She knew she was being silly, but she didn't seem to be able to stop herself.

"Who would like to go first?" Mrs. Jeffries asked.

"I will," Luty volunteered. "I found out a few bits that might turn out to be useful." She told them about her meeting with Edmund Slater. When she'd finished, she helped herself to a slice of brown bread.

"So Bernadine Fox is a member of the family that used to own Olive Kettering's house?" Ruth said slowly.

"Edmund says she is, but truth to tell"—Luty shoved her knife into the butter pot—"I'm not sure he knew what he was sayin'. By the time we got to that part of the conversation, he'd had a lot to drink."

"Really, madam," Hatchet exclaimed. "I don't think pouring liquor down a man's throat to get information out of him is very nice—or, apparently, very effective."

"Fiddlesticks." She glared at her butler. "I didn't put a gun to his head and force him. I offered him hospitality and he took it. Besides, this is murder we're talkin' about here, so the social niceties don't apply."

"I agree with Luty," Wiggins added. "Like she said, she didn't force him to drink the stuff."

Mrs. Jeffries didn't want them sidetracked by a debate on what was or wasn't acceptable behavior in ferreting out information. She had a feeling they'd all violated generally accepted principles of good behavior when the occasion called for it. "I think we can assume that Mrs. Fox is somehow related to the family that used to own the house. It would certainly explain why Olive Kettering rented the carriage house flat to her, especially if the families have known one another for years. Who would like to go next?"

"I will," Ruth offered. "I didn't learn much more than we already knew." She hesitated. "And I'm very sorry to have to say this, but I'm not so sure her servants were all that innocent of stealing from her. I'm not saying they are guilty. Only that it's possible. But if they did take her things, it wasn't because they were thieves but only because they were so angry at her. My source told me that the staff disliked her so much that they played tricks on her, especially when they found out the poor woman was starting to hear things in the middle of the night."

"What kind of tricks?" Mrs. Jeffries asked.

"Nasty ones," she said. "If Miss Kettering had been harsh with the scullery maid, the girl wouldn't wash the vegetables properly, and when the upstairs maid was in a tiff, she'd shake the dust rags into Miss Kettering's clothes cupboard so she'd sneeze."

"Cor blimey, you must 'ave a right good source to find out that sort of details." Wiggins shook his head in admiration.

"My source is a relative of a woman from my group. Mavis came by earlier today to leave me some pamphlets for our next meeting. I happened to mention the Kettering murder and she told me that her cousin worked there until last month but she quit when she was offered a position in a dress shop. The girl lodges with Mavis and when she read about the murder in the newspapers, she confided that she was glad she'd left because of all the terrible things the staff did to Miss Kettering."

"She thinks the killer might be one of the servants?" Mrs. Jeffries clarified.

Ruth frowned thoughtfully. "I asked Mavis that specifically and she said her cousin was sure that none of them had actually done the deed, but the girl was of the opinion that if the police found out about the nasty tricks the staff was playing on their mistress, they might be tempted to lay the blame for the murder on one of them."

"If it were anyone but our inspector, she'd be right to be scared," Wiggins declared. "That's the sort of thing that Inspector Nivens would do in a heartbeat. Speakin' of him, I've not heard the inspector mention him recently. What's 'appened to the fellow? 'As he left the force?"

"No, more's the pity," Mrs. Jeffries replied. "But ever since our inspector kept silent about the way he'd withheld evidence on that case last year, he's been behaving himself."

"That won't last long," Smythe muttered. "Nivens is like a bad penny; he'll turn up and try stickin' his nose into our inspector's cases soon enough. Mark my words."

Inspector Nigel Nivens had been dogging their inspector for years, insinuating that Witherspoon had help on his cases and wasn't the brilliant detective everyone thought he was. The household disliked him intensely.

"Why don't you go next, Wiggins?" Mrs. Jeffries suggested to the footman. "Did you have much luck today?"

"I think so. I had a chat with Olive Kettering's scullery maid, Lila Perkins." Unlike Luty, who'd freely admitted she'd gotten her source drunk, Wiggins didn't tell them he'd plied the woman with gin. He was a bit ashamed of that part of it, despite what he'd told himself as he'd bought the woman those last two drinks. He told them everything he'd learned from Lila. When he'd finished, he turned to Ruth and said, "But Lila never mentioned they'd been playin' tricks on Miss Kettering."

"Maybe she didn't know the extent of the mischief," Ruth suggested. "And we don't know for certain that Mavis' cousin was talking about the entire Kettering staff. It might have just been one or two members of the household."

"That Reverend Richards sounds like he knows which side his bread is buttered on," Betsy observed. "Miss Kettering was worth more to him alive than dead."

"We don't know that," her husband argued. "We've not found out who inherits her money. She might 'ave left it all to the Society of the Humble Shepherd.'"

"Servant," the cook corrected. "But I don't understand why Richards would think that havin' his wife in a wheelchair would get him more contributions. It wouldn't make me open my purse any wider."

"But it would some people," Mrs. Jeffries said thoughtfully.

"And she's supposed to be a beautiful woman as well," Wiggins added. Lila had told him that as they left the pub. Her exact words didn't bear repeating, as she insisted that men tended to think with a certain part of their anatomy instead of their brains whenever they saw a pretty face. He'd turned red and he hoped he wasn't blushing now.

"A beautiful woman in a wheelchair would make a lot of men feel a bit more generous," Betsy murmured.

"Nonetheless, this Reverend Richards does sound like a confidence trickster," Hatchet said.

Mrs. Jeffries looked at the footman. "Are you finished?"

He nodded.

"I'll go next, then," Mrs. Goodge said quickly. "An old acquaintance of mine dropped by the kitchen today and I got a bit of information out of her." She told them about Doris Atherton's visit. "So you see, from what Doris told me, Dorian Kettering really isn't very interested in money, so I doubt that he'd have any reason to want his cousin dead," she concluded.

"But you just told us that your source claimed the only time he ever raised his voice was when he had Miss Kettering over to dinner," Wiggins pointed out.

"So maybe she wasn't murdered over her money but because she was such a mean woman and he was fed up with her."

"You don't kill people you're fed up with," Mrs. Goodge argued. "You stay away from them." She had no idea why she felt compelled to defend Dorian Kettering, but she'd found herself liking the man that Doris had described. She didn't want to think he was a killer.

"But they were family, so how could he cut her out of his life?" Betsy added. "After all, if he did that, he'd be no better than she was. You said yourself that Dorian Kettering was furious with her because of the way she treated their niece. That was the reason for their most vicious arguments."

"True," the cook admitted grudgingly, "but I think it's important that we establish the fact that a member of Dorian Kettering's former household believes he wasn't interested in her money. But nonetheless, I'll concede you've made some good points and there could have been other reasons he might want her dead. Anyway, that's all I've got."

"I didn't find out anything today," Smythe said quickly. He'd wasted half the day on a futile trip down to the docks; specifically, he'd gone to have a word with Blimpey Groggins, one of his prime sources when they were on the hunt. But Blimpey wasn't for hire this week; he was home nursing a bad cold and wasn't expected back to the pub for another three or four days. Smythe was going to have to do his snooping on his own and he was a bit downhearted over the matter. He wasn't as good as the others at getting people to talk. "But I've got some ideas for tomorrow and I'm determined to find out something useful."

"Of course you will." Betsy grabbed his hand under the table and gave it a squeeze.

"I didn't find out anything today, either." Hatchet shot Luty a sour look. "But I'll have something by tomorrow morning."

CHAPTER 5

Inspector Witherspoon sighed happily as he sank into his favorite chair. "I must say, this has been the most unusual case."

Mrs. Jeffries handed him a glass of Harvey's. "Most of your cases are unusual, sir." She took her own glass and sat down opposite him. "And you do an excellent job of solving all of them. Now, sir, what is odd about this particular one?"

Witherspoon took a quick sip of sherry before he replied. "Thus far, everyone we've interviewed has been, well, I'm not certain how to put it, but I suppose the best description would be that they've all been most peculiar individuals."

"In what way, sir?"

"The victim was a rich woman who was very much disliked by a number of people, including her own household staff," he explained. "Now, that, of course, is frequently to be expected when someone is murdered, at least with the cases that I seem to get, but the difference between most cases and this one is that thus far, almost everyone I've interviewed isn't in the least hesitant to tell me why they disliked Olive Kettering."

"I should think that might make solving the murder a bit easier," she suggested.

"It should, but it really hasn't." He frowned and put his glass down on the table next to his chair. "Everyone I've interviewed has been very candid about their feelings toward the victim, but that hasn't helped me find any hard evidence which points to the killer. I'm beginning to wonder if this is going to be the one that gets away from us."

"You mustn't say that, sir, it's still very early days," she said calmly. "You're always like this at the start of an investigation."

"Like what?" he demanded.

She had to be careful of how she answered here; she could tell he was a bit confused by the unexpected honesty of the suspects he'd spoken with thus far. She didn't want him worried because this case was going a bit differently from most of his others.

The inspector's confidence in his abilities as a homicide detective had grown enormously over the years, but he was still very prone to self-doubt. She considered it her duty to keep reminding him that he was a brilliant detective and that Rome, so to speak, wasn't built in a day. "Well, sir, it's as if you let your mind, or your 'inner voice' as I like to call it, go wandering off to gather information and see connections that are invisible to most of us. That's what you do at the beginning of all your cases, so, consequently, one part of you can't see that you're making any progress at all, but you are. That's why you've been so very successful as a detective, sir; you're clever enough to let your inner voice have its own way, and in return, you always solve even the most complex of cases. This one won't be any different, sir. You'll find out who murdered Olive Kettering."

Witherspoon stared at her for a long moment and she wondered if she'd laid it on a bit too thick. Then he smiled. "You give me too much credit, Mrs. Jeffries, but I daresay it does give one pause when one feels half of one's reason has gone off on a jaunt."

Relieved, she laughed and took a sip of sherry. "Now, what sort of odd interviews did you have today, sir?"

"Several of them. I interviewed Olive Kettering's niece and her husband." He told her about his visit to the Cameron household. "As I said before, he wasn't in the least bit shy about telling us how much he loathed his wife's aunt."

"But he was in a sick bed when she was killed, is that right?" she clarified.

"That's what he claims, but tomorrow we're going to have a quick word with the neighbors. I think it's a good idea to see if any of them have seen him out and about recently."

"That's very clever of you, sir. But Mrs. Cameron didn't hate her aunt; she only had a quarrel with her. I wonder if she was angry enough to threaten Miss Kettering."

"Constable Barnes asked her that specific question and she claims she didn't," he answered. "And to her credit, she seemed genuinely sorry that she'd lost her temper. But as we've seen before, people aren't always what they seem, and she could have been acting remorseful for my benefit."

"She'd accosted her aunt to ask for money," Mrs. Jeffries murmured. "From what you've said, she was desperate. Her husband is dying and Olive Kettering refused to help her."

"Put that way, it does sound like a motive for murder," he agreed. "But then again, after we left the Cameron residence, we went to see the Reverend and Mrs. Richards, and frankly, if it wasn't for the fact that Mrs. Richards is in a wheelchair, I'd say she had an equal motive for killing Miss Kettering."

"What kind of motive, sir?" Mrs. Jeffries was thinking fast. She had to come up with some way to let him know what Wiggins had told them today, that Olga Richards was no more crippled than the inspector himself.

"Jealousy." He took another sip from his glass. "I'll admit that jealousy isn't a motive that I understand particularly well, but as a policeman, I've seen what kind of rage the green-eyed monster can provoke, and believe me, Olga Richards was so jealous of Miss Kettering that she could barely contain herself. Which is odd, really, considering that Mrs. Richards is one of the most beautiful women I've ever seen and Miss Kettering was a rather elderly spinster lady—" He broke off and blushed. "I'm sorry, that was a terrible comment to make, but I didn't mean any disrespect to Miss Kettering—"

Mrs. Jeffries interrupted. "Of course not, sir, you were simply using a descriptive comparison to make your point. Do you know why Mrs. Richards is confined to a wheelchair?"

"No, I don't. I was curious, but I couldn't think of a

way to ask that sort of question without being rude," he replied.

"Well, whatever the poor woman's affliction, I'm sure she's not in that contraption because she wants to be," she murmured. "I do hope she hasn't come down with one of those awful illnesses that are more the making of the mind than an actual ailment."

"What do you mean?" he asked, his expression curious.

"You know, sir—it's like that time poor Mrs. Winston from up the street hurt her knee and she was confined to a wheelchair. By the time her knee healed, she was so frightened she'd trip or fall and hurt herself again, she convinced herself that she'd not got well at all. But the whole neighborhood knew she was perfectly capable of walking because her maid told us she saw her walking about in her room," she explained. As Mrs. Winston was safely dead and had no relatives lingering in the neighborhood, she felt quite safe telling this particular lie. "But as Mrs. Richards is a much younger woman than Mrs. Winston, I'm sure that isn't the case with her."

Smythe looked at his wife from across their parlor. She was sitting in her overstuffed blue and gray upholstered chair, her feet perched on a matching footstool and her head bent over her embroidery hoop. "You're awfully quiet tonight." He laid the *Illustrated London News* down on the table next to his chair. "Is something troublin' you?"

She raised her gaze to meet his. "I'm fine. Why do you ask?"

"Because I've been watchin' you ever since we came

home and I can tell you're upset. You've been workin' on that bit of embroidery for an hour now and you've not done more than ten stitches," he replied. "Now tell me what's botherin' ya and don't try tellin' me it's nothing. I know you too well, love."

She sighed and laid her hoop to one side. "I think Mrs. Jeffries and Mrs. Goodge are annoyed with me. They were a bit cool toward me at dinner."

His brows drew together in confusion. "Are ya serious, love?"

"Of course I'm serious." She stared at him reproachfully. "Didn't you see at dinner how both of them avoided looking at me?"

He'd no idea what she was talking about. "They treated you like they always do," he insisted. "You've done nothin' to offend either of them. Dinner was like it always is, everyone chattin' and havin' a nice time."

"I wasn't having a nice time," she insisted stubbornly. "How could I with the two of them acting like I had a bad smell?"

"Betsy, darlin', why would either of them want to hurt your feelings? They love ya. We're not blood, but we're family all the same."

"Family," she scoffed. "I suppose that's one way of looking at it. But it seems to me it isn't much of a family when they're just waiting to show you the door."

He gaped at her in disbelief. "Why would you say something like that? They'd never want to show you the door . . ."

"Maybe not right away, but we all know there isn't really enough work for more than one maid, and I don't need the job anymore, Phyllis does. It'll not be long before they ease me out so she can have my place." She felt her eyes flood with tears and blinked hard to hold them back. Even as the words left her mouth, she knew she was being silly and unreasonable, yet she couldn't seem to stop herself.

Taken aback, he wasn't sure what to say. He could tell by the expression on her face that she was dead serious. "Now why on earth would you think such a thing? There's plenty of work at Upper Edmonton Gardens for the both of you."

"You see!" she cried triumphantly. "You're admitting they're trying to give her my job."

"I'm admitting nothing," he shot back. "I'm just tryin' to tell ya there's enough work for the both of you. What have you got against Phyllis? Seems to me she's always tryin' to get on your good side so you'll be nicer to her. Just the other day I 'eard her offerin' to run your letters to the postbox and you just about snapped her head off. It's not like you to be so mean to someone, especially a poor girl who's just tryin' to earn a living."

"Poor girl," Betsy repeated as she jumped to her feet. "So now you're on her side."

"I'm on your side," he protested. He had no idea how what had started out as a husband's tender inquiry as to his wife's well-being had ended up in a shouting match. It wasn't like Betsy at all.

"No, you're not." She started for the door. "No one's on my side." With that, she stomped out of the room, slamming the door behind her.

Luty was so bored she could scream, but she kept a polite smile on her lips as she surveyed the dancers in the vast ballroom. She enjoyed a party as well as the next person, and if she'd come here tonight purely for social reasons, she'd be out on that dance floor kicking up her heels. But she'd come to get information, and so far she'd not found one person who wanted to talk about murder. Sometimes she didn't understand what in tarnation was wrong with some people.

"Luty, my goodness, what on earth are you doing here?" a woman's voice boomed out of the crowd.

Turning, Luty saw Alice Wittington charging toward her. Alice was a tall, portly woman with bright red hair piled on top of her head in complicated waves and curls. Diamonds hung from her earlobes, sparkled on her fingers, and were draped around her ample neck. She wore a beaded blue taffeta scoop-necked gown and held a glass of champagne in one hand.

"Howdy." Luty grinned broadly. She liked Alice. She didn't have her nose in the air and she treated others decently. "It's good to see you. I thought you were in Italy for the winter."

Alice waved her hand impatiently. "Oh, I was, but Edward kept having stomach problems because of all the garlic in the food, so we came home early. How are you? It's been ages since I've seen you."

"It has been a long while." Luty laughed. As she'd not had much luck tonight, she might as well be sociable and spend some time with her friend. "The last time I saw you was at the Huffington dinner party last summer. Now, that was a lively evening."

"Only because Edward started arguing politics with Lord Rivington. Honestly, that hidebound old fool makes anyone who disagrees with him sound as if they're one of those revolutionaries. But I don't think putting a legal limit on the number of hours a day that a man can be worked is all that radical, do you? Of course you don't; as I remember, you jumped into the fray on Edward's side of the argument. That was very brave of you, considering that by then everyone at our end of the table was accusing him of being a socialist."

Luty laughed and shook her head. "As I recall, your Edward held his own."

"He always does." Alice grinned, tossed back her champagne, and handed her empty glass to a passing waiter. "Have you eaten? The Palmers usually have a wonderful buffet."

"I haven't had a bite," Luty admitted. "And I am getting a bit peckish. I hope they have roast chicken."

"They'll have everything," Alice promised. "And after we've heaped our plates as high as we can, we'll go off and find a nice quiet corner so we can visit."

Five minutes later, the two women were sitting at the most secluded of the small round tables in the dining room. On the opposite wall, a long buffet table was loaded with food and drink. Waiters moved quietly between the tables, filling glasses and picking up dirty plates.

Luty moved a silver candlestick from the center of the table to the edge. "I like to look at people when I talk to 'em," she explained to Alice. "And these things just git in the way. Isn't it awful about that Kettering woman getting murdered?" She picked up her fork, speared a piece of chicken, and popped it into her mouth.

Alice nodded in agreement as she sliced through a piece of roast beef. "It is terrible, though in all honesty she wasn't a very nice person. Not that that justifies someone taking her life. Gracious, if everyone went about murdering all the disagreeable people in London, the city would be empty."

Luty swallowed her food. "You knew her?"

"We have—or had—mutual friends," Alice replied. "I'd met her on a number of social occasions and, as I said, she wasn't very personable."

"Was she rude?"

Alice's forehead creased in thought. "I wouldn't call her rude or impolite. She always observed the proper social etiquette. But she never smiled and she had a very sharp tongue. The woman had absolutely no sense of humor whatsoever, which I think is very sad. If one can't laugh in this life, one might as well give up the ghost. Oh dear, I should learn to watch my tongue; I suppose that's exactly what she's done."

"I wonder what had soured her so on life," Luty mused. "From the gossip I heard, she had plenty of money and her health was good."

"Who can say?" Alice shrugged. "Perhaps she'd been disappointed or betrayed in love when she was young. She certainly went through this world looking for the worst in everyone and everything. The only way she could keep servants was by paying more than the going rate, and she left her local parish church, St. Matthew's, because the vicar there insisted on using church funds to feed the poor rather than send Bibles to the Far East. No one was at all surprised when she joined that odd religious group."

"Odd religious group?" Luty repeated. She knew perfectly well what Alice referred to, but she was playing dumb. On their last case, it had been pointed out to her that a number of people in London had realized she was helping Witherspoon with his murders. She'd resolved to be more discreet.

Alice picked up her champagne glass. "It's the Society of the Humble or some such name."

"I've never heard of it." Luty forked a marinated mushroom. "Is it a real church?"

Alice laughed. "I don't know precisely what it is, but I do know that the man who runs it, the Reverend Richards, has made a career out of bilking unhappy middle-aged women out of their money."

"Really?" Luty's eyes widened. "My goodness, how'd ya find that out?"

She laughed. "Oh, I have my sources and, unlike most people in this town, I'm not ashamed to admit I love gossip. But that's neither here nor there. What I do know is that Samuel Richards is as handsome as the devil and charming to boot." She leaned closer. "Ten years ago, he ran another religious society, only it wasn't called the Society of the Humble, it was something else." She took a quick sip of champagne. "It wasn't here in London, either, it was in Manchester. There was a woman there name Adeline Franklin, and, like Olive Kettering, she was single, middle-aged, and rich. She suddenly had a heart attack and died. When the will was made public, it was found she'd left her entire estate, a considerable fortune, to Richards and his group."

"And I take it he's gone through that cash already," Luty suggested.

"Oh no, not at all." Alice shook her head. "He never got so much as a sixpence. Adeline Franklin had heirs— two nephews—and once they found they'd been disinherited, they took Richards to court and charged that he'd taken advantage of their aunt when she wasn't in her right mind. They won."

"Was Miss Franklin out of her head?" Luty asked bluntly.

"Probably not." Alice smiled wryly. "But let's face it, Luty, judges in this country are almost exclusively from the upper strata of society. They don't like it when money is left out of the family, so to speak. It sets a dangerous precedent and gives people ideas."

Luty laughed. "You mean it might make people think they can leave the money to whomever they damned well please."

"Precisely." Alice grinned broadly. "And the upper class will never let that happen, not in our lifetime."

"Should I start on the upstairs, then?" Phyllis asked Mrs. Jeffries. "The bedrooms all need to be done, especially the rugs. I noticed the one in the inspector's is a bit worse for wear . . . Do you think Wiggins can help me bring them down so I can give them a good beating?"

Mrs. Jeffries, who was sitting at the kitchen table working on the household accounts, put her pencil down. Her gaze flicked to Mrs. Goodge, who was measuring flour into a bowl, and then back to Phyllis. "Please do the upstairs, but don't bother with the rugs. I'd prefer we wait until the weather is a bit warmer. It takes ages to haul them down, and this time of year the weather is simply too unpredictable to risk it. Just when you're ready to take them outside it'll start to rain. But there's plenty to do up there. Clean the inspector's room first, then you can polish the wall sconces on the upper floors. There's a new tin of brass polish in the linen cupboard. After that, you can have a go at the cobwebs forming on the second- and third-floor ceilings."

"Yes, Mrs. Jeffries." Phyllis started to bob a curtsy,

then caught herself, giggled, and hurried off. In her previous household, she'd had to do a lot of bowing and scraping. Here, all she had to be was polite, but old habits were hard to break.

As soon as they heard her footsteps fading, Mrs. Goodge sighed and put the lid on her flour canister. "I hope you have a long list of tasks we can give the girl to keep her occupied; otherwise, she's going to realize that, except for us, she's the only one in the house."

"I know." Mrs. Jeffries reached for her pencil again. "I'm amazed she hasn't asked where everyone else has got to."

"She has asked." The cook put butter into the bowl. "She noticed that Betsy and Wiggins were both gone and asked me where they were. I told her you'd sent Wiggins out to run some household errands and that Betsy was out looking for new material for the dining room curtains. I said that you liked Betsy to do that sort of thing because she had a good eye for color and fabric."

"Oh dear, did she believe you?"

"I think so, but at some point, no matter how sensible our explanations sound, she's going to realize that everyone is gone right when the inspector has a case."

They'd had their morning meeting before Phyllis arrived. It had run longer than usual because they'd wasted time waiting for Luty and Hatchet, who it turned out weren't able to come because some friend of Luty's had shown up unexpectedly. Unfortunately, the messenger they'd sent to inform the others of their absence had gotten held up by traffic. Betsy, Wiggins, and Smythe had left moments after Phyllis stepped through the back door and into the kitchen.

"Perhaps it would be best if we told her the truth,"

Mrs. Jeffries mused. "You're right, sooner or later she's going to figure it out for herself."

"Let's discuss it with the others and see what they think. I've noticed she and Wiggins seem friendly. Maybe she's said something to him about the situation." She picked up a knife and began slashing her butter into small pieces.

"That's a good idea."

"Did you notice that Betsy's eyes were red and Smythe looked as if he'd lost his best friend? I do hope those two aren't having difficulties."

Mrs. Jeffries had noticed. She'd also noticed that despite Phyllis' cheery hello to Betsy, she'd barely gotten a nod in return. "They're probably just getting used to being a couple," she commented. "It's always difficult at the beginning of a marriage."

"I wouldn't know." Mrs. Goodge laughed and put her knife down. "The 'Mrs.' on my name is merely a courtesy title. But getting used to being married shouldn't cause Betsy to be so cold to poor Phyllis. She's barely civil to her."

"I have noticed, and honestly, I've no idea what's really causing her attitude. At some point, we're going to have to have a chat with her about it. It's not fair to Phyllis, especially as she's trying so hard to win Betsy over."

"I don't know what's got into Betsy. This isn't like her at all." Mrs. Goodge looked at the carriage clock on the sideboard. She didn't want to be rude, but she had a source coming by any moment now and she really wished Mrs. Jeffries would go upstairs to work on the accounts.

"Betsy is a kind and generous girl; I'm sure she'll

come to her senses on her own." Mrs. Jeffries closed her account book and got up. "But we may not have a choice. As you said, Phyllis needs her position, and when we're on a case, we need her help to keep the house up and running properly. Let's see how the next few days go and then we'll make a decision."

Mrs. Goodge raised her eyebrows. "You think we'll have it solved in a few days?"

"I'm hoping," Mrs. Jeffries said with a laugh. "I'll take the account books upstairs and then I'm going out myself."

"Going on the hunt?" She poured some cold water into the bowl.

"Of course. I like to get out and do my fair share as well." She grabbed the book and started for the back stairs. Samson hissed at her as she went past.

"You do more than your fair share," the cook muttered as she went back to her task.

Olive Kettering's solicitor, Harry Howard Johnston, was in an office on the ground floor of a building on Edgware Road in Paddington. A clerk ushered Witherspoon and Barnes into the solicitor's office.

Bookshelves filled with black-bound books and box files covered three of the four walls. Two uncomfortable-looking straight-backed chairs were in front of a huge mahogany desk, and a faded Oriental rug covered the floor. Pale light filtered in through long narrow windows that faced the street.

"I've been expecting you, Inspector." Harry Johnston, who was behind the desk, stood up to greet them. He was a tall, slender man with thinning gray hair, spectacles, and a huge mustache. "Please come in and sit down. We're all most upset by Miss Kettering's untimely death. She was a longtime client of this firm. I certainly hope you catch the maniac that murdered her. It's disgusting that someone can commit such a crime in broad daylight."

"We'll certainly do our best to catch the perpetrator," the inspector replied. "As I'm sure you're aware, I do have a number of questions for you. To begin with, are you the only person who handled Miss Kettering's legal affairs?"

"As far as I know, our firm handled everything for her." He waited until the two policemen were settled in the chairs and then sat down himself.

"And how long has she been a client?"

"Since she came to London," he replied. "She was originally from Yorkshire. She sold the family estate about fifteen years ago and bought her current residence. But we didn't act on her behalf in that matter; our firm was already representing the original owners, the Fox family."

Barnes took out his notebook. "So another firm handled the purchase of her house, is that correct?"

Johnston nodded. "Yes. When Miss Kettering came to London, it was Jeremiah Fox that recommended us to her. Apparently the two families were well acquainted with one another and at one time were even related. But that was years ago."

"Is Mrs. Bernadine Fox a member of that family?" Witherspoon asked.

"She is. She was taken in and raised by Jeremiah Fox when her parents died. As a matter of fact, the Kettering house used to belong to her branch of the family.

She married Jeremiah's oldest son when they came of age and she lived in the Fox family home in Hampshire until it was sold. She's known Olive Kettering since they were children. I expect that's why Olive let her rent the flat over the carriage house."

"Can you tell us who inherits Miss Kettering's estate?" Witherspoon shifted on the hard seat.

Johnston flipped open a brown file folder and pulled out the top sheet of paper. "It's very simple, Inspector. Except for a few bequests to some charities and two legacies, her estate was split into three equal parts. One third goes to her cousin, Dorian Kettering; one third goes to her niece, Patricia Kettering Cameron; and one third goes to the Reverend Samuel Richards so he can continue the work of the Society of the Humble Servant." Johnston's lip curled as he said the last word. "I must tell you, Inspector, I strongly advised her against leaving her money to Richards, but she insisted, and as she was of sound mind, I had no choice but to do as she directed. It was, after all, her money."

"Why did you give her such advice?" the inspector asked curiously. "If I may say so, from what I've heard of Olive Kettering, she wouldn't take kindly to being told what to do."

"She didn't." Johnston laughed. "But I know my duty and I knew I was taking a risk by giving her unasked-for advice. She didn't appreciate my efforts to protect her interests; as a matter of fact, she got so angry that she threatened to dispense with the services of our firm."

"Then why did you speak up?"

"Because Samuel Richards is a confidence trickster." His lips flattened into a thin line. "I tried to tell her, but she wouldn't listen. He's no more an ordained minister than I am. I wrote to that Bible college he claims he attended in Canada and they've never heard of him. But Miss Kettering refused to hear a word against him. So I tried a different approach and told her that if she wanted to leave her money to a religious institution, there were a number of legitimate and worthy enterprises that would put her legacy to good use."

"I see," Witherspoon said. "Mr. Johnston, we were told that Miss Kettering had disinherited her niece because she didn't approve of her marriage."

Johnston laughed again. "That's what she told Mrs. Cameron, but she never went through with it. Blood is thicker than water, Inspector, and despite her anger at Patricia, she couldn't bring herself to cut her off completely. She practically raised the girl. I know their estrangement broke her heart."

"Then why didn't she reconcile with her?" Barnes interjected. "Mrs. Cameron told us she invited her aunt to her wedding and made several other attempts to mend the trouble between them."

Johnston hesitated and then sighed. "Miss Kettering could be very stubborn, especially if she'd been, as she put it, betrayed. Look, I oughtn't to mention this, as Olive told me this in confidence, but she's dead so I don't think she'd mind all that much if I told you the real reason she kept her distance from Patricia. You know that Patricia married an artist?"

Witherspoon nodded. "We've interviewed both of them."

"What you probably didn't know is that the Camerons and the Ketterings used to be neighbors. They lived on adjoining estates and, years ago, Olive Kettering was engaged to Patrick Cameron, Angus' uncle. Like Angus, Patrick was an artist as well. Supposedly, he did a painting of Olive and, well, let's just say she was shocked when she saw how he'd portrayed her. She demanded he destroy the work, he refused, and the engagement was broken off. Her family attempted to buy the painting but by then Patrick and the painting had departed for parts unknown. Shortly after that, the Camerons sold out and moved to Edinburgh. But that's the real reason she was upset over Patricia's marriage to Angus."

"I can't say that I blame her," Barnes muttered. "But did she ever tell her niece why she was so opposed to her marrying into that family?"

Johnston shook his head. "I tried to get her to discuss it with Patricia, but she claimed she didn't have to explain her actions to anyone. In truth, Constable, I think she was too embarrassed to tell the whole truth. But that's all water under the bridge, as they say. As it stands now, Patricia Kettering Cameron will be a rich woman."

"How much is a third of the estate worth?" Witherspoon asked.

Johnston glanced down at the paper on his desk. "Including property, stock shared, and cash in the bank, she's going to inherit over half a million pounds, as will Dorian Kettering and Samuel Richards."

The inspector pushed his spectacles up his nose. "She owned property other than her current residence?"

"She owns a number of commercial buildings in the city. I'm under instructions to sell all the property except for the house and add the proceeds to the estate before it's split."

"Why aren't you selling the house as well?" the inspector asked.

"The house is going directly to the Society of the Humble Servant." Johnston sniffed disapprovingly. "That's part of Richard's share of the estate. He gets less cash than the others but he gets the house. It was Miss Kettering's wish that the society would move its premises to her home. But I imagine now that Richards has got his hands on the property, he'll sell it faster than you can blink your eye. He only uses the society to bilk frightened people out of their hard-earned money."

"What about Mrs. Fox?" Barnes asked. "Was she mentioned in Miss Kettering's will?"

"She gets one of the legacies, but it's only a few hundred pounds a year," he explained. "She'll be devastated when she finds out she's got to leave. Olive told me that Mrs. Fox was thrilled to be able to come back and live on her childhood property."

"Who gets the other legacy?"

"The other legacy goes to her housekeeper, Maura McAllister."

The café in Chelsea was filled with workingmen, shop assistants, clerks, and day laborers having their morning tea. Wiggins made his way to the narrow table by the window and put the plate of buns down in front of the young lad.

"This is nice." Adam Bentley licked his lips. "I've been here before."

"'Ave you, now?" Wiggins sat down.

"When my brother come home from the army, he brought me here. But all we had was tea."

"'Elp yourself." Wiggins nodded at the plate of buns. Adam had brown hair and eyes, a pale narrow face with a few red spots on his cheeks, and a frame as thin as a train rail. Wiggins had seen him coming out the servants' entrance of the house where Dorian Kettering rented rooms. Coming up with a story to get the lad here had been easy. "You're the one doin' me a favor. If I don't figure out who I was supposed to give this note to, I'm goin' to get the sack." Looking grave, he pulled an envelope out of his jacket pocket and then, as soon as Adam saw it, he shoved it back inside. "But I can't for the life of me remember the name my guv told me when he sent me here. Thank goodness I found you."

"I forget names sometimes, too." Adam helped himself to a sticky bun. "But Mrs. Dearborn claims it's not so much forgettin' names as it is I don't listen properly." He stuffed it into his mouth and chewed hungrily.

"My guv says that about me, too." Wiggins grinned and reached for his teacup. "But I do remember them talkin' about how the fellow was a single man."

"All the men living at the lodging house are single." Adam swallowed and frowned. "Mrs. Slater won't rent to married men or to ladies. She claims they're too much trouble."

"Which ones, married men or ladies?"

Adam laughed. "Both I guess." He started to reach for another pastry and then stopped and looked at Wiggins.

"Go on, 'elp yourself. Like I said, you're the one doin' me a kindness." Wiggins had the feeling the boy would tell him anything as long as he was getting food. He suspected this Mrs. Slater wasn't overly generous with the rations for the help. "'Ow long 'ave you worked at the lodging 'ouse?"

"Two years, since I was twelve." Adam helped himself to another bun. "But I'll not be there much longer. My brother is getting out of the army next month and we're going to America."

"Won't your brother have to serve his reserve time?" Wiggins asked, referring to the six-year standard reserve time of a twelve-year enlistment. He asked the question to make sure the lad wasn't just telling tales or making things up as he went along.

"He would normally, but he's being discharged because there's something wrong with his chest. That's why when Dick comes home, we're goin' to America, to California. It's warm and dry there and that's what the doctors say that Dick needs."

"California's a long way off," Wiggins muttered. He couldn't tell if the boy was being truthful or whether he was clever enough to come up with the right answers.

"We've got an uncle that lives there," Adam replied. "And the voyage out will take a long time. It'll give Dick a chance to get his strength back. He's already bought the tickets."

"Warm weather would be nice, wouldn't it?" Wiggins nodded. "You was sayin' all the men that live at the lodging house are single?"

"That's right. Mrs. Slater claims it's a posh lodging house so she can be choosy about her tenants."

"How many tenants are there?"

"Four. There's Mr. Jones and Mr. Kettering—they've got rooms on the second floor—and Mr. Grimaldi and Mr. Rees, who are on the third floor. Do you know what your fellow looks like?"

"I've never seen him." Wiggins frowned and crossed his arms over his chest. "But I do recall the guv tellin' his friend that the man was out in that storm we had a couple of days back."

Adam scratched the tip of his nose. "Mr. Grimaldi has been in Bristol on business ever since last week and Mr. Jones was at his office that morning. So it must have been Mr. Kettering or Mr. Rees. They're the only two that don't go out to work regularly."

"Kettering, Kettering," Wiggins repeated. "That name sound familiar. I'll bet that's the man."

"Mr. Kettering is a nice gentleman." Adam took a quick slurp of tea. "He reads a lot. I know because I help him lug books up and down the stairs and I take messages for him. He pays well."

"What kind of messages?"

Adam shrugged. "You know, like to the telegraph office or notes he wants delivered. He sends me to Brook Green a lot. He's got a relation that lives there." He broke off and made a face. "She's not so nice, though. Last summer no one answered when I knocked on the front door so I went around to the back and I accidentally tripped and fell into a flower bed. This woman come runnin' out of the back house, screamin' and shoutin' at me like I'd done it on purpose. I tried to explain that I had a note for the mistress, but she was so angry she slapped it out of my hand." He looked down at the tabletop. "She scared me so bad I dropped it and I run off."

"Did you tell Mr. Kettering what happened?" Wiggins asked softly. He could see the boy was embarrassed.

"'Course I did," Adam declared. "And I tried to give him his money back as well but he wouldn't take it. He just smiled at me and said he was sorry that I'd had the misfortune to meet his cousin in such a manner."

* * *

Smythe rounded the corner and walked toward the hansom cab stand down the road from the Shepherd's Bush railway station. His pockets had plenty of coin and he was determined to find out something useful to add to their case. It would help keep his mind off Betsy.

He slowed his steps as the memory of the previous night's argument came into his mind. He didn't understand what had upset her so much. One moment, she'd been right as rain, and the next, she was hissing like an angry cat. He didn't understand what he'd done. He'd hoped that a good night's sleep would smooth things over between them, but this morning she'd been in an even worse mood. There were dark circles under her eyes, as if she'd not slept, and she'd obviously lost her appetite because she'd barely touched her breakfast. He'd no idea what to do next. This wasn't like his Betsy. To top it off, when they'd gotten to Upper Edmonton Gardens, she'd barely spoken to Phyllis and he'd been too afraid to do much other than give the poor girl a fleeting smile.

He stopped when he reached the small wooden structure where the drivers took their breaks and brewed tea. Two rigs were tethered to the post by the road. One of the horses, a big bay, gave a snort as if to say he was wasting his time. His spirits lifted and he patted the animal's nose and then gave a short, sharp knock on the door frame before pulling the tarp to one side and stepping into the shed.

There were two drivers inside, both of them holding mugs of tea. They stared at him in surprise.

"Sorry to burst in on you gentlemen, but it's important I speak with you," Smythe said. "I know you're busy but I need some information. I'm prepared to pay you for yer time."

"What kind of information?" The driver closest to him, a burly man with a handlebar mustache, asked.

"My employer left a packet of letters in a rig and it's urgent I find 'em."

"Where was your guv picked up?" the second driver asked.

"It's a lady and she was picked up near Brook Green."

"When did this happen?" the one with the mustache asked and took a sip from his mug.

"That morning we had the bad storm."

"Not in my rig," he replied with a shake of his head. "I wasn't even working that morning. The weather was so bad I didn't bother to take it out until the rain had let up."

"Nor mine," the other man added. "Sorry, but much as I'd like to earn a bit of extra coin, I can't help ya."

"Was anyone else working around the area?" Smythe asked. Blast a Spaniard, he shouldn't have blurted out a specific question. He should have been a bit more vague.

"Mickey Leadbetter was working," the second driver said. "And Tom Duggan. Another bloke was in as well, but I don't know his name. But none of us picked up many fares that morning; it was too miserable out and half the roads were flooded. I ain't heard of anyone finding any letters."

"Where could I find Leadbetter and Duggan?" he pressed.

The clean-shaven man put his mug down on the small rickety table. "Your best bet would be to come back later this afternoon. Leadbetter and Duggan both come in around three."

"Or you can try the Dragon's Head Pub," the other one added. "They usually stop in there for a pint at lunchtime."

CHAPTER 6

"Good day, Inspector, Constable." Dorian Kettering nodded politely at the two policemen as he came into the drawing room of his lodging house. "Mrs. Slater says you wish to speak with me. This isn't a very convenient time. I must leave soon to meet with the vicar. Mrs. Cameron and I are going over the details for Olive's funeral. It's tomorrow morning."

"Would that be the Reverend Samuel Richards you'd be meeting with?" the inspector asked.

"Hardly, sir." Kettering didn't bother to mask his contempt. "The Society of the Humble Servant will not be involved with my cousin's funeral. She'll be buried properly in St. Matthew's churchyard."

"Are you inviting them to the funeral?" Barnes asked. He studied Kettering's face as he posed the question, hoping to see a reaction. They'd come here after learning that, unlike what Kettering had implied when the inspector first interviewed him, he was enough in Olive Kettering's good graces to still be in the will. Samuel Richards was an heir as well, and in the constable's experience, it wasn't impossible that heirs would join in a conspiracy to murder the victim. But the way Kettering's lip curled at the mention of the fellow's name would be hard to fake.

"I'm hoping that awful man and his wife have the decency to stay away from her services altogether, but I can hardly stop them from coming into the church," Kettering declared. "They won't, however, be invited to the reception. Now, as I said, I'm in a bit of a hurry."

"We'll be as brief as possible, sir," Witherspoon said. "May we sit down?" Both policemen had risen from their seats when Kettering entered the room.

"Of course, Inspector, I'm sorry, please make yourselves comfortable." He sat down in a balloon-back chair across from them. "Now, what can I do for you?"

"Mr. Kettering, are you aware that you're one of Miss Kettering's heirs?" Witherspoon watched him carefully as he asked the question. He wasn't particularly skilled at reading expressions, but he thought it worthwhile at least to try to ascertain if the man was surprised by the news.

Kettering's face didn't change. He shrugged. "I'm a bit surprised. As I mentioned when we first spoke, Olive and I weren't on good terms. Since I returned from abroad, we've had a number of rather heated arguments. She certainly led me to believe she'd cut both Patrica and me out of her estate. The truth is, it was impossible to know who was in or out of her will. She was always changing it."

"According to her solicitor, she's only made one change in years," Barnes said.

"And I've no doubt that I can easily guess what change that was." Kettering pursed his lips.

Just then, the drawing room door opened and the middle-aged woman who'd let Witherspoon and Barnes into the house swept into the room. Bernadine Fox was right behind her. "Mr. Kettering, you've a guest," she said. "I told her you were indisposed, but she insisted on seeing you."

"Of course I did," Bernadine Fox said irritably. "We're old friends." She deftly stepped around Mrs. Slater and moved toward the settee.

Witherspoon stared at her. She seemed much younger today than when he'd first met her. The dress she wore was a bright, vibrant blue that highlighted the color of her eyes, and the cut was different, conforming more tightly to her person and giving her an altogether more pleasing silhouette. He was no expert on women's hair, but today's style was looser, with curls dangling prettily around her temples and waves framing her face. Her hat was a simple bonnet in a darker blue with a veil that trailed halfway down her back.

All three men rose to their feet. Mrs. Slater gave them a sour look and withdrew, closing the heavy double doors behind her.

"Bernadine." Kettering came toward her with his hands outstretched. "How nice of you to come for a visit. But you shouldn't have ventured out in this miserable cold."

"It's not cold at all, it's bracing and it does me good to get out and about." She grabbed his hands and together they sank down to the couch. "And of course I'd come. I know that you're planning Olive's funeral and it must be dreadful for you."

"Patricia is helping me." Kettering released her fingers. "So it hasn't been too awful."

"Patricia?" She drew back in surprise. "Gracious, I'm amazed she's willing to do anything after the way Olive treated her."

"Bernadine, surely you don't mean that," he chided her gently. "Despite their differences, they were once very close."

"I'm only speaking the truth." She smiled to take the sting out of her words. "Olive was very harsh with Patricia. I saw them having a terrible argument on Brook Green just a day or two before the murder. Olive stomped off in a rage and Patricia followed her all the way to the house, pleading and crying and demanding that she help her. But Olive wouldn't so much as look at her. She simply went inside and slammed the door in her niece's face. It was terrible, Dorian, absolutely terrible."

"Where were you when this was happening?" Witherspoon asked softly.

"I was coming from my dressmaker's and I'd started across the green when I saw Patricia—Mrs. Cameron—accosting Miss Kettering. I stayed a little ways behind them and then I ducked behind a tree so Patricia wouldn't see me after Olive went inside. Mrs. Cameron would have been embarrassed if she'd realized someone had witnessed the incident."

Witherspoon wasn't sure what to ask next. Patricia Cameron's version of this incident had been decidedly different.

Mrs. Fox turned her attention back to Kettering. "What other arrangements have been made?"

"I'm meeting with the vicar in a bit to pick out the hymns and set the time—"

"What about the reception?" she interrupted. "That's going to be the difficult one to manage."

"I've spoken with Mrs. McAllister and we'll have the reception at the house."

"But what about the food?" Mrs. Fox frowned. "The house has no cook."

"Mrs. McAllister has obtained a suitable cook from an agency, so it should be fine."

"Is Patricia acting as hostess?" she asked. "Or do you need me to do it?"

"Patricia will," he replied. "She's been very good and she is genuinely upset by her aunt's death." He glanced at the two policemen as he made the last statement and then cut his gaze back to Mrs. Fox. "But it was very good of you to offer. I was going to come around to the carriage house this evening and tell you the plans, but as you're here, you've saved me a trip."

"Nonsense, you must still come over, we'll have dinner together. My girl is quite an adequate cook." She fixed her gaze on Witherspoon. "I do hope you're quite finished with Dorian. He has quite enough to contend with now and you ought to be out finding the maniac that murdered Olive."

"Bernadine, that's alright." Dorian gave them an embarrassed smile. "They're only doing their job."

"I assure you, Mrs. Fox, we're doing our very best to catch the person who committed this horrible crime," Barnes said.

"We're almost finished," Witherspoon commented.

"We were telling Mr. Kettering what we'd learned about the disposition of Miss Kettering's estate."

"Oh, Dorian, how awful for you. I'm sure she didn't mean to disinherit you and I know she loved you. She loved both you and Patricia; you were all the family she had in the world. I'm sure you can both contest the will." She reached over and patted his hand. "Olive really wasn't in her right mind. I can testify to that, so you should speak to the solicitor immediately."

"That's kind of you to say, Bernadine, but I'm fine. My circumstances are modest but so are my wants and needs." He smiled awkwardly. "There was nothing wrong with Olive's mind and she has a perfect right to dispose of her estate in any way she sees fit."

"But she wasn't in her right mind," Bernadine insisted. "She was seeing things and hearing things that simply weren't there. All of the servants have been complaining for months of how oddly she's behaved."

"Mr. Kettering hasn't been disinherited," Witherspoon interjected. "He gets a third of the estate and Mrs. Cameron gets a third as well. Miss Kettering never followed through on her threats to leave her family out."

Mrs. Fox turned to look at Witherspoon. "Are you certain of that, Inspector?"

"According to Mr. Johnston, Miss Kettering's solicitor, except for a few minor bequests, one of which goes to you," he replied, "the estate is evenly divided into thirds. One third for Mr. Dorian Kettering, one third for Mrs. Cameron, and one third for the Reverend Samuel Richards and the Society of the Humble Servant."

"The Society of the Humble Servant," she snorted in derision. "They oughtn't to get so much as a penny.

Dorian and Patricia still ought to go to court. He's no right to her money."

"It's not just the money he's getting," Witherspoon added. "His share of the estate includes the house."

Betsy had never felt less like smiling in her entire life. She stood outside Bramley's Fine Furnishings and Fabrics and wondered what on earth had happened to her. Only a few days ago, she'd been as fit as a fiddle. Oh, she'd been a bit put out by Phyllis and her eager puppy-dog manner—all that bowing and scraping the girl did got on her nerves—but she'd been nice and polite.

But since they'd gotten this new case, she felt as if a stranger with the world's nastiest disposition had taken over her character.

She'd been mean to her husband, ignored Phyllis' greeting, snapped at Wiggins, and generally been a right little madam to everyone. Tears sprang into her eyes, but she blinked them back. Crying wasn't going to help, even though at the moment she wanted to weep buckets and she was so hungry she could eat a horse.

Enough, she told herself firmly. There was work to be done, and if she was going to do her fair share, she'd have to put her own misery aside and do what she'd come here to do. She took a deep breath, grabbed the handle of the draper's shop, and stepped inside. The place was empty, so she stopped just inside the doorway. The young clerk behind the counter looked at her and she gave him her best smile. She wasn't just here to pry a bit of information out of the lad, she was actually going to buy something for her own home.

"May I help you, ma'am?" the clerk inquired.

Betsy swallowed. She'd never done this before. Growing up, her family had lived in places that came with a few sticks of furniture and, most of the time, there hadn't been curtains in the places she'd lived. But she'd gone with Mrs. Jeffries to buy household items for Upper Edmonton Gardens and so she straightened her spine, lifted her chin, and said, "I'd like to buy some curtains, please. They're for a bedroom."

"Of course, madam." He smiled eagerly and came out from behind the counter. "If you'll follow me, I'll show you the materials we have available. Is there any particular fabric you'd like?"

"A lightweight material would be best; it's for one of the smaller bedrooms," she replied. He hurried across the wide room toward a round table and chairs on the far side. Behind the table, rolls of cloth were mounted on the wall. Betsy followed him. She was surprised that this was suddenly so very easy. But perhaps that was what having a handbag full of money could do for you.

"Is there a particular color you wish to see?" He pulled out a chair for her.

Betsy sat down. Her mind was working furiously, trying to come up with a way to get him headed down the path she wished to go. Perhaps she shouldn't have spent so much time pitying herself and a bit more preparing a reasonable story. "I saw a lovely set of drapes in a house very near here. As a matter of fact, that's why I came. The mistress of the house said she'd found the fabric in this very shop. I'd love to find material of the same color."

"Of course, madam." He smiled graciously and then gestured toward the bolts of cloth. "What color is it? Do you see it here?"

She took her time and pretended to study the fabric.

"No, I don't, but I'm sure this shop did the curtains so you must have it. I believe it was a pale coral fabric."

"Perhaps it would help if you told me where you saw the curtains," he suggested.

"Oh dear, this is awkward. They were in Miss Olive Kettering's morning room and now that the poor woman has been murdered, I feel awful even mentioning the subject." She started to get up.

The clerk, frightened of losing a sale, waved her back to her seat. "Don't be upset, madam, life does go on and you do need curtains. But honestly, Miss Kettering isn't one of our customers."

"But I was sure that's where I saw them," she protested. Drat, now she'd have to start over somewhere else.

"Are you certain you didn't see the curtains in Mrs. Fox's flat?" he countered. "We did make some lovely ones for her drawing room; they were an elegant blue and cream striped silk."

"My gracious." Betsy closed her eyes and shook her head. "I'm such a silly ninny. Of course it was those lovely blue and cream ones I adored, not the coral. How could I have made such a mistake! Thank goodness you've such a wonderful memory."

He beamed proudly. "That's quite alright, madam, we all get confused at one time or another."

"You're too kind and you're obviously very intelligent if you can recall all the names of your customers off the top of your head." She smiled flirtatiously and didn't feel in the least bit guilty about it.

"Thank you, madam." He blushed with pleasure. "But Mrs. Fox is one of our best clients. She comes in frequently. Is she a friend of yours?"

"Not really," Betsy admitted. She was glad she'd worn the expensive cloak that Smythe had bought her for Christmas. Apparently the man hadn't noticed she was wearing that most telltale item of servant's clothing, her lavender broadcloth skirt. She reached under the table and made sure the edges of her cloak covered it completely. "I don't know her very well at all. But I had tea there and noticed how lovely the drawing room was furnished. Has she been coming here long?"

"She's been a client for about five years." He went over to the bolts on the wall and pulled down a roll of dark blue cotton. "Is this the sort of color you had in mind? It's a bit darker than what we did for Mrs. Fox, but very much in the same shade."

"I'd like something a bit lighter," Betsy replied. "Mrs. Fox must redecorate quite often, then."

He nodded and went to a set of drawers built into the wall next to the fabric bolts. "She gives us a substantial amount of business." He glanced over his shoulder and then looked at Betsy. "That's one of the reasons we put up with some of her antics."

Betsy glanced in the direction he'd just looked toward and noticed a closed door leading to the back of the shop. She realized he loved to chat but was worried about being caught by his boss. She gave him another bright smile. "Oh, do tell. What kind of antics?" she whispered.

"Mrs. Fox is very difficult to please. Mind you, lots of our clients are particular and there's nothing wrong with that," he assured her. "But Mrs. Fox likes old-fashioned materials. Those curtains you liked, she made us copy an old set of drawing room drapes that have been out of fashion for ages. She came in with a bit of cloth that must have been forty years old. We had to send all the way to Paris to get the fabric and it took forever. On top of that, when we went to hang them, they were too big for the windows in the carriage house. Turns out she'd given us measurements for full-sized windows, you know, like the sort one would find in a drawing room. It took forever to keep pinning the wretched things so they'd fit."

"Why didn't you just bring them back here and cut them down to size?" she asked.

"That's precisely what I suggested we do." He sniffed disapprovingly. "But Mrs. Fox was adamant we hang them that day." He pulled out a drawer, reached in and yanked out a bound volume, and brought it to the table. "I've got some samples here. We ought to be able to find just the perfect shade of blue for your curtains." Using his index finger, he flipped the book open at the half-way point. Small squares of material, all in gorgeous shades of blue and many in intricate woven patterns, were pasted onto the heavy paper. "Not all of these are lightweight materials, just the two bottom rows."

"They're beautiful," Betsy gasped. For a brief moment, she forgot she was here to get information. All she could think of was how lovely the fabric was and how wonderful any of them would look in her flat.

"They're very expensive, but very much worth the price," he commented.

"Price isn't important," she muttered. She caught herself as the words passed her lips, stunning her because she'd never uttered such a sentence in her life. The fact that it was true didn't lessen the shock to her system and brought her firmly back to the task at hand. "But of course I don't want to be overly extravagant. My husband expects me to be a prudent manager. Was Mrs. Fox's husband upset with her?"

He blinked at the sudden change in subject, then his expression brightened. "She's a widow and, judging from the way she spends, she's got plenty of money. We never had a problem getting her to pay her bills. When she wanted a particular fabric, it didn't seem to matter to her how much it cost." Again he glanced toward the closed door. "She came in two weeks ago and ordered some lace table runners. It's such an old pattern that we're sending to Belgium to have them specially made."

"But you can buy lace table runners anywhere," Betsy said. She was beginning to suspect she was wasting her time. All she'd learned so far was that Bernadine Fox liked old-fashioned fabric. Too bad this shop hadn't made the drapes or the linens for the Kettering house. But the day wasn't a total waste of time; she had found the right material for her curtains. She glanced down at a lovely cornflower blue silk on the bottom row. The fabric would go perfectly with the white chenille bedspread and the lace doilies in the back bedroom.

"True, but she was adamant about what she wanted—and willing to pay for them. She wasn't even upset when Mr. Bramley—he's the one who always serves her when she comes into the shop—pointed out that it might take up to three months to get the runners here."

Betsy smiled politely. "I believe I've found my fabric." She reached into the pocket of her cloak, pulled out a folded piece of paper, and handed it to him. "Here are the measurements. I'll need two sets of curtains. How long will it take to get them made?"

He took the paper from her hand. "We can have them for you this time next week. Will that do?"

"That will be fine." She smiled and got to her feet. "Do you require a deposit?"

"We do, ma'am," he replied. "If you'll step up to the counter, I'll do the invoice."

She nodded and followed him back to the front of the shop. She hoped this wouldn't take too long. If she hurried, she still had time to get to the fishmonger's and the greengrocer's.

The small office at the far end of the casualty ward smelled of carbolic soap and disinfectant. Mrs. Jeffries stood across from the matron's desk and kept her smile firmly in place, despite her disappointment.

"An appointment would have been best; it would have saved you the trouble of coming," the matron chided gently. "When Dr. Bosworth returns from Scotland, I'll let him know you were here. Perhaps there's someone else who can help you. We have many fine doctors on staff."

Mrs. Jeffries had come to St. Thomas' Hospital in the hope of seeing the household's good friend Dr. Bosworth. He'd helped them on many of the inspector's cases. He'd studied and worked in America for a number of years and had some interesting and, to her mind, very accurate views about corpses. Apparently he'd had many opportunities to study them, as there had been a rather large supply on hand when he'd been in San Francisco. Bosworth maintained that a thorough study of death wounds could elicit an enormous amount of information if interpreted correctly. If he could manage to get a look at a victim's body or even to read the post-mortem report, he could often determine what kind of murder weapon had been used in the killing.

Bosworth's views weren't widely accepted, but they were based on precise observations and that was good enough for Mrs. Jeffries. He'd been proved correct many times in the past, and right now Mrs. Jeffries was so muddled about this case, she'd take any help she could get.

"It's not a medical problem," she replied quickly. "Dr. Bosworth is a family friend and I simply stopped in on the off chance that he would be available. But do tell him I was here. My name is Mrs. Jeffries."

The matron inclined her head and then quickly got to her feet, her gaze moving to the doorway. "Dr. Pendleton, may I help you?"

Mrs. Jeffries turned to see a short, chubby fellow with black hair standing in the doorway. He wore a surgeon's smock and, to her eyes, he didn't look old enough to have left school, much less be a qualified physician.

He gave her a friendly grin. "No hurry, Matron, I can wait my turn. You can finish your business with this lady."

"Mrs. Jeffries was just leaving," the matron replied. "She stopped in to see Dr. Bosworth and, of course, he's in Scotland at the moment."

She could take a hint. "Yes, of course. I must be on my way." She nodded her thanks and turned toward the door. As she stepped past the doctor, he said, "Just a moment, did you say your name was Jeffries?"

Surprised, she stopped. "That's correct."

"I'll be right back, Matron," he said. He took Mrs.

Jeffries' elbow. "I'd like to speak to you a moment. Let me escort you out."

Intrigued, she let him lead her out into the hallway. The corridor was empty when they stepped out through the double wooden doors. He released his hold on her elbow and turned to face her. "I'm Phineas Pendleton and Bosworth is a friend of mine. He's spoken to me about you and I suspect I know why you've come to see him today."

"And why is that?" she replied warily.

"You don't give anything away, do you?" He laughed. "Bosworth said you were a smart one. But look, we both know you're here because of that Kettering murder. Now, now, don't look so worried. I can keep a secret. As a matter of fact, that's how I know who you are. Bosworth mentioned you when I went to him for help on my first postmortem for the police. I was appointed the police surgeon for Clapham three months ago and he helped me a great deal. We were able to correctly identify the murder weapon for the police. When I heard that Inspector Witherspoon had caught the Kettering murder, I was able to get my hands on the postmortem report and I had a bit of a look-see. If you can wait for a few minutes, we'll go have a cup of tea and I'll tell you what I think." Without waiting for an answer, he started back the way they'd just come. "I'll just go have a quick word with Matron and then we'll go up to the canteen. You wait right here."

Mrs. Jeffries did as she was told.

Bernadine Fox stared at Witherspoon in disbelief. "She actually left the house to those lunatics?"

"I'm afraid so," the inspector replied.

"That is very surprising, Inspector," Kettering said. "Olive was very involved with the society, but she wasn't a fool. At current London prices, her home is worth a fortune."

"It's priceless," Mrs. Fox exclaimed. "The house is well over two hundred years old. It was built by a royalist during Cromwell's reign as Lord Protector."

"It doesn't look that old," Witherspoon blurted out.

"The façade's been redone a number of times," she snapped. "But that's not the point. Those people will have absolutely no idea about how a property of such historical significance should be treated."

"Obviously Miss Kettering didn't feel that way," Barnes said softly. "Or she'd not have left it to them in her will."

"Olive had no sense of history, either." Bernadine sighed heavily. "But I suppose that what's done is done. I should have thought those sort of people would be more inclined to want money rather than property. I suppose the reverend is now going to be my landlord."

"You can't be thinking of staying in the carriage house," Dorian protested.

She shrugged but said nothing.

"Mr. Kettering, can you tell us where you were on the morning your cousin was murdered?" Witherspoon asked. "Now that you're a direct beneficiary of Olive Kettering's estate, we'll need to clarify a few facts."

"But I didn't know I was going to get anything from Olive," he complained. "She'd told me she'd disinherited both myself and Patricia."

"When did she tell you this?" Barnes asked.

"I don't recall the exact date, but it was sometime

before I went to America," he replied. "We were having dinner at my house."

"Here, you mean?"

"No, Inspector, at my old house on Bretton Road. I gave up the lease when I sailed to New York, and when I came back I realized I didn't need a whole, huge house so I took rooms here. But I can furnish you with the names of my servants; I'm sure several of them must have overheard us arguing. They'll confirm that I'm telling the truth, that I genuinely thought I'd been disinherited."

"He *is* telling the truth," Mrs. Fox interjected. "Olive was always going on and on about cutting people out of her estate. It was actually one of her favorite subjects."

"If you could give us those names, sir," Witherspoon pressed, "we'll contact them. But again, sir, where were you on Tuesday morning?"

He frowned, got up, and walked to the window. "I'd prefer not to say," he finally stated.

Witherspoon saw Bernadine Fox's eyes widen in surprise. Truth to tell, he was a bit taken aback as well. "I'm afraid I must insist, sir," he replied.

Kettering turned, grabbed the lapels of his coat with both hands, and simply stood there.

"Dorian," Mrs. Fox said, turning fully toward him, "don't you think you'd better answer the question? You don't want them thinking you had anything to do with Olive's death."

"Of course I had nothing to do with it," he said brusquely. He looked at the two policemen. "I was visiting a sick friend that morning."

"May we have the name of this friend?" Barnes noticed that Kettering's cheeks had flushed. He was beginning to see why the man was being so stubborn—he didn't want to say who he'd been visiting in front of a lady like Mrs. Fox. The constable ripped a sheet out of his notebook and stood up. "Why don't you write it down for us, sir, and that way we can verify your statement." He held out the paper and his pencil.

Kettering grabbed them and gave the constable a quick, grateful smile. "Yes, of course, that would be best." He went to a table near the fireplace and wrote on the paper.

"You could just tell them, Dorian," Mrs. Fox suggested as she craned her neck to try to see what he was writing. "Surely that would be simpler."

Witherspoon finally understood. "We'd prefer it written down," he said quickly. "It makes it easier for us."

"In that case, I'll take my leave." She got up and crossed the room. When she reached the doorway, she paused and looked at Dorian Kettering. "Dinner is at eight; please don't be late."

"Oh, this is wonderful." Myra Manley smiled broadly as she handed Hatchet a cup of tea. "Reginald will be green with envy that he missed you and that I got you all to myself."

Hatchet laughed. He was in the morning room of the elegant Mayfair mansion of Myra Haddington Manley, the wife of his old friend Reginald Manley. Reginald was a not-very-successful artist who'd married Myra Haddington when they were both well into middle age. Reginald was charming and handsome, and, despite having been subsidized for years by rich women, since his wedding he'd devoted himself solely to his wife. Hatchet had no doubt Reginald would spend the rest of his days as an attentive and loving husband.

Myra was middle-aged and slightly bucktoothed and had more than a few strands of gray in her brown hair. Her skin was perfect, her carriage erect, and, as always, she was elegantly dressed. Today she wore a deep purple dress, with shiny black beading on the lapels of its fitted overshirt and pale lavender lace on the high-necked collar.

"You flatter me, Myra," he replied. He'd come to see them because between the two of them, they had a wide knowledge about everyone who was anyone in London. "And I absolutely love it."

"You're in luck." She poured herself a cup of tea. "I don't have much information about the Ketterings, except for what you probably already know—that the family is rich as robber barons and seems to get smaller with each generation—but I do know something that might prove useful."

"At this point, I'll be grateful for anything I can get." He took a sip from his china cup.

"I understand that Olive Kettering was very involved with a religious group called the Society of the Humble something or other."

"Servant. It's the Humble Servant." He gave an encouraging nod. "You know something about them?"

"I know about the wife of the founder, Olga Richards. She was born Olga Emmering-Todd." She reached for the sugar tongs and delicately added two lumps. "We went to the same school. She's a good deal younger than I am, of course, but we also moved in the same social circles. I was a grown woman when she was presented to society and, gracious, what a stir that caused."

"What do you mean?" He leaned forward.

She smiled and picked up her spoon. "Olga was

probably the most beautiful woman I'd ever seen. She'd walk into a room and every head would turn to stare at her. Her family wasn't extravagantly wealthy, but they had plenty of money." She broke off and her eyes got a faraway look as she recalled the past. "She was expected to make a brilliant marriage and managed to become engaged to Lord Beltran's youngest son. But the engagement was abruptly canceled and Olga suddenly disappeared from society. Her family claimed she had health problems and she needed a warm climate. It was put about that she'd been sent to the south of France, but no one believed them."

"What did people think had happened?" Hatchet knew good and well that despite a family's efforts, there was always gossip.

"Not what one would think." Myra stirred her tea as her expression grew thoughtful. "She didn't get in the family way or anything like that and she did go to France, but it wasn't because of her health. The rumor going about was that she'd lost her temper in a fit of jealousy and stabbed her fiancé. It's worth noting that right after this was supposed to have happened, Jonathan Beltran walked around with his arm in a sling, but, being ever the gentleman, he kept his silence and the story eventually died down."

"How long ago was this?" Hatchet asked. He wanted to get as many facts as possible.

"It's been a long time." Her brows drew together in thought. "I don't recall the exact time, but it has to have been fourteen or fifteen years ago. But I do know that I wasn't surprised by the story."

"Why not?"

"Even as a schoolgirl, Olga Emmering-Todd had a

reputation for a terrible temper. She once pushed a maid so hard, the girl fell down the steps and ended up needing medical attention. The Emmering-Todds paid the girl's family off and that was the only reason that Olga got to stay in school, but no one would stay in the dormitories with her, so she had a private room."

"When she went to France, how long was she gone?" Hatchet asked.

"She didn't come back for five or six years. When she arrived back in London, she was in a wheelchair and married to the Reverend Samuel Richards. Supposedly, she'd fallen and damaged her spine."

"What about her family?" Hatchet asked. "Weren't they a bit surprised by her choice of a husband?"

Myra took a sip of tea before she answered. "Her family had lost most of their money by the time she and Richards came back to London, and her father had died. I think her mother was simply grateful Olga had a husband and she was now his problem."

"Aha," a deep baritone voice said from the doorway. "I've caught you."

Myra's face lighted up with pleasure as she turned and looked at her husband. "You're back early."

"The better to catch that thieving Hatchet trying to steal my wife," Reginald Manley teased as he came toward them. He was a tall, slender man with fine features and dark hair sprinkled with gray. He dropped a kiss on his wife's cheek and sat down.

"Drat, foiled again." Hatchet grinned broadly.

A maid carrying a tray with another cup came in and put it on the table. Myra reached for the teapot. "We've been talking about Olga Richards," she said as she nodded her thanks to the maid.

"I can do better than that," Reginald bragged. He looked at Hatchet. "The minute I heard your friend was handling the Kettering murder, I started asking questions."

Slightly alarmed, Hatchet choked on the sip of tea he'd just taken.

Reginald threw back his head and laughed. "Don't worry, old man, I know how to be discreet; and furthermore, I've a bit of a reputation as a gossip, so my asking questions about a woman who was just murdered is considered very natural."

"He is a gossip," Myra agreed. "But then again, so am I. I suspect that's one of the reasons we were so attracted to each other. We used to have contests to see who knew the most salacious rumors going about London. I must say, Reginald always won."

"But you gave me an excellent run for my money." He reached for her hand and raised it to his lips and lightly kissed her fingers.

"Forgive me," Hatchet apologized to Reginald. "Of course you're discreet and I was being a fool. Now, what have you heard?"

"Probably not much more than you've already found out," Reginald replied. "You know, of course, that the Ketterings sold the brewery that bears their name some years ago and got a mountain of money for it."

Hatchet nodded and then gave the two of them a quick summation of the other information they'd learned about the victim and the other suspects in her circle.

"It appears you already know quite a bit," Reginald said. "But I'll bet you didn't know Angus Cameron was seen getting out of a hansom cab right down the road from the Kettering house on the morning of the murder."

"Gracious, how did you find that out?" Myra gazed admiringly at her husband.

"It was easy; Harley Plummer, an artist friend of mine, dashed over to the cab just as Cameron got out. If you'll recall, there was a terrible storm that morning and Harley was desperate to get out of the wet. He and Cameron almost knocked one another down. Harley said he was surprised to see Angus out and about. He's been so ill recently."

"That's right," Hatchet exclaimed. "Of course—Angus Cameron is an artist. You're bound to know him."

"Cameron's a very talented painter, but not a very lucky one," Reginald said. "And it's not just poor health which has plagued the fellow. He's had one disaster after another with his work."

Hatchet's spine tingled. Disasters and murder often went hand in hand. "What kind of disasters?"

"He's had two exhibitions here in London, and both times, something awful has happened. The first gallery that showed his work got broken into and his entire collection was so badly vandalized they were worthless. Someone had slashed every painting in the place with a knife."

Hatchet leaned forward. "Do you remember when this happened?"

"It was just before he got married. He was so distraught he almost postponed the wedding. But that wasn't the worst of what happened to Cameron. He spent the next year working on another collection and managed to find another gallery willing to give him a show." Reginald looked directly at Hatchet. "Do you know how difficult it is to find a gallery to give you your own exhibition?"

"Not really," he admitted. "You're the only artist I know."

"And how many of my shows were you ever invited to?" Manley asked softly.

"Point taken." Hatchet laughed. "But I did see some of your paintings—"

Reginald interrupted him with a wave of his hand. "Yes, but I never had my own showing. Occasionally I'd do a piece some gallery owner would agree to hang on his wall to see if he could sell it. My point is that Angus Cameron was and is talented enough to have had two exhibitions, and both times something happened to stop the public from seeing or buying his work."

"What was the second disaster?" Myra asked.

"That one was even worse than the first," Reginald grimaced. "Cameron worked out of a small studio he'd rented in a commercial building in Wandsworth. The night before the paintings were to be moved, the building caught fire and every single one of his paintings was destroyed."

"The whole building burnt down?" Hatchet asked.

Reginald shook his head. "Luckily, the fire brigade got there very quickly and put the fire out. But unfortunately for Cameron, they weren't able to save his studio. It was gutted."

"Do they know what caused the blaze?" Hatchet drained the remainder of his cup.

"According to Angus Cameron, the cause of the fire was Olive Kettering." Reginald smiled slyly. "He told his friends he thought she was out to ruin him. She never accepted his marriage to her niece. He was convinced she'd hired someone to burn his work."

"But fires happen all the time," Myra protested.

"Yes, but this one seemed to have been centered on his studio." Reginald shrugged. "It was the only part of the building that was destroyed. Cameron claimed that the only combustible in the room was turpentine, which he kept in a sealed metal can."

"If he was suspicious of his wife's aunt, why didn't he go to the police?" Hatchet asked.

"There was some sort of history between the Cameron and the Kettering families," he replied. "So that might have been why he hesitated to take legal action."

"Did he suspect that Olive Kettering was responsible for his first show being ruined as well?" Myra asked curiously.

"Oh, you clever woman, how did you guess?" He grinned broadly. "He was convinced Olive Kettering was responsible for both incidents but he'd no proof."

Hatchet frowned. "But Olive Kettering was a genteel woman from an upper-class family. I can't see her skulking about in the night with a knife or a box of matches. That sort of thing is far more difficult to do than one would think."

"She's also a rich woman," Myra pointed out. "And, believe it or not, with very little effort one can hire that sort of work done."

"But why would she try so hard to ruin the poor fellow?" Reginald mused softly. "That's the more interesting question. Why did she hate him so much?"

"Probably because she thought Angus Cameron had stolen her most precious possession from her," Myra speculated. "Patricia Kettering's parents died when she was a child and Olive practically raised her. Perhaps Olive saw her niece's actions as a betrayal. But then again, perhaps there's another reason she didn't want the Camerons marrying into her family. Now that she's been murdered, I don't think anyone will ever know for certain."

"True," Hatchet agreed. "But I'm wondering why a man supposedly at death's door got out of a sickbed and ended up at Brook Green. Angus Cameron had a powerful motive for wanting Olive Kettering dead."

CHAPTER 7

Mrs. Jeffries took her seat and reached for the teapot. From the air of excitement around the table, she suspected everyone had something to share. Good, she thought, she was still befuddled by this case, so any additional information was very welcome. She was also rather proud that she'd have something very solid to contribute to the conversation. "Who would like to go first?" she asked as she began to pour.

"I'll go," Betsy volunteered. She felt much better now. Her nerves had settled and she'd even managed a cheery hello to Phyllis when she'd come in this afternoon. "I don't think that what I found out is very important, but apparently, Bernadine Fox has plenty of money." She told them everything she'd learned at the draper's shop.

"Cor blimey, why would anyone care who made their lace table runners?" Wiggins exclaimed. "Fancy sending all the way to Belgium."

Betsy shrugged. "She's very particular in how her house is decorated. But that's not all I found out. I had a bit of real luck at the fishmonger's. The clerk there told me that on the morning of the murder, he saw the Reverend Samuel Richards crossing the road in front of the Kettering house."

"What time did he see him?" Smythe asked. He was relieved that his wife seemed to be her usual cheerful self.

"He thinks it was between ten and ten thirty that morning, but that's as close as he could guess."

"Where did Richards say he was that morning?" Mrs. Goodge looked at the housekeeper. "I mean, in his statement to the inspector."

Mrs. Jeffries' brows drew together in a small frown. "He claimed he was home working on a sermon and that he'd last seen Miss Kettering at dinner the evening before she was murdered. But the inspector also mentioned that because of the storm, Olga Richards said that their servants weren't able to get to the house untiil almost noon, so the inspector hasn't confirmed Richards' statement."

Smythe looked at Betsy. "How did your clerk at the fishmonger's know it was Richards?" He didn't doubt the accuracy of his wife's reporting, but he knew that young male clerks could exaggerate a bit when they were trying to impress a pretty lady. "The Kettering neighborhood is two miles from the Richards house so I doubt the good reverend buys his fish that far from home."

Betsy was ready for that question. "His sister goes to services at the Society of the Humble and he's even gone a time or two himself. The Reverend Richards is making a bit of a name for himself."

"Yes, and the local vicars aren't all that happy about it," Ruth added. "Oh, sorry, I didn't mean to interrupt."

"Not to worry, I'm finished. I just want to say I think it odd that Richards was skulking about near the Kettering house the very same morning that the woman was murdered."

"We'll have to be sure to give the inspector another nudge in that direction," Mrs. Jeffries stated. "Perhaps he'll need to ask Richards for a more thorough accounting of his whereabouts at the time of the murder."

"I think he got distracted by Olga Richards and her jealous outburst," the cook suggested.

"Yes, I suspect that's exactly what happened," the housekeeper replied. She looked at Betsy. "Exactly where was this fishmonger's stall? It wouldn't hurt to have Constable Barnes have a quick word with that clerk, just to be on the safe side."

"It's on the corner of Faroe Road, just opposite the draper's shop," Betsy said.

Mrs. Jeffries nodded her thanks and then said, "Who would like to go next?"

"I'll take a turn," Luty offered. "I didn't hear much, but I did find out that the Reverend Samuel Richards is used to getting the short end of the stick. A few years back he was all set to inherit a bucket of money from a lonely woman in Manchester, a woman very much like Olive Kettering. You know, single, middle-aged, and rich. She died suddenly of a heart attack and willed him her entire estate. But before the estate was settled, there was family that took him to court and he ended up losing everything. He didn't get so much as a penny."

"How could he lose if he was named in the lady's will?" Wiggins helped himself to a slice of bread. "I mean, wouldn't her wishes be the ones that the courts would 'onor?"

"Don't be so innocent." Mrs. Goodge chuckled. "Once someone is dead, all the power shifts to the family. Outsiders generally get nothing."

"That doesn't seem right," Betsy protested. "People ought to be able to leave their money to anyone they please."

"Of course they should," Mrs. Jeffries interrupted. They didn't have much time and she didn't want them distracted by this sort of discussion.

"Courts always take a hard look at anyone outside the family gittin' the money," Luty declared. "It's the same way in the States. I expect it's been like that for thousands of years. Anyways, that's all I found out. It don't sound like much, but I like to think that every little bit helps us."

"Indeed it does," the housekeeper agreed.

"As Madam is finished, I'll go next if it's all the same to everyone," Hatchet said. He told them about his visit to see the Manleys. When he'd finished, he helped himself to a slice of cake and picked up his fork.

"Cor blimey, it sounds as if half of London was skulkin' about near the Kettering house that morning," Wiggins exclaimed. "And here we all thought that Angus Cameron was too ill to get out of his bed."

"Perhaps it was his excursion out in the storm that forced him into his bed," Mrs. Goodge murmured.

"What I find interestin' is that everyone involved in this case seems to have a bit of a secret life," Wiggins continued excitedly. "You know, like from one of them novels." He read a lot of novels and had once considered trying his hand at writing his own book, but that was before he'd decided to become a detective.

"What do you mean?" Betsy asked curiously. Over the course of their cases, she'd realized that the footman's insights were valuable.

"Well, it looks like this Mrs. Richards has a bit of a past, what with her pushin' maids down staircases and stabbin' her fiancés, and now we find out that Angus Cameron might have been skulkin' about the Kettering neighborhood in the middle of a fierce storm even though he's supposedly at death's door. And what about Mrs. Fox? From what you've told us, she's an odd one as well. Imagine sending all the way to Belgium for a couple of lace runners; it don't make sense. None of them people in this case make sense. I think the whole lot of 'em are a peculiar bunch and, what's more, I think it's got something to do with the Kettering house itself. Today, I spoke to a lad that took messages there for Mr. Dorian Kettering, and he told me about how he'd gotten yelled at because he'd accidentally fallen in a flower bed. Seems Miss Kettering had come running from the house screaming her head off. Poor lad was so frightened, he dropped his note and run off."

"Most people have a secret life of one sort or the other," the cook muttered.

"I'll go next." Smythe glanced at the clock. "We'd best hurry. It's gettin' on and the inspector's going to be here any minute now. Luckily, I've not got much to report. I spent most of the day trying to find any cab drivers who might have taken one of our suspects to the Kettering neighborhood, but I didn't have any luck. Which is downright strange, considerin' that it looks like 'alf our suspects was there that mornin'. But I'll keep tryin'."

Mrs. Jeffries glanced at Ruth. She shrugged and shook her head. "I'm afraid I've not done as well as the others. All I heard was that the local vicars aren't happy to be losing parishioners or collection monies to the Society of the Humble, but there's nothing they can do about it. I know it's not much, but I'm hoping to learn something useful soon. I'm going to a tea party and there's sure to be lots of gossip there."

"You've done as well as the rest of us," Wiggins declared. "We all 'ave days when we don't find out much of anythin'."

"I agree," Mrs. Jeffries assured her. "You've certainly done your fair share. Now, if no one else has anything to report, I'll tell you what I found out. I went to St. Thomas' Hospital this afternoon to have a quick word with Dr. Bosworth, but unfortunately, he's in Edinburgh at a medical conference. But my trip wasn't wasted because I ran into another physician, a Dr. Pendleton, who apparently has taken Bosworth's principles to heart."

Mrs. Goodge's eyes narrowed suspiciously. "Has Bosworth been talkin' about us to this fellow?"

"He has," she admitted. "But only because Dr. Pendleton has recently been appointed police surgeon for Clapham and he went to Bosworth for some help and advice. Apparently, our names came up . . ."

"You mean someone else knows what we're doin?" Luty yelped.

"Really, Mrs. Jeffries, do you think that's wise?" Hatchet added.

"Cor blimey, 'alf of ruddy London is goin' to be onto us if we're not careful," Wiggins exclaimed.

"Mrs. Jeffries knows what she's about," the cook cried impatiently. "If she got any information out of this Dr. Pendleton, we ought to give her a chance to tell us without second-guessin' her decisions."

"Thank you, Mrs. Goodge," Mrs. Jeffries said. "I'm not surprised by your reactions," she said to the others. "It does seem as if more and more people are now privy to the fact that we help the inspector, but the truth is, it's almost impossible to ask questions without some individuals realizing what we're doing. Dr. Pendleton did have something to say. He managed to get a look at the postmortem report on Olive Kettering, and he's of the opinion that her assailant was standing less than two feet away from her when the fatal shot was fired. Additionally, there were bruises on her hands and on her arms."

"Did he have any idea what that might mean?" Betsy asked.

Mrs. Jeffries shook her head. "I asked him that very question and he didn't really know. His best guess was that she slammed into something and was moving at such a quick pace, she couldn't stop. It's not much, I know, but it might prove useful eventually."

They broke up and, moments later, the inspector's hansom cab pulled up out front.

Mrs. Jeffries hurried upstairs to greet him. "Good evening, sir," she said cheerfully as she took his hat and coat. "Have you had a successful day?"

Witherspoon thought for a moment. "You know, I'm never really sure if I have or not," he admitted. "Though

I will say it was a very busy day. Let's have a glass of sherry and I'll tell you all about it."

Five minutes later, he was cozily ensconced in his favorite chair and she was sitting across from him. "Now, sir, do tell me about your day," she suggested as she took a sip of her drink.

"We spoke with Olive Kettering's solicitor," he began. He paused and took a sip from his glass. "As we expected, she was a very rich woman." He told her the details of his meeting with Harry Johnston.

When he'd finished, Mrs. Jeffries said, "So she hadn't disinherited either Mrs. Cameron or Mr. Dorian Kettering. I wonder if they knew they were still in the will."

"Mr. Johnston certainly didn't tell them," Witherspoon replied. "He seems a very ethical solicitor. He even tried to stop Miss Kettering from leaving a third of her estate to Richards." He told her about Johnston's investigation into Samuel Richards' past.

"So the Bible college in Canada had never heard of him," she mused thoughtfully.

"They hadn't, but apparently that didn't bother Miss Kettering. She simply got angry at Mr. Johnston and told him to stop interfering in her affairs." He took another sip of his sherry. "The only change she made to her will in fifteen years was adding Richards and the Society of the Humble."

Mrs. Jeffries thought this might be a good time to give the inspector a gentle push. "I wonder if that has ever happened before . . ."

"What?" he asked. "If what has happened before?"

"If Richards has preyed upon some other lonely rich woman and ended up being named in her will," she explained. "After all, Olive Kettering's lawyer called the man a confidence trickster. Perhaps Mr. Johnston had heard rumors about Richards, rumors that hinted the fellow had done something like this previously."

"If that were the case, why wouldn't Johnston tell us what he'd heard?"

"He's a lawyer, sir. Perhaps he might have been concerned that repeating unsubstantiated rumors might cause problems in the administration of the Kettering estate. Perhaps by using the term 'confidence trickster' he was hinting for you to check more closely into Richards' past."

"That could well be the case." Witherspoon nodded thoughtfully. "It's certainly worth looking into, but I've no idea where to start. He did live in Manchester before coming to London."

She jumped at that opening. "That's brilliant, sir, that's exactly where you ought to look. If he did this sort of thing before, that's where it would have been. A fox doesn't stray too far from its own lair." He'd gone precisely where she wanted him to go and now all she had to do was ensure that he continued on the path to learning the gossip they'd dug up in the past few days. It wasn't going to be easy, but it wasn't impossible, either.

"Thank you, Mrs. Jeffries." He beamed. "You're far too kind. After we left the solicitor's office, we went and had a word with Mr. Dorian Kettering. While we were speaking to him, Mrs. Fox arrived." He put his empty glass on the table as he spoke.

Mrs. Jeffries got up and poured the both of them another sherry, listening as he told her the details. It was a lot of information and she wanted to be certain she took it all in. She put his now full glass down next to him and took her seat. "So Dorian Kettering was visiting a 'friend.' That's very interesting."

Witherspoon grinned. "Mrs. Fox thought so as well—she craned her neck so hard to try to see what Kettering was writing that I feared she was going to topple off the settee. The constable and I are going to see this Mrs. Williams tomorrow and see if she can confirm Kettering's whereabouts at the time of the murder."

"But didn't you tell me the funeral is tomorrow? Aren't you going?" she asked. "You generally go to the victim's services."

"Oh yes, we'll be there," he assured her. "We'll stay discreetly in the background. We'll go to see Mrs. Williams beforehand. I doubt she'll be getting ready to attend Miss Kettering's service. Then I suppose we'll start another round of interviews." He sighed heavily. "Honestly, Mrs. Jeffries, there are times when I've no idea what to do next."

"Now, you mustn't tease me, sir." She forced herself to laugh. He didn't see that he was making any progress and so was getting worried. "You know exactly what you're going to do after you speak with Mr. Kettering's lady friend."

"I do?"

"Certainly. To begin with, there are your inquiries in Manchester, and then didn't you mention that you were going to have a closer look at Mrs. Richards' background."

His expression changed and he began to smile. Witherspoon often had moments like this in a case, moments where his doubts about his abilities as a detective overwhelmed him. All it took to get him out of that state of mind was a bit of prodding. "Yes, I believe I did say something to that effect. After all, we've no real evidence she's absolutely confined to that wheelchair. Perhaps a word with her servants might be in order. And after that, I believe I'll have another word with the Camerons. From what Mr. Johnston told me, there's been some bad feeling between the Camerons and the Ketterings for years. Perhaps Mr. Angus Cameron knows where that painting his uncle did of Miss Olive Kettering might be stored. As we both know, Mrs. Jeffries, old sins cast long shadows."

The house was dark and silent. Mrs. Jeffries took her mug of cocoa into the drawing room and walked over to the window. She pushed the heavy curtains aside and stared out into the night. It was already past eleven o'clock, but she was wide awake. A bit of fog drifted in and a lone hansom cab went past. She propped the curtain against her shoulder and took a sip of cocoa. Nothing in this case made sense. Every bit of information she learned was interesting, but thus far nothing had helped her see a pattern or determine the identity of the killer. Essentially, everyone who knew Olive Kettering had a good reason for wanting her dead. Well, not everyone. Bernadine Fox was going to lose her home and be forced to move, as the house now belonged to the Society of the Humble, so she had no motive for wanting Olive dead.

Another carriage went past and she sighed, wishing that she could make sense of something useful in this case, but she couldn't. Angus Cameron had been seen near the Kettering house at the time of the murder and he had a motive. He blamed the victim for the loss of his life's work. Perhaps as he faced his own decline, he'd decided to put an end to Olive's interference. And what about Olga Richards? She was insanely jealous and not confined to a wheelchair. She could walk. Perhaps she'd finally had enough of Olive Kettering interfering in her life and her marriage. From what they'd heard, Olive had begun insisting that the society meet at her house, not the Richards home. She paused as a thought occurred to her—was it perhaps the case that Olga didn't go to the meetings at the Kettering home?

She sighed and got to her feet. She'd left a candle burning in the hall so she could make her way to the door. What about the servants? They all loathed the woman, but that was commonplace here in London— and how often did anyone ever commit murder just to be rid of a terrible employer? Anyway, these days it was not as hard as it once was to find another position.

She'd reached the hall, so she picked up the candle and started up the staircase to her room. Someone had shot Olive Kettering in broad daylight in her own back garden. Just as she reached the top of the stairs, she realized something important. Why was Miss Kettering out in the garden? Gracious, how could she have forgotten such an important fact? Olive Kettering had run out in the middle of a storm. Why? What had scared her so badly and, more importantly, had whatever frightened her been the result of her own mental state or had someone deliberately set about to terrify the poor woman? And what about the bruises on her hands and arms. Could they have happened because she was running for her life?

She shook herself. Unless she was able to speak to

the dead, she'd never know the answers to either of these questions. Olive's reasons for running out in the middle of a storm had died with her. At least for the time being.

She continued on to her room, stepped inside, and leaned against the closed door. She took a deep breath and relaxed her body as everything she'd learned today whirled about in her head. She stood there for a long time, hoping that one of the facts or bits of gossip would help an idea take shape or begin forming some kind of pattern. But nothing happened and she finally pushed away from the door and went toward her bed. She refused to give in to despair. She was going to find the key to solving this case sooner or later. No killer was so very clever that he or she could commit the perfect crime and fool everyone. Regardless of how smart a murderer thought they were, there was always some mistake that gave them away. It was simply a matter of time before one of them stumbled across the clue that would point to the assailant. Perhaps tomorrow they'd find out something that would help them figure out who'd murdered Olive Kettering.

"This is the place, sir." Constable Barnes pointed to a modern, three-story redbrick house in Hammersmith. Harding Road was part of a newly built neighborhood of town houses. Barnes was in a chipper mood. He'd had a word with Mrs. Jeffries this morning and she'd passed along quite a few bits and pieces. Now all he had to do was to make sure to pass them along to the inspector.

"Good, it's still early enough that we should catch her before she goes out for the day. Let's just hope Mrs.

Williams isn't still having her breakfast." Witherspoon started up the short stone walkway. "Williams is the name, isn't it?" He frowned.

"That's the name, sir." Barnes moved ahead of the inspector up the short flight of steps to the door. He banged the brass knocker.

A few moments later, a young maid opened the door. Her mouth gaped open at the sight of them, her gaze fixing on Barnes' uniform. "Uh . . . uh . . . may I help you?" she finally asked.

"We'd like to speak to Mrs. Williams," Barnes replied.

She bobbed her head and opened the door wider. "Please come inside. I'll tell the mistress you're here."

They stepped into the house and the girl hurried off down the corridor to a set of double doors and stepped inside. A second later, she stuck her head out and motioned for them to come forward.

"Mrs. Williams will see you," she called as she shoved the doors wide for them to enter.

"Thank you." Witherspoon led the way into a beautifully furnished but modestly sized drawing room. Pale yellow paint covered the top half of the walls and the bottom half was paneled in white-painted wood. Dark green silk curtains hung at the two windows and green and yellow table runners and gold and silver–fringed shawls covered the various tables and cabinets filling the room. Portraits of people in old-fashioned dress, seascapes, and still-life paintings hung on the walls.

A dark-haired woman was sitting on a couch by the fireplace drinking tea. "Do come in, Inspector. I'm Emily Williams. My maid says you wish to speak to me."

"I'm Inspector Gerald Witherspoon and this is Constable Barnes," he replied. As he drew closer he could see that she was a rather attractive woman, well into middle age and just a bit on the plump side. She wore a high-necked white blouse and a dark blue skirt. A blue shawl was draped over her shoulders. "We would like to ask you a few questions and we'll try not to take up too much of your time."

"I appreciate that." She gestured toward the love seat. "I do have a very busy day planned. Please sit down and make yourself comfortable." She looked at the tea tray on the table next to her. "Would you care for a cup of tea?"

"No, thank you," Witherspoon replied as he sat down opposite her. Barnes took his notebook out of his pocket before taking his own spot at the end of the love seat.

She smiled politely. "Actually, I've been expecting you ever since Dorian told me about his cousin's murder."

"Did you know Miss Kettering?" Witherspoon asked. He was somewhat relieved that she was so cordial.

"I met her on several occasions," Mrs. Williams responded. "But we weren't friends. I didn't approve of the way she treated people. She could be very harsh."

"In what way, ma'am?" Barnes asked.

She paused for a moment before answering. "She abused the power she had over those who depended on her." She nodded toward the closed drawing room door. "My maid, the one who let you into the house, used to work for Miss Kettering. Poor Agnes was tossed out into the street without so much as a reference because she accidentally broke a serving platter. Olive Kettering claimed to be a Christian, but I don't believe she had an ounce of real kindness in her heart."

"When did this happen?" Witherspoon glanced at Barnes, silently signaling that they had better have a word with the maid before they left.

"Oh, it was three years ago," Mrs. Williams replied. "Luckily, Dorian happened to be there the night it happened and he knew Agnes to be a fine, hardworking girl. He also knew I was looking for additional domestic help, so as soon as everyone's back was turned, he slipped down to the kitchen and gave her my address. She came along to see me and I hired her. Honestly, Inspector, depriving someone of their livelihood over a piece of china is cruel."

"Yes, I rather agree with you," the inspector said. "Did you feel that Miss Kettering was equally harsh with her relatives?"

She laughed softly and put her empty teacup on the table next to her. "If you're referring to fact that she's disinherited her remaining family, then yes."

"Mr. Kettering told you he'd been disinherited?" Witherspoon eased back in the seat.

"Of course. Dorian and I are very close friends. We have very few secrets from one another," she said. "Olive also cut her niece out of her will because she didn't approve of the man she married. As I said, Inspector, Olive Kettering abused the power she had over those around her."

Witherspoon wondered if Kettering and Mrs. Williams were the sort of close friends that he and Lady Cannonberry were or whether their relationship was a bit more intimate. He could feel a blush climb his cheeks so he quickly forced his mind onto another subject. "Mrs. Williams, did Mr. Kettering ever give you a specific reason for his cousin's actions?"

She frowned. "I'm not certain I understand your question. Are you asking why she disinherited him?"

"That's precisely what I'd like to know," he replied. Mrs. Williams was either a very good actress or she genuinely thought Dorian Kettering had been disinherited. "Mr. Kettering wasn't very specific about what had so angered Miss Kettering. He merely said they had some strong differences over religion."

"That was part of the reason." She nodded her head. "But it wasn't the only one. Dorian wasn't shy about sharing his opinion of that group she'd become involved with, the Society of the Humble Steward . . ."

"Servant," Barnes interrupted softly. "It's the Humble Servant." He wondered why so many people kept getting the name wrong. "Sorry, didn't mean to interrupt you, ma'am."

She smiled and waved her hand to indicate she'd not taken offense and continued speaking. "As I said, he wasn't shy about sharing his opinion about that bunch, especially that Reverend Richards person. That angered Olive greatly. Plus, she was furious when he went to the United States and then she became even angrier when he came home and tried to share his new ideas with her. Miss Kettering was far more comfortable believing in a vengeful God rather than a loving one, but the real issue between the two of them was far more personal and it's a very delicate subject, one that I'm not comfortable sharing with you."

Witherspoon was stunned and couldn't think of what

to say next. Constable Barnes had no such compunc-
tion. "Mrs. Williams," he said softly, "this is a murder
investigation and, frankly, Mr. Kettering is very high on
our list of suspects."

"But Dorian wouldn't ever kill anyone," she protested.

"Then tell us everything you know so we can make
sure he isn't arrested," the constable urged. "After all,
'by the truth, ye shall be free.' Isn't that what the Bible
says?" He hoped he wasn't misquoting here. He never
paid attention to the readings at church on Sundays.
"Surely if Mr. Kettering is innocent, the truth can only
help him."

She bit her lip and her eyes filled with tears. "I suppose you're right. But it's such a sad episode and, oh, I
feel wretched repeating it."

"We're all adults, Mrs. Williams," Witherspoon
murmured. "I assure you, unless what you have to tell
us would be pertinent to convicting the guilty party
in a court of law, whatever you tell us will be kept
confidential."

She looked down at her hands. "He was disinherited
because of me," she whispered. "Oh, he tried to tell me
that it had nothing to do with me and everything to do
with his lunatic cousin wanting complete control over
everyone's life, but I knew the truth. It was because of
me."

"I'm afraid I don't understand. There isn't anything
illicit about two adults having a friendship," Witherspoon pressed. "You're a widow . . ." His voice trailed
off. Perhaps she wasn't widowed.

"My husband died ten years ago," she said quickly
as she guessed his thoughts. "But that had nothing to do

with Olive's reaction. She wanted Dorian to marry some-one else. Someone she thought more suitable. She kept hinting that he was getting on in years and that it was his duty to take a wife so he could set an example for others. When he finally told her he had no intention of ever mar-rying, she was enraged. They had a horrible argument and she told him she was cutting him out of her will."

"Olive Kettering knew that you and Mr. Kettering were close friends?" Barnes asked. He watched her carefully. Whether she understood it or not, Emily Wil-liams might have just put herself on the suspect list. They only had her word that Kettering hadn't decided to leave her in order to get back in his cousin's good graces and her will. A middle-aged woman desperately in love and being abandoned by that lover might be tempted to take matters into her own hands. And he suspected that Emily Williams loved Dorian Kettering very much.

"Oh yes, Dorian was discreet about our relationship, but he certainly didn't hide the fact we were seeing one another. When Olive began pressuring him to marry, and he wouldn't, she accused him of wanting to marry me instead of a suitable woman from his own back-ground. Which is ironic, really, as I have no wish to be married again."

Witherspoon drew back in surprise.

She laughed. "Don't look so stunned, Inspector, not every woman wants to be married. I had one good mar-riage and my husband was a good man. However, I like my freedom, and as much as I love Dorian, it suits the both of us to stay independent. He tried telling that to Olive, but she wouldn't listen. From what Dorian tells me, once the woman gets an idea in her head, she sim-ply won't let facts get in the way of her opinion."

Witherspoon nodded. "Mr. Kettering said he was here with you on the morning of the murder?"

"That is correct," she replied. "We'd planned on going to a lecture at the British Museum and then having luncheon at Piero's Restaurant. But with the weather being so terrible, we changed our minds and stayed in."

"What time did Mr. Kettering arrive?" Barnes asked.

She frowned slightly. "I don't recall the exact time—I don't remember looking at the clock—but it must have been about nine. That's when he was scheduled to arrive for our outing. The lecture was at ten and we wanted to give ourselves plenty of time to get there. I don't recall that he was late."

"What lecture were you going to hear?" Barnes asked. That was the sort of fact that was easy to check.

"It was one being given by Mr. John Parrington, the archaeologist who's been working in Turkey. Dorian wanted to hear him because he recently excavated one of the first Christian churches ever built," she replied. "But as I said, the weather was so awful we were both afraid it might have been canceled and we didn't want to risk going all that way for naught. So we spent the morning together here and he left right after luncheon. Now, if there isn't anything else, I do have another appointment."

Witherspoon glanced at the constable, who gave a barely perceptible shake of his head. "We've no more questions." He got to his feet. Barnes closed his notebook and stood up as well. "Thank you for your help, ma'am," Witherspoon said politely.

"You're quite welcome, Inspector." Emily Williams rang for the maid. "The maid will see you out."

"Thank you, ma'am. Would it be alright with you if I used your cloakroom to wash my hands?" Barnes requested.

"Of course." She smiled graciously and turned her gaze to the open doorway where the maid waited. "Please show the constable to the cloakroom and then see them out. I'm going upstairs to get ready to go out. Please send one of the street boys to fetch me a hansom. I'll need it in fifteen minutes," she instructed as she got up.

The maid nodded and motioned for the two policemen to follow her. The inspector stopped in the foyer while Barnes followed the maid down the hallway toward the cloakroom. Witherspoon gave a polite bow of his head as Emily Williams went past him and up the staircase.

While he waited for the constable to reappear, the inspector spent his time studying his surroundings. The foyer, while modest in size, had walls covered with the palest of pink silk wallpaper, which he knew was very expensive. White marble tiles covered the floor, and on the wall opposite the door was a huge mirror in an elaborate gold leaf frame. He was no expert, but the paintings on the drawing room walls had looked very decent and he'd also noted two Dresden figurines, a table full of porcelain snuffboxes, and a set of silver candlesticks.

Apparently, Emily Williams had plenty of money of her own.

"Sorry to keep you waiting, sir," Barnes apologized as he strode up the hall with the maid on his heels. He nodded to the girl as they reached the foyer. "And thank you, Miss Agnes, you've been very helpful."

She grinned, opened the door, and they took their leave.

As soon as they were down the walkway and out of earshot, Barnes said, "I had a quick word with the maid, Inspector, and Mrs. Williams isn't being completely honest with us."

"Ah, I suspected you had a reason for wanting to 'use the cloakroom.'" He chuckled. They'd reached the pavement. "Let's go up to the corner. We'll have better luck getting a hansom up there. What did the maid tell you?"

"At first she confirmed Mrs. Williams' account and said that Mr. Kettering had arrived at nine," he said. "But then we chatted a bit about how foul the weather had been that day and she let it slip that when Kettering had come to the house, he'd come in the back door because he wasn't just wet, his coat and trousers had been covered in mud."

The inspector thought for a moment. "Covered in mud, that's odd." He raised his arm and waved at a cab that was dropping a fare in front of the bank building farther up the street.

"That's what I thought," Barnes agreed with a nod of his head. "It might have been raining cats and dogs but the most likely place he could have gotten mud on him was in Olive Kettering's back garden. So I pressed Agnes just a bit harder and she finally admitted that it was almost ten o'clock when Dorian Kettering arrived, not nine."

"And the two properties are close enough together that, even on foot, he could have murdered his cousin and gotten here by ten," the inspector said. "I don't suppose that the maid thought to ask Kettering how he'd gotten so muddy?"

"Agnes told me that when he came in, he said he'd taken a shortcut through the park because there weren't any cabs about," Barnes said. "Which could be true, sir. Park grounds are dreadfully muddy at this time of year."

"But if it were true that he got muddied coming through the park, why did Mrs. Williams lie to us about the time he arrived?" The inspector frowned. "Why not just tell us it was almost ten o'clock and not nine?"

"Perhaps, sir, because she's afraid he might have actually committed the murder." The hansom pulled up and Barnes looked at Witherspoon expectantly. "Where to, sir?"

"The Society of the Humble Servant," he replied. "Your comments this morning on the way here have set me to thinking. I'd like to have another word with the Reverend and Mrs. Richards. Honestly, Constable, one minute we've no real suspects and the next we find out that everyone we've spoken to has been less than honest."

Barnes gave the driver the address and then swung in next to Witherspoon. "Do we have time to get there before we need to get to the funeral, sir?" he asked.

Witherspoon pulled his watch out of the inner pocket of his overcoat. "It's only just half past nine and the funeral isn't until eleven thirty. I think we can manage it. St. Matthew's Church isn't far from the Richards house."

"Mrs. Fox is a decent enough sort," the maid commented as she cast a shy glance at Wiggins.

"'Ow many staff does she 'ave?' Wiggins asked. He'd gone to Brook Green hoping to find one of Olive Kettering's servants to talk with when this young lady had come around the corner of the house. He couldn't believe his good luck and so he'd followed her. She'd meandered across the green and he'd had a devil of a time keeping far enough back so she wouldn't see him. She'd sat down on a bench on the far side of the green and he'd stopped nearby and dropped to his knees, pretending to look for a lost sixpence. After spending a few moments crawling around on his hands and knees, she'd finally asked him what he was doing and he'd made contact.

Her name was Rosemarie Lewis and she was a housemaid for Bernadine Fox. Her brown hair was tucked neatly under her black straw bonnet and her eyes were brown, her complexion pale, and her features thin and sharp. Wiggins guessed she was about sixteen. She was out this morning instead of taking her usual afternoon out because her mistress was going to a funeral. Chatting her up and getting her to agree to come for a cup of tea had been dead easy.

"Mrs. Fox has a flat over the carriage house," Rosemarie replied. "So I'm the only help that lives in, but she doesn't make me do everything. Once a fortnight, we get a cleaner in to do the heavy work. Mrs. Fox is right particular about her things. She's always getting the rugs cleaned and having the curtains aired. They're heavy as the very devil as well, so getting them up and down takes ages. I couldn't do it on me own."

They'd reached the café. Wiggins opened the door and escorted her to a table by the door before going to the counter to get their tea. He was annoyed with himself. He'd forgotten that the Kettering servants would be getting ready to go to their late mistress's funeral today and wouldn't be outside the house running errands. He supposed he ought to consider himself lucky he'd even managed to find Rosemarie Lewis. But he didn't think she'd have much to tell him. She couldn't have much to do with the Kettering household, he reasoned, since she wasn't being forced to go to the funeral. But she seemed to be a nice girl and he'd not hurt her feelings. It just niggled him that he was wasting time. Still, maybe he'd learn something useful. After all, Bernadine Fox had been the one to find the dead woman and raise the alarm.

The counterman gave him two cups of tea and he took them to the table. "'Ere you are," he said, putting one in front of Rosemarie. He took his seat. "It sounds like your mistress is a good sort to work for, then; that must be a relief to you. Some places aren't so nice."

"I know," she agreed. "I don't just do the housework—Mrs. Fox lets me do the cookin' as well. That's my ambition, you see, to become a proper cook. Mrs. Fox says that'll take years and years and that I'd need to get experience workin' in a big house. She says when she was growin' up in the Kettering house, they had two full-time cooks and three scullery maids. Isn't that amazing? She says that back in her day, they used the old ballroom on the second floor as a dining room and that the scullery maids had to use a secret passage to get up there from the kitchen so the food would still be hot. Mind you, sometimes I think she can be as fanciful as poor Miss Kettering, because when I asked her where the secret passage was, she told me she'd never said any such thing."

Wiggins opened his mouth to ask a question, but she didn't give him a chance. She kept right on speaking. "But Mrs. Fox treats me decently and pays well. Not like those poor girls that worked for Miss Kettering."

"Who's Miss Kettering?" he asked quickly. Cor blimey, she was really a talker.

"She's the lady who owns the main house and she was just murdered," she explained with the air of someone passing along a great secret. "Surely you've read about it in the papers. We've had the police around for ages asking questions and making a nuisance of themselves."

"Oh yes, now I remember. She's the poor lady that was murdered in her back garden."

"Poor lady, my foot," Rosemarie snorted. "She was a terrible woman. She was mean and nasty to everyone—"

"Were you there when it happened?" he interrupted.

"I was at a funeral that morning and that was her fault, too," Rosemarie declared. "Poor Mrs. Grant— she was Miss Kettering's cook—she was right nice to me, helpin' me with my cookin' and sharin' recipes. She died of a stomach ailment because that old witch didn't call the doctor in on time. So I was in Kent at her funeral. Olive Kettering couldn't be bothered to go. Like I said, she was awful, especially to her servants. I don't know why Mrs. Fox and Miss Kettering were such great friends. They were nothing at all alike. But they must have been friends because Mrs. Fox sent off all the way to Holland for that expensive cocoa—Mrs. Fox kept asking Miss Kettering how she liked the taste and all she'd ever say was that she couldn't tell the difference between good English cocoa and that Dutch stuff! Talk about being rude! Honestly, you'd think she'd at least have had the decency to tell a little white lie and pretend she liked the stuff."

CHAPTER 8

"It's cold in here," Witherspoon muttered to Barnes. They were at the Richards house and the tired-looking young maid who had answered the door had bid them wait in the rows of hard seats used for the society's religious services. "I don't think they bother to heat this part of the house." He stopped speaking as the door opened and Samuel Richards appeared.

"Good day, Inspector, Constable." He nodded to them as he approached. "I'm rather surprised to see you. Especially today. Poor Olive's services are this morning."

"We know; we intend to be there," Witherspoon replied. "Are you going to the funeral?"

Richards raised an eyebrow. "But of course I'm going. She was a member of my flock and I was her spiritual adviser. She would have wanted me there."

"But we've had it on good authority that the family doesn't want you or any member of your group at the services," Barnes said. He'd decided to put the cat among the pigeons and see what happened. Angry people often lost control of their tongues.

"The family has no say in who can come into a church," Richards snapped. "Now, I'm in a hurry, so what is it you want?"

"We've only a few more questions, sir," Witherspoon said. "We'll try to be brief."

Richards sighed heavily. "I would appreciate that. Now, can you please get on with it?"

Olga Richards suddenly appeared in the doorway. "What do they want?" she asked, addressing her husband.

"They're almost finished," Richards said to her before turning his attention back to the policemen. "Now, what else is it that you need to ask us? This has been a very distressing day and I'd like some time to meditate and pray before we need to leave."

"Where were you on the morning that Miss Kettering was murdered?" Witherspoon asked.

"I've already told you, I was right here, writing a sermon." He folded his arms over his chest.

"Are you certain of that, sir?" Barnes added.

Richards drew back a bit. "I don't know what you can possibly mean by that comment. Of course I'm sure. I know exactly where I was."

The inspector glanced at Mrs. Richards. He was hoping her expression might help him decide if her husband was lying. But she was staring impassively straight ahead, her face giving away nothing. He looked back at Richards. "Mr. Richards—"

"Reverend Richards," he interrupted. "Please use the proper address when speaking to me, sir."

"Then we'll address you as Mr. Richards," Barnes said. "Considering that the Bible college in Edmonton has never heard of you and certainly didn't grant you a degree."

Richards was taken aback but quickly recovered. "That's nonsense. Obviously your people must have made a mistake when they checked my credentials."

"No, sir, they did not," Barnes replied evenly. "You've no more right to use the word 'reverend' in front of your surname than I do."

"I don't have to stand here and be insulted," he sputtered.

"That's correct, sir, you don't have to stand here," the inspector interjected. "We can always have this conversation at the station."

Richards' mouth gaped open in stunned surprise. "Get on with it, then—what do you want to know?"

"If you were here on the morning Miss Kettering was murdered, why do we have a witness that claims they saw you at the Kettering house?" This was a bit of a shot in the dark. The inspector didn't have a witness per se, but Barnes had told him that one of the local constables had been told that Richards had been spotted near the murder scene.

"Your witness is lying." Olga Richards wheeled herself forward. "My husband was here with me that morning."

Richards smiled at his wife. "Of course I was," he agreed. "Just as I told you, Inspector."

"Can anyone else confirm this?" Barnes asked. "One of your servants, perhaps?"

"Very clever, Constable. I've already told you that neither of the servants were here that morning." Olga lifted her chin defiantly. "So you'll have to take my word for it."

"And you can vouch for the fact that your husband was here the entire morning," Witherspoon pressed.

"I've said he was, haven't I?" she replied irritably. "Now, we're busy so I'll thank you to leave."

"We're not through with our questions, ma'am," the inspector said. Even though she'd been rude and he was a bit embarrassed, after thinking about what Mrs. Jeffries had said, he had to ask the question. It would be difficult, after all, he was a gentleman, but for the sake of justice, it had to be asked. "Er, Mrs. Richards, this is rather awkward, but we've heard a rumor that you're not completely confined to your, er . . . uh . . ."

"Are you confined to your chair or can you walk?" Barnes asked bluntly.

Witherspoon gave him a grateful smile.

She stared at them for a few moments, her expression calculating. "I do have some mobility, but I tire quickly. Now, if you're through with your questions, I'd like you to leave."

Smythe stood just inside the door of the Dragon's Head Pub and took a good look around. It was a busy workingman's pub with plain wooden benches along the walls and a few rough-hewn tables. As it was lunchtime, the bar was crowded with people in for a quick pint before going back to their labors. He started across the room, thinking he'd push his way in, but just then two men at the far end left so he quickened his pace and got to the empty spot before it was snatched by someone else.

The barman, a big, burly fellow in a stained apron, was midway up the counter. "What'll you 'ave?"

"A pint," he called. While the barman got his drink, he listened to the people around him, but the place was so noisy all he could hear was a babble of voices.

"Here you go." The barman slid his glass in front of him and Smythe handed him some coins, taking care to put down far more than the cost of the beer.

The man picked up the money and his eyes widened in surprise, but before he could say anything, Smythe said, "I'm 'opin' you can 'elp me. My employer left some important papers in a cab over on Brook Green and I'm tryin' to track 'em down." He was careful to use the same story here that he'd used with the drivers at the cab shack. "I was told there were a couple of drivers who were out that morning and that they often stopped in 'ere for a pint at lunchtime."

The barman glanced at the coins in his hand again and then back at Smythe. "You know their names?" he asked.

"Leadbetter and Duggan."

"Duggan's not been in today, but Leadbetter's sitting over there." He nodded toward one of the tables. "He's the one in the brown coat."

Smythe nodded his thanks, picked up his glass, and went to the table. Three men, all of them wearing bowlers and heavy overcoats, looked up as he approached. "Are you Mr. Leadbetter?" he asked, focusing his gaze on the man closest to him.

The fellow regarded him warily before he answered. "I am. Do I know you?"

"No, but you might 'ave met my employer. She was

in your rig the other day," Smythe replied. "Can you spare me a couple of minutes?"

"You alright, then, Mickey?" one of his companions asked. He kept his gaze on Smythe.

"I'm alright," Leadbetter said to his friends.

"We'll be shoving off, then," the man said as he and the other man pushed away from the table and got to their feet. "See you later, Mickey."

Smythe waited until they were out of earshot before he slipped onto the stool and pulled a half crown out of his pocket. It was a lot of money, but he wanted some answers if there were any to be had.

Smythe laid the coin on the table and Leadbetter's eyes widened. "If that's what you're offerin', then ask all the questions you want," he muttered. "Uh, if I don't know the answers do I still get the money?"

"It's your time I'm buyin'," he replied. "Now, what I'm wantin' to know is if you picked up a fare and took it anywhere near Brook Green on the morning we 'ad that terrible storm."

Leadbetter's heavy brows drew together in thought. "There were two fares that mornin'," he said slowly. "I remember because it was such a miserable day and a lot of drivers weren't even takin' their rigs out. I didn't take either of them to Brook Green, but both of them were dropped near there. Will that do ya?"

"Can you give me a few more details? You know, where you picked 'em up and where you took 'em?"

Leadbetter scratched his chin. "A bloke waved me down and I took him to Randolph Road—that's just around the corner."

"What did 'e look like?" Smythe took a sip from his glass.

"I don't remember too much; it was pourin' with rain and he 'ad an umbrella. But he was a young man, I know that much."

"Where'd you pick 'im up?"

"At Shepherd's Bush station," Leadbetter said. "I dropped him in front of an estate agent's on Randolph Road. I saw him go inside the office."

Smythe nodded. It didn't sound like this fellow was one of their suspects. "And the second fare?"

Leadbetter grinned broadly. "Now, that one I do remember. She was one of the prettiest women I've ever seen. She waved me down on the Uxbridge Road. She was standing there, trying to 'ang onto this huge umbrella and wave me down at the same time. She seemed a fragile sort of lady, so I got down and helped her into the rig. She was carryin' a small carpetbag and it was soaked through. I took her to where Randolph Road dead-ends on Brook Green."

The end of Randolph Road was almost directly across from the Kettering house. "Did you see where she went when she got out of the cab?"

He shook his head. "Once she got out and paid me, I just wanted to get the rig out of there. By then the roads were startin' to flood."

"Do you remember what time you dropped her?"

"It was still pretty early in the day," he replied. "Probably around a quarter past nine or thereabouts. But I can't say for certain. I didn't look at my watch."

From the cabby's comments, Smythe suspected he knew who this woman might be, but he wanted to know for sure. There were lots of beautiful women in London. "You said the lady was very pretty. What did she look like?"

He laughed. "Oh, she was a beaut, she was. Blue eyes and dark hair. That's a combination you don't see too often. She had lovely skin."

"About how old was she?" he pressed. All the inspector had told Mrs. Jeffries was that Olga Richards was beautiful. He needed as detailed a description as possible. "And what was she wearing?"

"I'm not too good at guessin' ladies' ages," he said, frowning, "but I'd say she was in her thirties. As to what she was wearing, she had on an overcoat and beneath it I think she was wearin' something in a maroon color. But that's all I can recall. Frankly, by the time we got to Randolph Road, I was too busy tryin' to keep the rig on the road to pay too much attention to her clothes."

Danny Taylor was a tall, wiry fellow with thin blonde hair, bright blue eyes, and a weathered complexion that spoke of hours of outside work. "Why would you be offerin' to buy me a pint?" he asked, his expression wary.

They were in the public bar of the Hanged Man Pub just off Brook Green and Wiggins was glad he'd put plenty of coin in his pockets this morning. "Because I'm a private inquiry agent and I think you might have some information that might 'elp my client."

Taylor leaned against the bar. "What kind of information?"

"Just ordinary bits and pieces," Wiggins replied. He pushed up to the counter and waved the barman over. "I saw you comin' out of the Kettering house and I was hopin' you weren't some toff that wouldn't 'elp a workin' bloke make a living."

"I'm not a toff," Taylor replied. "I was there for a funeral reception. My employer was just murdered."

"What'll you have?" the barman asked.

Wiggins looked at Taylor expectantly. "A pint for me, please," the gardener finally said.

"I'll have the same," Wiggins told the barman.

"So what do you want to know about?" Taylor asked.

"I'm makin' inquiries about your household. You know, the murder," he replied.

"I thought that's what the police were for." Taylor nodded his thanks as the barman gave him his beer.

Wiggins paid him, picked up his pint, and nodded toward an empty table by the door. "Let's move over there. It's a bit more private-like."

They went to the table and sat down on the bench seats. "The police aren't the only ones with an interest in who might have killed Miss Kettering. Can you tell me if anyone has been actin' funny since the murder?"

The moment he asked the question, he wanted to kick himself. What a stupid thing to say. But Taylor seemed to take the inquiry seriously. His forehead wrinkled in thought. "The servants didn't like her, especially now that poor Mrs. Grant up and died. She was the cook and everyone in the household more or less held Miss Kettering responsible for her death. She wouldn't send for the doctor when the cook took ill, can you believe it?"

"That's terrible," he replied. Cor blimey, he already knew all this. "Uh, was there anyone in particular that seemed to have a grudge against her?"

Taylor took a sip. "Well, that Mrs. Richards didn't like her much, but she kept a civil tongue in her head."

"Then how do you know this Mrs. Richards didn't like her?"

Taylor shrugged. "Because she was always pullin' faces and rolling her eyes when Miss Kettering wasn't looking. Last week, I saw her stick her tongue out at Miss Kettering as they were leaving the house. But most people didn't like Miss Kettering. I can't say she was my favorite person, either. She made me move out of my nice warm room in the carriage house just because I'm a single man and Mrs. Fox was living upstairs in the flat." He broke off and snorted. "As if Mrs. Fox would ever look at the likes of me! That woman's got her nose in the air so high it's a wonder that bugs don't fly up her nostrils."

"Miss Kettering made you move out?"

Taylor nodded. "She was a right religious sort of woman and didn't think it was proper for a single man to be living on the property where there were single females." He rolled his eyes. "It was bloomin' inconvenient. But I didn't 'ave much choice. Mind you, I thought it was stupid that she made me leave when all and sundry could get into that place whenever they wanted."

"What do you mean?"

Taylor grimaced. "There were plenty of single men in the Society of the Humble, but she let them have the run of the place. Her cousin comes and goes as he likes and he's not a married man, and that Mrs. Fox, she's got a key to the back door. So I ask you now, what was so awful about letting me keep my little room in the carriage house?"

"Doesn't sound to me like there should have been anything wrong with you stayin' on the property," Wiggins replied. He'd no idea what to ask next but he needn't have worried about it, as Danny Taylor apparently liked the sound of his own voice.

"I'm a decent sort of bloke and it wasn't as if my family was newcomers to the property. My granddad was the head groundsman there when Mrs. Fox was just a slip of a lass. She lived there as a girl, you know. Three generations of my family has served that household, but once Miss Kettering got the idea that a single man was a walking sin, there was no changin' her mind and I was told to get out."

Ruth picked up her teacup and took a sip from the elegant china. She surveyed the room, trying to see where her quarry had finally settled. She spotted her sitting in a pink satin corner chair on the far side of the ballroom. Ruth stood up and made her way among the tables toward Evangeline Howard. She was in the home of Rosalind Wilson, a rich, elderly cousin of her late husband, and she rarely accepted the woman's invitations. Ruth didn't really care for her very much. Rosalind was overbearing, narrow-minded, and mean to her servants. But Ruth was desperate to help solve this case, because poor Gerald was working so very hard. So she'd accepted the tea invitation in the hopes that she could use the occasion to find out a bit more about their suspects or their victim.

Lady Howard, eighty if she was a day, smiled broadly as she saw Ruth approaching. "Oh, goody, I was hoping you'd come see me. My rheumatism has been bothering me so I couldn't come to you." She waved at an empty chair at the nearest table. "Pull that over and sit down so we can have a chat."

Evangeline Howard was Rosalind Wilson's opposite

in every way. Kind, generous of spirit, and, most importantly, very supportive of women's rights, she was a delightful companion and Ruth was glad she was here this afternoon.

"Are you still friends with that police detective?" Evangeline asked as Ruth pulled the chair next to her and settled into her seat.

"I am," she replied.

Evangeline's eyes widened in pleasure. "Then I must tell you, I know some of the principals in this latest murder. You know, Olive Kettering. The lady who was shot in her own garden. Your inspector got that case, didn't he? I thought he got all the rich ones."

"He did," she replied. "Did you know the victim?"

"I knew her, but not well. She was far too serious a person for my liking."

"Would you care for anything, madam?" asked a waiter pushing a tea trolley loaded with plates of pastries as he paused by their table.

"I'll have an éclair and a couple of those petit fours." Evangeline pointed at what she wanted.

The waiter nodded, loaded up a small china plate, and put it down in front of her. "And you, ma'am? Would you like something?" he asked Ruth.

"An apple tart, please," she said. "Thank you," she said as he served her and then moved off to the next table. "Now, you were saying something about Olive Kettering."

"I was saying she was a very serious person," Evangeline said. She picked up her fork and cut into her éclair. "By that I meant that she was narrow-minded and perhaps the sourest personality that I've ever met. This is odd, really, because both she and Bernadine Fox were once gay and high-spirited young girls."

"You knew them as girls?" Ruth took a bite of her tart.

"Not well, but we traveled in the same social circles. I was quite a bit older, of course, but I remember that Olive Kettering was once besotted with a young artist. At one point they were engaged, and then all of a sudden it was called off and no one ever knew why." She shook her head. "But you're not interested in ancient history, are you? That won't help your inspector solve the murder."

"Actually, it does help to find out these things," Ruth replied. "You're an intelligent woman, you know that old sins cast long shadows."

Evangeline laughed in delight. "They most certainly do. Well, if you're interested in the past, you've come to the right place. I also know a bit about Dorian Kettering, Olive's cousin. They're as unlike one another as chalk and cheese. He was always a lovely man, the sort of person any mother would want for their daughter, except that his branch of the family hadn't any money. Olive's people were the ones that owned the brewery."

"Dorian's family had nothing?" Ruth pressed.

Evangeline thought for a moment before she answered. "At one point, I believe they were part owners of the business, but there was some sort of trouble and Dorian's parents had to sell their shares cheaply in order to hang on to the family farm. I don't recall the details, it was years ago. Dorian would only have been a child when his family lost their money."

"Do you remember who benefited from the transaction?" she asked.

"It would have been Olive's parents; both of them were very shrewd businesspeople and the rumor always was that Olive was equally shrewd. The gossip I heard was that she managed her investments so well she more than doubled what she inherited."

Ruth nodded thoughtfully. Children were very impressionable, and she wondered if Dorian might have blamed his cousin for what her parents had done to his family. As she'd just said a few moments ago, old sins cast long shadows.

"Of course there was always a strain of madness in that family," Evangeline mused.

"The Ketterings?" Ruth murmured. "Really? What kind of madness?"

"Oh, not just the Ketterings, the Fox family as well—they're all related to one another and have been for the last three hundred years or so." Evangeline laughed again. "Old Campion Fox—that's Bernadine Fox's great-grandfather—supposedly kept a servant girl he'd fallen in love with imprisoned in the cellar. She was finally set free when her brothers stormed the house and got her out. Then Esme Fox, Campion's daughter, fell in love with a young Quaker man and followed him all over England. He had to move to someplace called Pennsylvania in the United States to get away from her. And Bernadine, of course, was supposedly in love with a young man back when she was younger, but the fellow had no money so she was forced to marry one of the distant Fox cousins." She paused and took a quick sip of her tea. "The Ketterings aren't much better. The gossip I heard is that before Olive became a religious fanatic she was a bit of a libertine; and Dorian is equally fanatical, only at the other end of the spectrum. Honestly, you'd think people would have better sense than to use God as a weapon against one's own family. It's not healthy, I tell you."

Betsy flew through the back door of Upper Edmonton Gardens and skidded to a halt, narrowly missing crashing into Phyllis, who was on her way out. "Watch where you're going," she snapped.

"Oh dear, I didn't hear you come. I'm ever so sorry," Phyllis cried.

"You shouldn't be the one apologizing," Mrs. Jeffries said and stepped out of the dry larder. She'd gone there to get a sugar cone for Mrs. Goodge and she'd seen the whole incident. She'd had enough. It was time to put an end to this nonsense. "Betsy should. She was the one that came running through the back door with no regard to the fact that another person might be in the hallway."

"Oh, it's alright, Mrs. Jeffries." Phyllis laughed nervously and edged toward the door. "I don't want to make a fuss."

Betsy merely gaped at the housekeeper, her expression stunned.

"No, it's not alright," Mrs. Jeffries retorted. "And expecting common courtesy from others isn't making a fuss. You have the right to be treated with the same respect as everyone else in the household."

"I'm sorry, Phyllis," Betsy stammered. "Mrs. Jeffries is right, I was rude."

"That's alright, Betsy." Phyllis smiled hesitantly. "I'm fine. Uh, I'll just be off. I'll see you both tomorrow." She gave a quick wave and hurled herself out the back door.

The two women stared at one another for a long moment, both of them more than a bit taken aback by what had just happened. Mrs. Jeffries broke the silence. "I didn't mean to embarrass you, Betsy, but you were most definitely in the wrong."

Betsy said nothing; she didn't trust herself to speak. She knew the housekeeper was right, that she'd behaved horribly, but the reprimand had stung. Tears welled in her eyes and she blinked hard to hold them back. She took a long, ragged breath as the hall suddenly narrowed and darkness swam toward her. She put out her hand to steady herself, but it was too late; her knees crumpled and she fell to one side, landing hard against the wall.

"Betsy, oh, my goodness." Mrs. Jeffries leapt toward her, grabbing her around the waist before she actually hit the floor. "Betsy, Betsy, are you alright?" Gently she pulled her up and leaned her against the wall. "Oh, my gracious, are you alright? You scared me to death. Stay here while I go get Wiggins and Mrs. Goodge. We'll carry you into the kitchen."

Betsy's face had drained of color and her eyes had rolled up before Mrs. Jeffries realized the girl was going to faint. Betsy wasn't one to have a fit of vapors because she'd been reprimanded, and this meant that something was most definitely wrong. Mrs. Jeffries was genuinely scared. The idea that one of her family—and she did think of all of them as family—might be ill was terrifying.

"Don't go," Betsy said. "I'm fine. I've only fainted." She grabbed the housekeeper's hand. "Please don't tell anyone. I'm fine. I just got light-headed for a moment." She knew that if Smythe heard about this, she'd be stuck in the ruddy kitchen. She wasn't having any of that, not when they had a murder to solve.

"Betsy," Mrs. Jeffries pleaded, "you can't ask me to—"

"Yes, I can," she interrupted. "You're right, I've been a right cow, and I'm very sorry. But please don't punish me by telling Smythe. You know what he's like. He'll have me confined to my bed if he thinks there is something wrong."

Mrs. Jeffries stared at her in shocked surprise. "Punish you! I would never do that. You're like a daughter to me and I'd never hurt you. But you were wrong to treat Phyllis in such a manner . . ."

"I know, I know, and I swear I'll not do it again. I don't know what's got into me. Phyllis is a nice girl and, more than anyone, I should understand what it's like to be an outsider. I don't know what's wrong with me these days, but I give you my word, I'll be nicer from now on. Just don't say anything to Smythe," she pleaded.

"Oh dear, Betsy," Mrs. Jeffries said softly. "There is something wrong. I think you're ill. I won't say anything if you promise you'll go see a doctor."

"I promise." She pushed away from the wall. "But it's nothing. I was in a pub this afternoon and I had a drink. It's gone straight to my head." That was only partially true; she'd had a sip of gin, but the taste was terrible and she'd not finished it. "And I've not had much to eat today, either."

Wiggins stuck his head in the hall. "Are you two comin' in for our meeting? Mrs. Goodge says I can't have a slice of cake until everyone's 'ere, and it's seedcake, that's my favorite."

"We're just coming." The housekeeper turned and gave him a smile. "I asked Betsy to help me bring in a few supplies from the dry larder. Mrs. Goodge needs to do more baking tomorrow to feed her sources."

"I hope the others get 'ere soon," Wiggins muttered as he retreated to the kitchen. "I'm bloomin' 'ungry."

"Thank you, Mrs. Jeffries." Betsy gave her a brilliant smile. "You won't be sorry. I'll be as sweet as sugar to Phyllis."

"Betsy!" Mrs. Jeffries shook her head in exasperation. "I don't like the way you treated the girl, but that's not my main concern right now. I'm worried about your health."

"I'm fine." Betsy turned as they heard people at the back door. "Don't worry, it was the gin and the empty stomach," she hissed as Smythe, followed by Luty Belle and Hatchet, entered, "but if it'll make you feel better, I promise I'll go see the doctor."

A few moments later, they were all gathered around the table.

"Can I 'ave a slice of cake now?" Wiggins asked plaintively. "I'm so 'ungry I could eat a 'orse."

"Help yourself, lad." Mrs. Goodge shoved the plate toward him and then glanced at the carriage clock on the pine sideboard. "But we'd best not dillydally. Everyone was late today and if we don't hurry, the inspector will come walking in the front door before we're finished."

"Who would like to go first?" Mrs. Jeffries asked brightly. She was relieved to see that some of Betsy's color had come back to her cheeks. She was even more relieved to note that Smythe didn't appear to notice anything wrong with his wife.

"If no one objects, I'll pass along the gossip I heard

today," Hatchet offered. "As we know, Bernadine Fox grew up in the Kettering house, but what we didn't know was that Dorian Kettering lived in a house just down the road. It's been torn down for years, but according to my source, when the two of them were young, they were together constantly. When Dorian Kettering's family lost their home, he was sent north to stay with Olive's family."

"How old were they when they were separated?" Betsy asked.

"Very young," Hatchet replied. "My source thinks they might have been in their early teens. I'm afraid that's all I found out today."

"I'll go next," Wiggins volunteered. "I got right lucky today. I found two people to talk to about our suspects." He grinned at the cook. "That's why I was so starved when I come 'ome—I didn't 'ave anythin' to eat at lunch." He told them about his meetings with Rosemarie Lewis and Danny Taylor. When he'd finished, he reached for another slice of cake.

"I'll go next," Betsy said. "I had a chat with one of Patricia Cameron's neighbors today and she said that Mrs. Cameron was home on the morning that Olive Kettering was murdered." She didn't mention she'd followed the woman to a local pub and bought her several glasses of gin to keep her talking. Sometimes it was best to avoid too much detail.

"How did she know that?" Mrs. Jeffries asked curiously.

"Because they were both in the chemist's right after he opened for business and that was at half past nine. Then the rain started and Mrs. Cameron walked Mrs. Potts back to their block of flats. She said that

Mrs. Cameron had gone to the chemist's to get her husband some medicine."

"But how does this Mrs. Potts know that the Cameron woman didn't go out again? The Camerons don't live that far from the Kettering house," Luty observed.

Betsy laughed. "Mrs. Potts collects the rent for the landlord, and the tenant on the top floor is behind. She had her front door open because the tenants had gone out that morning and she wanted to catch them and demand the rent when they came back. That's all I've got."

"That's plenty, love." Smythe smiled at his wife. "If your source is right, then we know that Mrs. Cameron couldn't be the killer. Mind you, I found a hansom driver that did take a fare to Brook Green that morning and, from his description, I believe the woman he let off was Olga Richards." He told them the rest of what he'd learned from Leadbetter. He finished just as the clock chimed.

"Oh dear, we're running out of time." Mrs. Jeffries looked at Ruth. "You found out something, didn't you?"

"Yes, but I'll make it very quick." She told them about her meeting with Evangeline Howard as efficiently as possible while taking care not to leave anything out.

When she'd finished, Mrs. Jeffries shook her head. "You've all found out so much information, yet there are still so many things we don't know."

"Like what?" Mrs. Goodge demanded.

"Well, like the gun, for instance," the housekeeper replied. "Now, before you all start telling me that the weapon is probably at the bottom of the Thames, remember this—guns are expensive and none of our suspects, save for Bernadine Fox, had much money. So

I ask myself, would one of these people, the Camerons or the Richardses or Dorian Kettering, toss away something they could sell? I think we ought to suggest that the inspector send a few lads out to some pawnshops and see if anyone has recently pawned a small handgun."

"Wouldn't it just be easier to hint that the inspector should search the Kettering house again?" Ruth asked. "I mean, it seems to me if your original contention is correct—"

Mrs. Jeffries interrupted. "What contention is that?"

Ruth frowned slightly, as though she couldn't tell if the housekeeper was being serious. "Uh, well, if what you told us this morning is correct, you know, about Olive Kettering not wearing a coat, then it sounds as if she came running out of her house because she'd no time to put one on. Doesn't that imply she was being chased by the killer?"

The light went on in Mrs. Jeffries' mind. "Oh, my gracious, you're right. I've been asking myself over and over why she was out in the garden and the answer was right under my nose. She was chased out. That would explain the bruises on her hands and arms. She probably banged into things as she was running."

Just then, they heard the clatter of a hansom pulling up in front of the house. Wiggins leapt up and rushed to the window. "It's the inspector," he called.

Everyone got to their feet and grabbed their outer garments. "We'll be back tomorrow morning," Luty called as Hatchet hustled her toward the back door.

"And I can be here as well," Ruth said as she slipped her shawl over her shoulders and rushed after the other two.

Mrs. Jeffries nodded and raced for the stairs and the

door. Blast, she thought as she ran up the backstairs. She'd almost had it, she'd almost seen how the pieces had fit together. But it was gone now. Completely gone. She couldn't even remember what it was that had sparked the brief flash of insight where it all made sense.

She hid her annoyance behind a smile as the inspector came in the front door. "Good evening, sir. How was your day?"

"It was very busy, Mrs. Jeffries." He handed her his bowler. "Do we have time for a glass of sherry before supper?"

"Of course, sir." She hung up the hat and took his coat.

A few moments later, he was ensconced in his favorite chair, sipping his drink. "Ah, this is very nice. Gracious, we had such a busy day. As you know, Olive Kettering's funeral was today. I must say, considering that very few people claim to have liked the poor woman, there was a large number at her service."

"Perhaps even those that weren't fond of her wanted to pay their respects," she murmured.

He nodded agreeably. "A good number of her neighbors were there and, of course, her servants."

"What about Samuel Richards and his lot?" she asked.

Witherspoon grinned. "They were there as well. As a matter of fact, I thought I was going to have to break up some fisticuffs involving the good reverend. The Ketterings made sure the funeral reception was private and neither Richards nor anyone else from the Society of the Humble was invited. Olive Kettering's solicitor was there, of course, and as he was leaving the church, Richards asked him about the estate. Honestly, Mrs. Jeffries,

Dorian Kettering was standing right behind the two of them, and when he heard Richards' question, I thought he was going to attack the man. Luckily, another fellow stepped between them."

"What did Richards ask?"

"Two things." Witherspoon took a quick sip of sherry. "First of all, he wanted to know when the will was formally going to be read to the heirs and, second, he wanted to know what would happen if one of the principal heirs died, specifically, what would happen to their share of the estate."

"So he knew he was going to inherit," she mused. "And the other two heirs claimed they didn't. That's very interesting."

"What was even more interesting was Johnston's answer. I think the fellow was so surprised at being asked such a question he blurted out that if any of the principal heirs died within six months, their share would go to the other two. In other words, they wouldn't own their inheritance outright for six months." He pursed his lips. "Frankly, I was rather stunned that a solicitor would be so indiscreet, but Mrs. Fox was absolutely incensed. She told Mr. Johnston in no uncertain terms that he ought to keep family matters private and not be standing in a churchyard publicly blabbing about Olive Kettering's estate. She was waving her umbrella about so wildly I feared she was going to do the poor fellow a serious injury. But Mr. Johnston is very spry for a man his age and managed to leap out of her way."

Mrs. Jeffries laughed. "It does sound like you had quite a day, sir."

"The funeral, exciting as it was, was only one small part of it." He put his empty glass down on the table.

"Before the service, we went to see Mrs. Williams, Mr. Dorian Kettering's friend. After that, we went to the Society of the Humble to have another interview with Mr. and Mrs. Richards."

"Let me get you more sherry, sir," she offered as she got up. "I want to hear all about it."

"I'll finish up here," Mrs. Jeffries told the cook. "Dinner was very late today and you look tired."

Mrs. Goodge's eyes narrowed suspiciously. "You just want the kitchen to yourself so you can have a think, don't you? You're beginning to see the pattern, aren't you? You're beginning to see how it all fits together."

"A few bits and pieces are coming together," she admitted. "But between what we learned from everyone at our meeting today and everything I heard from the inspector, I'm not sure I'm on the right track. But you do look done in and you should go and rest. With Betsy and Smythe living out and Phyllis leaving before supper, there's a lot of little chores that you've taken on. I saw you taking those empty crocks to the larder—you should have had Wiggins do that for you."

Mrs. Goodge waved her hand dismissively. "I'm fine. Speaking of Betsy, did you say something to her? I noticed she was awfully quiet this evening."

"She was rude to Phyllis today and I made her apologize, but I'm going to talk to her again tomorrow morning. I'm going to speak my mind and find out what's the cause of all this foolishness." Mrs. Jeffries winced inwardly. She didn't like keeping secrets from the cook, but she knew Mrs. Goodge would worry if she told her everything that had happened in the hallway this afternoon. She had decided to have a talk with Betsy. She couldn't concentrate on solving this murder as long as she was so worried about the maid and her odd behavior.

Mrs. Goodge nodded. "Good. I don't mind telling you, I've been concerned about the girl. But I am tired so I'll take you up on your kind offer and go to my room." She yawned and headed for the door, stopping at the stool where Samson was perched. "Come along, lovey. It's nighty-night time."

Samson gave a pretty little meow, shot Mrs. Jeffries a glare, and then hopped off the stool and hurried after the cook.

Mrs. Jeffries moved slowly around the room survey-ing the small chores that still needed to be done. They all could have waited until Phyllis came in tomorrow, but she'd learned that dull, routine tasks tended to free up her mind. A stack of soiled tea towels were piled on the end of the worktable. She picked them up and turned toward the hallway. Her mind cast back to what Wiggins had said he'd heard from the gardener: *Her cousin comes and goes as he likes and he's not a mar-ried man, and that Mrs. Fox, she's got a key to the back door.* She dumped the towels into the small wicker bas-ket kept by the stairs and leaned against the newel post as the inspector's words echoed in her mind: *Constable Barnes had a quick word with the maid and, despite what Mrs. Williams told us, Agnes finally admitted that Kettering hadn't arrived at Mrs. Williams' house until almost ten o'clock.*

She shoved away from the post and went back to the kitchen, crossing the room and heading for the dish rack by the sink. There were only a few odds and ends left. But she'd put them away. Betsy had washed the blue and white salt cellar. Mrs. Jeffries took it off the bottom row, picked up the small lamp she'd left burning off the worktable, and went to the dry larder. Ideas, insights, and snatches of conversation from their meetings whirled about in her head as she went down the hall. Olive Kettering was running for her life and, surely, the killer had to have been in the house. But who was it? She pushed open the door, stepped inside, and put the lamp and the salt cellar on the small worktable. She pulled a tin of salt off the bottom shelf and then just stood there, staring off into space. Who benefited from Olive Kettering's death? Two of the heirs claimed they didn't even know they were still in the will and the third obviously knew he was. It didn't make sense, it simply didn't make sense. She pried open the lid of the tin and reached behind her for the cellar.

There has to be something I'm missing, she thought as she scooped the salt into the vessel. Either something that's hidden so cleverly no one could find it, she told herself, or something that's so obvious you don't even see it.

CHAPTER 9

The next morning, Mrs. Jeffries was awake and down in the kitchen well before anyone else in the household. She took a sip of tea and stared across the room at the pale light seeping in through the window. She hadn't slept well at all; her mind simply wouldn't quiet. Between her domestic worries and the details of this case, she doubted she'd had more than two hours' rest and it had all been for naught, at least as far as the murder was concerned. That flash of insight she'd experienced yesterday hadn't come back and that, of course, was her own doing. She knew good and well that thinking too hard and trying to connect all the pieces was the worst thing to do! But she hadn't been able to stop herself.

But the sleeplessness had resulted in something useful. In the wee hours of the morning, she'd made a decision. There was one problem she could take care of today and, despite her misgivings, she was going to do it.

There was a knock on the back door, startling her and almost causing her to knock over her mug of tea. Getting up, she hurried down the hall and unlocked the door. It was still very early, so she cracked it open an inch to see who was there. "Constable Barnes, you're here awfully early. Is anything wrong?" She backed up and waved him inside. "Come in, come in, it's freezing out there. I've made tea."

"I could do with something hot." He stepped across the threshold and moved aside so she could shut the door. They started up the corridor. "I wasn't going to stop, I was going to leave you a note, but when I got here I saw the light on so I knew someone must be up. Lucky for me it wasn't the inspector." He chuckled as they came into the kitchen.

Mrs. Jeffries pointed to the table. "Sit down, I'll get us some tea and you can tell me what this is all about." She was suddenly very happy. Barnes coming by at this time of day had to mean he had something of importance to report.

She poured his tea, refreshed her own, and handed him his mug as she slipped into her chair. "Now, what were you going to leave a note about?"

He took a quick drink before he spoke. "I meant to mention it to the inspector yesterday, but we were so busy that I completely forgot until late in the evening. I was so annoyed at myself for forgettin' something which might be important that it kept me awake most of the night."

"I know precisely what you mean," she agreed. "This case seems to be keeping all of us up. I didn't sleep much, either. Now, what was it?"

"It was a conversation I overheard at the funeral yesterday." He took another quick sip. "Sorry, but this is warm and it was ruddy cold outside. I'm sure the inspector told you about the ruckus between Richards and Dorian Kettering."

She nodded. "He did and he also mentioned how indiscreet the solicitor was and how angry Mrs. Fox became."

"She'd have been even angrier if she'd heard what the servants were mumbling about her." Barnes grinned. "I made it a point to walk out of the church behind them and, believe me, all of them were complainin' that now that Miss Kettering is gone, Mrs. Fox is acting like she owns the place. I expect her nose will be out of joint quite a bit when the Society of the Humble takes possession of it. But that's not what I came to tell you. As we left the church, I heard one of the maids telling Mrs. McAllister that she thinks she's catching the same thing that poor Miss Kettering had before she died."

Mrs. Jeffries stared at him curiously. "What does that mean?"

"It was hard to hear very clearly—remember, we were leaving the church and everyone was crowded in the center aisle—but I think the girl was referring to Miss Kettering's complaints that she heard people walking in the house at night," he explained.

"I didn't hear everything she said," he continued, "but I did hear Mrs. McAllister tell the girl not to worry, she thinks it's just the house making strange noises as old houses do, because only the night before, she'd heard someone walking about herself." He leaned back in the chair and shrugged. "I know it doesn't sound like a very important piece of information, but I tell you, Mrs. Jeffries, it kept me awake half the night and I don't know why."

Mrs. Jeffries said nothing for a moment, she simply stared off at a spot somewhere over Barnes' shoulder. "I know why. The house was built by a royalist during Cromwell's reign," she murmured.

Barnes' brows drew together in confusion. "Sorry, I don't understand what you're getting at. What's that got to do with the servants starting to hear things?"

She wasn't sure she understood it, either, but suddenly she was sure she was on the right track. She took a deep breath. Explaining her idea wasn't going to be easy, and if she was wrong it might cause the constable a great deal of embarrassment. "You'll need to get the inspector to search the Kettering house again, and this time, if my idea is correct, you'll need to be exceedingly thorough."

Mrs. Jeffries stood in the shadows beneath the oak tree in the communal garden and watched the path. She pulled her cloak tighter against the chill and hoped they'd hurry up and get here; it was cold and their morning meeting was due to start soon. She wanted to have a word with Betsy beforehand.

They appeared suddenly out of the midst from the far side of the garden. They came down the path hand in hand. They walked silently, as couples that are very easy with one another can do. Mrs. Jeffries waited till they were almost at the tree before she stepped out. "Good morning."

"Mornin', Mrs. J." Smythe grinned cheerfully. "What are you doin' out 'ere?"

"Good morning, Mrs. Jeffries." Betsy gave her a timid smile.

"I was waiting to speak to you." She kept her attention on Smythe. "I need your help. We've got to air the attic out—there's terrible smell up there—and Wiggins has gone up to open all those little windows at the top."

"He'll never get 'em open on his own." Smythe shook his head. "They're stuck. It'll take the two of us to pry 'em loose."

"That's what I told him." Mrs. Jeffries nodded eagerly. "But he said he wanted to try it on his own and I didn't want to hurt his feelings—Wiggins does like to think he's very strong. Would you slip up there and help him? You can tell him I sent you up because I didn't want him late for our morning meeting."

He nodded, gave Betsy's hand a squeeze, and hurried toward the house.

As soon as he was out of earshot, Mrs. Jeffries turned to Betsy. "I need to speak with you." She took her arm and led her toward the wooden bench under the tree.

"But the bench will be wet," Betsy protested half-heartedly.

"No, it won't. I've wiped it down with a towel. Now sit down."

Betsy flopped down, folded her arms over her chest, and stared at the housekeeper defiantly. "Alright, I'm here. Now, what is it? If it's about Phyllis, I told you yesterday I'd be nice to her."

"It's not about Phyllis." Mrs. Jeffries noted that Betsy's face was pale, there were dark circles under her eyes, and she looked as if she'd lost weight. "It's about you."

Betsy straightened up, uncrossed her arms, and

balled her hands into fists. "I knew it, I just knew it. You're going to ask the inspector to give me the sack so you can give my job to Phyllis," she charged. "You think that just because Smythe is rich and I don't need the wages, you can take it away from me." Her eyes filled with tears. "But you can't. It's my place, Mrs. Jeffries. It's my place and I won't be driven off like I'm nothing."

The agony on the girl's face broke her heart. "Oh, Betsy, I'd never do that. You know I'd die before I'd hurt you. We'd never want you to go. If you'll recall, the one time you tried to leave, I'm the one that begged you to stay."

Betsy sniffed and wiped her eyes on her sleeve. "But I've said I'll be nicer to Phyllis, so if you're not going to sack me, what's wrong?"

"What's wrong?" Mrs. Jeffries sighed. "Oh, Betsy, I'm so worried about you that I can't think straight. And I'm not the only one. Mrs. Goodge is concerned and even Wiggins has noticed that something is amiss. Now listen, I'm going to speak my mind and if you don't like what I've got to say . . . well, there isn't anything I can do about that. Because what I've got to say is important. There's something wrong with you, and I'm not just talking about your attitude. You don't look well."

"I didn't sleep much last night."

"Neither did I," Mrs. Jeffries retorted. "And part of the reason why is that I'm so concerned about your health that it's all I can think about when I shut my eyes. I don't think you quite see yourself in a true light. One moment you're sweet as can be and the next you're snapping poor Phyllis' head off. Hasn't Smythe noticed it as well?"

"He has, but I told him the moods were because I was getting used to being married," Betsy mumbled. "I know I've been awful and I don't like it, either. It's just that for the last month, sometimes I feel like I'm all jumbled up inside. One second, I'll feel like I'm going to cry, and the next, I'll be so happy I could laugh like a loon."

"But why do you seem to dislike poor Phyllis so much?" Mrs. Jeffries asked. "That's what I can't comprehend and that is what is so worrying. You've only started acting this way in the last month or two. When Phyllis first arrived, you were very nice to her. What happened? That's what I need to understand. You're a kind, sweet woman and it's not at all like you to be mean to someone who is too scared of losing her position to fight back. You've never been a bully, Betsy."

Betsy covered her face with her hands and sucked in a long, hard breath. "I was scared she wanted to take my place," she finally murmured. "I know it's silly to feel that way—you'd never run me off—but every time I saw you or Mrs. Goodge or the inspector being nice to her, it made me feel like I wasn't needed. Or wanted. I'm so sorry and I won't do it again, I promise."

Mrs. Jeffries put her arm around Betsy's shoulder and with her other hand lifted her chin until they faced each other. Betsy stared at her. "I know you won't, but that's not my concern."

"What is the concern?" Betsy whispered.

"Sometimes, when people's behavior changes, it means there is something physically wrong. I know you've said you'll go to see a doctor, but I want your word of honor that you'll do it right away."

Betsy smiled tremulously and her eyes filled with

tears again. But then she began to giggle. "I give you my word."

Mrs. Jeffries drew back. "What is so funny?"

"I was going to the doctor anyway, but you see, there's really no need. I know what's wrong with me."

"Oh, you've medical training, now, do you?" This time it was Mrs. Jeffries who crossed her arms over her chest.

Betsy laughed out loud. "No, but I did have a nice long chat with my neighbor Mrs. Verner. She's not in the least shy about getting right to the heart of the matter."

"Does this Mrs. Verner have a medical degree?" Mrs. Jeffries demanded. Really, young people, sometimes they simply didn't know what they were about.

"No, but she does have three children." Betsy threw her arms around the housekeeper. "Mrs. Verner said that sometimes in the beginning your emotions can get the better of you and you can latch onto silly notions, like I did about Phyllis taking my place, but that all passes. Oh, Mrs. Jeffries, I'm going to have a baby."

Betsy ducked her head to hide her own smile. Mrs. Jeffries was having the very devil of a time keeping her feelings hidden, as it were, but she had no doubt the housekeeper would keep her word. Betsy had made her promise to keep her secret just a bit longer. She hadn't told Smythe yet and if her husband knew about the baby, he'd not want her dashing about London finding clues. She didn't want anyone else knowing before him, either. But it had felt good to tell someone, almost as good as it had felt yesterday evening when she'd spoken with Mrs. Verner and finally figured out was wrong . . . well, not wrong exactly. She helped herself to a slice of bread. Gracious, she was hungry this morning. Now she understood why she'd been acting like such a silly cow. Now, at the very least, she could keep herself in check when those childish feeling overwhelmed her. She wondered how much longer they were going to last.

"Cor blimey, what are you two grinnin' about?" Wiggins asked as he slipped into his place at the table. "Did Mrs. Jeffries figure out who our killer is? Which reminds me, there's a few bits that I forgot to tell yesterday. But it weren't really my fault because the inspector come home and we didn't get to finish our meeting properly."

"What did you forget?" Luty asked. "Somethin' important?"

Wiggins frowned and swiped at his shoulder to remove a cobweb that he'd picked up in the attic. "I'm not sure. You remember when I was tellin' ya about Rosemarie Lewis. She mentioned that Susan Edwards— she's the scullery maid at the Kettering house—"

"We know who she is," Mrs. Goodge said quickly. "Go on, we've not got all day and we need to save a bit of time for Mrs. Jeffries to tell us about Constable Barnes."

"Susan told Rosemarie Lewis that she'd felt bad when Miss Kettering had been murdered so she'd told Mrs. McAllister about how the cook had switched the cocoa. Mind you, in her next breath, Rosemarie said Susan complained that the cook hadn't shared the good drinking chocolate with any of them, she'd kept it all for herself. Rosemarie told her to stop being a ninny, that bein' as someone had murdered Miss Kettering, she didn't think anyone would care much about the stupid tricks the cook might have played."

"That's very interesting," Hatchet murmured.

"I'm not finished," Wiggins said. "Susan was worried she was going to get the sack because when she turned around, Mrs. Fox was standing there and Susan thought she might 'ave heard her."

"What does Mrs. Fox have to do with it?" Luty demanded. "She don't own the place. Besides, all of the servants are probably goin' to be let go when Richards and his bunch take over."

"But that's not goin' to be for a while," Wiggins argued. "And I think that the scullery maid was hopin' to get a few more weeks in her pay envelope before she was let go. Accordin' to what Susan told Rosemarie, the family is lettin' Mrs. Fox run the house."

"Mrs. Fox is right there, almost on the premises," Ruth commented. "It seems a sensible way to proceed. But why would the scullery maid fear getting let go because of the actions of the cook? That's what I don't understand."

"Because it was Mrs. Fox that sent the cocoa to Miss Kettering in the first place."

"Susan knew about the switch and she was probably frightened that Mrs. Fox would take her anger about the deception out on her," Mrs. Jeffries murmured. Suddenly, everything became crystal clear in her mind. She could see it all now. She knew exactly who the killer was.

What she didn't know was why.

But what if she were wrong? Oh dear, she'd been so distracted this morning by Betsy's wonderful news she'd only half listened to Wiggins. Drat. More importantly, what was she going to do about it? But perhaps she wouldn't have to do anything. She'd told Barnes what she suspected about the house. Surely that might yield some evidence. But what if it didn't? What if her original supposition was completely wrong?

"Right, then, are you through?" Mrs. Goodge asked Wiggins. "Because if you are, we need to hear what Mrs. Jeffries learned from the constable."

"I'm done." He grinned broadly, glad to have gotten that last bit of information off his chest. He, along with everyone else at the table, looked at the housekeeper expectantly.

Lost in thought, Mrs. Jeffries didn't notice she was now the center of attention. She stared off into space, her gaze unfocused as she tried to connect the pieces together. It made sense, yet it didn't make sense.

Hatchet cleared his throat. "Uh . . . Mrs. Jeffries, is everything alright?"

"Huh?" she muttered. "Uh, yes, I'm fine. I was just thinking."

"Do you know who the killer is?" Luty asked eagerly. "Usually when you go off all starry-eyed like that, you're getting ready to figure it out."

"Not as yet." Mrs. Jeffries smiled apologetically. She felt a bit bad about lying, because she had figured it out, but she wasn't sure. Oh dear, that didn't make sense. "But Constable Barnes came by with some very interesting information this morning and I think we're moving forward with this case." She hesitated and then plunged ahead with her idea about the Kettering house. She was relieved that none of them laughed. After all, secret staircases and hidden passages sounded so very melodramatic when one actually said them out loud.

Smythe leaned over and whispered in Betsy's ear. "Are you alright, love? You look pale."

"It's the light in here," she replied. "And I'm fine. Mrs. Jeffries, what did the constable tell you?"

Mrs. Jeffries told them what she'd learned. She paused for a breath and Wiggins interrupted. "Do you think the 'ouse is haunted, then?"

"No, of course not," she replied. "As a matter of fact, I think there's a very rational explanation for those footsteps and I said as much to the constable." She stopped as she realized the full implications of what Wiggins had said just a few minutes ago.

"She's doin' it agin." Luty leaned toward the housekeeper. "See, she's gettin' all dreamy-eyed. If she was younger, I'd say she was in love."

Mrs. Jeffries snapped out of it. "Wiggins, please go to the Kettering house straight away. You need to find Constable Barnes and tell him that it's imperative he search the cook's room."

"What's he lookin' for?" Wiggins was already on his feet. "And what if the inspector sees me? What do I say?"

"Tell Barnes to find the cocoa—that's the key to this whole case," she replied.

"Wiggins can't go," Smythe said. "'E's already talked to half the people that work there. I think I'd better go. No one has seen me before."

Wiggins started to protest and then realized the coachman was right. He sat back down. Then he leapt back up. "But I can go in case there's a message to bring back 'ere," he pointed out. "I don't 'ave to go to the 'ouse. I can lolly about on Brook Green and if Smythe needs something done, he can nip out and tell me."

Mrs. Jeffries agreed. "We've often had to dash about

when we're at this point in a case. Having you on hand there is a very good idea."

"Should I go as well?" Hatchet offered. "Young Wiggins can stay on the green and I can take Madam's carriage to one of the side streets to have at the ready if we've a need to get somewhere quickly."

"What about me?" Luty demanded. "Shouldn't I go? It's my carriage."

"Of course it's your carriage, madam," Hatchet said soothingly. "But if circumstances get a bit rough-and-tumble, I want you safely away from any danger."

"We can stop in Knightsbridge and I'll get my Peacemaker," Luty declared.

"That won't be necessary, Luty," Mrs. Jeffries said quickly. "I don't think anything is going to happen today. As a matter of fact, I'm sure of it. But I do think Hatchet's suggestion is a good one. It wouldn't hurt to have your carriage at the ready."

"Right, then, we'll be off." Smythe dropped a kiss on Betsy's forehead, pushed to his feet, and grabbed his coat. Wiggins and Hatchet followed suit.

As soon as the men had gone, Mrs. Goodge crossed her arms over her chest and focused her attention on Mrs. Jeffries. "You goin' to tell us who you think is the killer?" she demanded. "Or are you goin' to be like you usually are and keep us all in suspense until the last possible minute?"

"I only do that because I'm never sure of my conclusion," Mrs. Jeffries said defensively. "Honestly, I don't try to keep you in the dark deliberately." She winced inwardly. She was keeping a secret, a wonderful secret that would delight everyone in the household, but she couldn't say a word. Blast.

"I'm going to stay busy. It's the only way to make the time pass," Betsy announced as she pushed back her chair and stood up. "I'm going to polish the furniture in the drawing room and the inspector's study. Besides, Phyllis will be here soon and it won't do to have her finding all of us sitting here chatting."

Luty sighed heavily and turned her attention to the housekeeper. "How long do you think this idea of yours is goin' to take to bear fruit? Should I go home or should I stay here? I don't want to miss anything."

Betsy, who'd bent down to pull the polishing oil out of the bottom of the pine sideboard, straightened and looked at Mrs. Jeffries.

"I don't want to miss anything, either," Ruth stated. "But on the other hand, if you really don't think something is going to happen, I've some correspondence to finish. My women's group is soliciting funds from our sisters in America."

Mrs. Jeffries wasn't sure what to tell them. On the one hand, her idea could be completely wrong, in which case sitting around the kitchen would be a waste of everyone's time. On the other hand, what if Barnes found something? "I don't think anything is going to happen. What we could do is go about our business and meet here this afternoon for our usual time."

Luty got up. "Fine then, I'll go out and flag down a cab. I've got a couple more people I want to speak to about our case. No sense in stopping now if you ain't sure you know who did it."

"I'll walk you to the corner," Ruth offered. "And if you're going to keep at it, so will I. I've another source I can tap after I've written my letters."

* * *

A tall, wiry man stepped in front of Witherspoon as he and Barnes got out of the hansom in front of the Kettering house. "Are you the policeman trying to find who killed Miss Kettering?"

"I am. I'm Inspector Witherspoon and this is Constable Barnes. Who might you be, sir?"

"I'm Danny Taylor, I'm the gardener here. I was on my way in to get Mrs. McAllister, but then I saw the hansom stoppin' out front and I had a feelin' it might be the police. Mrs. McAllister said you'd probably be back once we laid Miss Kettering to rest."

Witherspoon grimaced. He'd meant to interview Taylor, but to date, he'd not found the time. "Mr. Taylor, the constable and I were going to come and speak with you, we simply hadn't gotten around to it as yet. But as you're here, is there something you want to tell us?"

"It's not so much telling you as showing you," he said hesitantly. "I've found something you ought to see."

Witherspoon winced. He hoped it wasn't another corpse.

Barnes, correctly reading his superior's facial expression, stepped forward. "Where is it, Mr. Taylor? Lead the way and we'll follow."

"It's in the back of the carriage house." Taylor pushed open the wrought-iron gate and started up the walkway. "I found it today when I was looking for some oil to keep the gate from squealin'." He led them up the walkway, around the main house, across the garden, and around to the back of the carriage house. He stopped in front of a wide door that was swung up on hinges into the ceiling. The space inside was wide enough for at least three carriages.

"This is where the rigs were kept," he explained. "But Miss Kettering sold all the vehicles years ago and got rid of the horses as well. Pity, really, they were nice animals. My dad was quite fond of them."

"Your family has been in service here for a long while?" Witherspoon asked. He craned his neck to see into the interior of the gloomy space, but he couldn't spot anything that looked like a body. Good, he hoped it stayed that way.

"Three generation of us," Taylor announced proudly. "Mind you, most of that time the Fox family lived here, not the Ketterings, but you'll want to see what I found this morning. It's this way." He went inside and they followed. The floor was swept clean and there were shelves along one side of the room. The other half appeared to have been partitioned off into two rooms. "This side is where the stable used to be. When I was a lad, the family had six horses, but they built up the stalls and turned them into rooms." Taylor stopped by the door nearest them. "This used to be mine. It was right nice."

"Your family lived there?" Barnes asked.

He shook his head. "We lived in a set of rooms in the main house when I was growing up, but when my parents died, I moved out here. But I've not lived here for a year. Miss Kettering asked me to leave. She didn't like having a single man on the place." He continued on toward the end of the corridor and stopped at the last door. "But what you need to see is in here. This is used as a storage shed." He opened the door and then stepped back. "Take a look in there, sir."

Witherspoon steeled himself and moved toward the opening. But Barnes moved faster. He stuck his head inside first and then disappeared into the small room. A moment later, he reappeared holding a burlap bag that had been tied at the top with a piece of thin rope. "Is this it?"

Taylor nodded. "Open it up, sir."

Barnes put the bag on the ground and untied the rope. He spread the sides open, revealing two silver candlesticks, a Dresden shepherdess figurine, a silver bowl, three spoons, a carved wooden box, and a stuffed parrot missing most of its tail feathers. Barnes looked at the inspector. "I think we've found the missing knick-knacks Mrs. McAllister told us about."

"I concur, Constable. Let's take them inside and see if she can identify them." He glanced at Taylor. "When did you notice this was here?"

"Today." He nodded toward the open door. "Like I said, I went to get oil for the front gate and found that bag. I looked inside. Frankly, I wasn't sure what to do. But then you showed up and made the decision easy."

"When was the last time you were in here?" Barnes got to his feet.

"Last week, Mrs. McAllister wanted some paraffin for the downstairs lamps. We don't use it much anymore, it's too dangerous. But Miss Kettering insisted that we have a lamp on each floor. She was always worried the gaslights wouldn't work."

"And I take it the bag wasn't there then?" Witherspoon asked.

Taylor shook his head. "No, nothing in that room but the oil and the paraffin."

"Does everyone in the household have access to the room?" Barnes tied the rope loosely around the top of the bag.

"No one does but me and Mrs. McAllister. We keep

it locked. But when I came here today, the door was standing open."

Witherspoon walked over, bent down, and examined the lock closely. "There's no indication that anyone tampered with it," he mused. "No scratches on the plate or on the wood."

"So whoever opened it must have had a key," Barnes said. He turned to Taylor. "Did Mrs. McAllister open it for any reason?"

"I doubt it. She generally asks me when she needs the lamps refilled and, like I said, we refilled them last week so she'd no reason to come out here. Besides, she's had her hands full with the service and the reception."

"Were you here when Miss Kettering was murdered?" the inspector asked.

Taylor didn't look offended by the question. "I was with the others at Mrs. Grant's funeral in Kent," he replied matter-of-factly.

"Have you seen anyone coming or going in this area in the past few days?" Barnes swept his arm in a wide arc.

"No one, at least not while I've been here. But I'm only here during the day. If you want to know what happens at night, you'll need to ask Mrs. Fox. She lives upstairs."

"You live off the property, is that right?"

"I've a room in a lodgin' house nearby. Miss Kettering did give me a raise to pay for the room, I'll give her that much."

Barnes put the burlap bag gently down on the ground and went to where the inspector stood by the open door. He studied the lock for a moment and then looked at Taylor. "These are old, aren't they?"

"Yes, when they built this room, they took the lock

off the butler's pantry and put it in here. Miss Kettering wasn't one to waste money." He turned and pointed to the room that used to be his. "She got that lock off the door to the library. She said there wasn't any reason to keep a library locked, most people wouldn't bother stealin' books."

"So if the locks are old, does that mean that Miss Kettering didn't change the locks when she bought the place?" Witherspoon asked.

"I don't think so, but Mrs. Fox might be the best one to ask, or Mr. Dorian Kettering; they both grew up here."

"We'll do that, Mr. Taylor, and thank you for your cooperation," Witherspoon said.

"If you need me for anything else, I'll be working on the other side of the house." Taylor nodded respectfully and left.

Barnes picked up the burlap bag. "Shall we go see Mrs. McAllister, sir?" He was very relieved. Mrs. Jeffries had made it clear that the Kettering house had to be searched again and he'd done some fancy talking himself to get the inspector here. "And should I send for some lads?"

"Lads?" Witherspoon looked puzzled. "Why?"

Barnes nodded toward the bag. "It's like you said, sir, there's more to this place than meets the eye. If the gardener can find a bag of stolen knickknacks, who knows what else is here? Your idea that we need another search is a good one, sir. These old houses have a lot of secrets."

Witherspoon nodded in agreement. "Ask the constable at the front to get us some help from the local station. I'll take the bag into the house and see if I can find Mrs. McAllister." Barnes handed him the bag and both men headed for the open doorway.

Witherspoon laughed softly and hefted the sack as he spoke. "Wouldn't it be ironic if these had been stolen by someone from the Society of the Humble? They'd have been stealing from themselves. They own this place now and everything in it."

They came out of the carriage house and went their separate ways. Barnes hurried to the front and Witherspoon started across the garden.

He reached the door and knocked. Mrs. McAllister herself opened up. "I saw you and the constable from the upstairs window. Do come inside, Inspector."

He stepped inside, holding the bag carefully in front of him to avoid damaging the contents. "I've something I must show you," he said as she closed the door.

She glanced down and moved in front of him. "So I see. Let's go in here." She pushed open the first door on the corridor. "This is our dining room. But it ought to be empty."

Witherspoon followed her. A long oak table, darkened with age, dominated the room. Shelves filled with mismatched china, crockery, mugs, and odd-sized serving platters were on the wall opposite where he stood. Gray linoleum, buckling in places, covered the floor.

The inspector put the bag on the table, flicked off the loosely tied rope, and spread it open. Mrs. McAllister, who'd moved to stand beside him, gasped. "Dear me, where on earth did you get those things?"

"Are these the objects that have been stolen from the house?" Covertly, he lowered his eyes and watched her expression. She wasn't one of the major heirs of the estate, but she was getting a legacy. He'd known people to kill for less. He was no expert at reading faces, but in his judgment, she certainly didn't look guilty, only surprised.

"They most certainly are." She clasped her hands together. "Where on earth did you get them?"

"The gardener, Danny Taylor, found them today. He saw us get out of a cab and showed them to us," Witherspoon said. "He found them when he went to get some oil for the front gate. They were in that little room at the back of the carriage house."

"But that's impossible, that room is always kept locked. How could anyone have gotten inside it?" she protested.

"That's what I wanted to ask you. Mr. Taylor said that you and he are the only ones with keys."

"That's true, but my key is right here." She pulled a round brass ring out of her pocket and held it at eye level for a moment. There were a dozen keys on it. She grabbed one of them by the tip. "This is my key and it's still safely on my ring. I can assure you, Inspector, I haven't been near that room in quite a long time. I never go out there."

"That's what Mr. Taylor told us," he replied. "Have you seen anyone on the grounds that shouldn't have been here?"

She smiled wearily. "Inspector, yesterday there were dozens of people here for the funeral reception. They were milling about all over the place. Even some of those wretches from the Society of the Humble managed to get into the house. I recognized them, but I didn't want another scene so I said nothing to Mr. Kettering."

Witherspoon nodded in understanding. "I imagine you or someone else in the household would have noticed if any of the funeral guests had been carrying a burlap sack. However, someone may have slipped out and unlocked the door for an accomplice. I forgot to ask Mr. Taylor if the outer door was open. Do you know?"

"It was closed. It is only opened when the gardener is working on the grounds and there was no work done yesterday."

"Is that door kept locked as well?"

"Yes, Miss Kettering wanted every door in the place kept locked," she replied.

"Then the bag must have been put there before yesterday," he mused. "I don't suppose we'll ever know, but at least these items have been returned to the household."

"Thank you, Inspector." She scooped up the bag. "I'll put these back in their proper places."

"Mrs. McAllister, how many people are in the house today?"

She looked surprised by the question. "Just the usual number, the servants and the cook from the agency. Why?"

"We're going to search the house again," he said. "We'll do our best to avoid disrupting your routine, but there will be a number of policemen about the place."

"I hope you find something, Inspector. I must say, I am feeling a bit more sympathetic to Miss Kettering. The night before last I was sure I heard footsteps walking about the house. But when I got up and looked, there was no one there."

"Where is your room?"

"On the floor above Miss Kettering's." She smiled sheepishly. "The rest of the servants are in the attic, but Mrs. Grant and I had rooms along the third floor corridor. I suppose I might have been overly sensitive. It's been strange having both the cook's room and Miss Kettering's room empty."

"I take it the cook from the agency doesn't live in?" he commented. He'd no idea how these things worked. He left domestic issues up to Mrs. Jeffries.

"No, she doesn't, and I don't know how much longer we can keep her on or what's going to happen to the household. The servants have been asking. They're all worried they're to be chucked out at a moment's notice. They've heard that she left the house to the Society of the Humble and they're worried. People have got to have time to find other places to work and live."

"I'm sure there's been some provision in Miss Kettering's will for domestic arrangements. Why don't you ask Mr. Johnston about it? Furthermore, it does take a while before an estate is disbursed."

"That's good to know." She smiled gratefully. "I'll have a word with him. He seems a decent sort of man; I'm sure that at the very least he'll be able to tell us how much time we've left here. I'm going to his office tomorrow morning for the formal reading of the will. I'll ask him then."

"I would advise you to get there a bit early so you can speak with him privately," Witherspoon suggested. "He may be more forthcoming out of the earshot of the other heirs. If you'll excuse me, I'd better see if the constables have arrived so we can begin the search. We'll try to stay out of everyone's way."

Mrs. McAllister hesitated. "You might want to have a word with Mrs. Fox before you start. She's in charge of the household until things get sorted out legally."

*   *   *

Wiggins spotted Barnes coming out the front gate of the
Kettering house. They were in Luty Belle's carriage and
Hatchet had instructed the coachman to drive by the
house before finding a suitable spot to wait along one
of the streets near the green. "Cor blimey, there goes
Constable Barnes. He's in a ruddy 'urry."

Hatchet banged on the ceiling, his signal to the driver
to stop, then he turned to Wiggins. "Jump out and get
the constable. Tell him we've a message from Mrs. Jeffries."

Wiggins waited till the rig slowed and came to a halt.
He flung open the doors, leapt to the ground, and raced
across the road.

Barnes heard running behind him and looked over
his shoulder. He smiled slightly, not at all surprised by
the footman's sudden appearance. He was used to this
sort of thing from the Witherspoon household. "Hello,
Wiggins. What brings you here?"

"We've got a message for you, Constable," Wiggins
explained quickly. He glanced toward the Kettering
house. "Get in the carriage and we'll take you where
you need to go. It's from Mrs. Jeffries."

"Right, then, let's hurry." Barnes crossed the road.
"I've got to get to the local police station before I can go
back to the house."

Bernadine Fox wasn't pleased to see him; Witherspoon
could see that from the way she glared at him. He was
standing in the center of her elegant drawing room. She
hadn't invited him to sit down.

"This is most inconvenient, Inspector," she complained. "There is much work to be done today. I told

Dorian and Patricia I'd do an inventory of the house for them. Haven't your people already searched?"

"True, but we need to do it again," he replied. "We'll do our best to stay out of the way. Can you tell me if you've seen any strangers hanging about the carriage house in the last few days?"

"Strangers, no, why do you ask?" She regarded him warily.

"We—or rather, the gardener—found a burlap sack filled with items from the household in the little storage room just below here."

"What items?" she demanded. "What are you talking about?"

"The knickknacks that have been stolen from the Kettering house this past year."

"They were a bit more than knickknacks, Inspector," she retorted. "Some of the items that are missing are very valuable and I know who took them. It was one of those wretches from the Society of the Humble. You really should search their premises. I'm sure you'd find all sorts of incriminating evidence if you did." Her eyes narrowed angrily. "I can't believe Olive was foolish enough to leave that confidence trickster a third of her estate. Well, we'll see about that. I've spoken with Dorian and Patricia about taking the matter before a judge and I think I've made them see reason."

"Be that as it may, ma'am, right at the moment, my concern is the return of the stolen goods." He couldn't put his finger on why this mattered, but he had a feeling it might be very important. "And whoever took them to begin with obviously decided to bring them back. They deliberately put them in a place where they'd eventually be found, the little storage room just below your flat.

I was wondering if you might have seen anyone or perhaps heard strange noises."

She thought for a moment and then shook her head.
"No, Inspector, I saw no one. But I'm a heavy sleeper, so
if they broke into the carriage house during the night, I
wouldn't have heard them."

CHAPTER 10

"I had the constables wait at the back of the house, sir," Barnes said to Witherspoon. "The local station gave us four men. Will that be enough?" They were standing in the foyer of the Kettering house. Barnes had gotten Mrs. Jeffries' message and then sent Wiggins back to Upper Edmonton Gardens with the news that the items stolen from the Kettering house over the past year had been found. He'd then gone to the Hammersmith station and requested assistance.

"It should be sufficient," Witherspoon replied. He wasn't precisely sure why he'd been so adamant the house be searched again, but as Mrs. Jeffries was always telling him, his "inner voice" hadn't let him down yet, so he should trust that he knew what he was about.

"This is an old house, sir," Barnes said. "Why don't I start belowstairs?"

"That will be fine." Witherspoon looked confused.

"But I don't see what the age of the house has to do with anything."

Barnes laughed. Since his meeting with Mrs. Jeffries he knew exactly what to say. He'd been mentally practicing to get just the right words. "You said it yourself, sir, if this place was built by a royalist in Cromwell's time, there might be secret passages about."

"I did?" Confused, the inspector made a face. "But I thought secret passages were done when the Tudors outlawed Catholicism."

"Those were priest holes, sir." Barnes started for the back staircase. "Different, yet, in one way, very much the same; a lot of royalists in Cromwell's time copied the idea. Cromwell did like to swing the axe, and when they came to arrest someone, a nice hiding place could come in handy. Where should I have the lads start, sir? The cook's room?"

"Yes, that'll be fine. Have two of them on the main corridor and two of them search the second floor. You and I can do belowstairs." Witherspoon hurried after the constable. If there were any secret passages to be found, he wanted to be in on it.

"Mrs. Jeffries, Mrs. Jeffries, are you in there?" Wiggins called as he charged through the back door. He was in a hurry. Fred, who'd been sleeping peacefully by the cooker, jumped up and raced for the hallway.

"I'm right here, Wiggins." Alarmed, Mrs. Jeffries looked up from the household accounts and shoved back from the table as she stumbled to her feet. Mrs. Goodge, who was sifting dry ingredients for a cake, dropped the sifter into the bowl with a loud crash, startling Samson, who was under the table waiting for a treat to fall his way, into scrambling out and running for the staircase.

Wiggins skidded to a halt as he flew into the kitchen, oblivious that he'd scared the cat, startled the dog, frightened the cook, and driven Mrs. Jeffries to her feet. "Cor blimey, things are startin' to 'appen!" he exclaimed. "The inspector 'as found all that stuff that's been nicked from the Kettering house."

"Wait, wait, don't say another word until I get there," Betsy shouted as she ran down the steps, her footsteps thumping in quick succession and making even more noise than Wiggins.

"Betsy, slow down. You'll hurt yourself," Mrs. Jeffries warned. "He'll not say another word until you're here."

"I'm coming, I'm coming," Betsy cried. Panting, she dashed into the kitchen, steadying herself on a chair as she almost went past the table. She smiled brilliantly. "I heard you come in," she said to Wiggins. "I didn't want to miss anything."

"Everyone sit down!" the cook yelled. She gave Wiggins a good glare. "You've scared my poor cat and almost given both Mrs. Jeffries and I heart failure. Unless someone is dead, you'll sit yourself down and tell us what's happened." She turned her attention to the maid. "And you'll not be running down any more stairs, young lady. That's dangerous and you can end up turning an ankle."

"Thank you, Mrs. Goodge," Mrs. Jeffries said.

"Sorry," Betsy said meekly as she pulled out her chair and took her seat.

"I'm sorry, too." Wiggins pulled out his chair as

well. "I was just excited and I do need to get back." He reached down and petted Fred, who was nudging him with his head. "Easy, boy, go back to your spot and lie down. I'll take you walkies tonight when I get back."

"Now, what was it you wanted to tell us?" Mrs. Jeffries asked.

"You know all them knickknacks that was pinched since the Society of the Humble started meetin' at the Kettering house? They were found right there on the property. Constable Barnes wanted you to know about it right away." He repeated everything that Barnes had told him, making sure that he didn't skip even the smallest detail. When he finished, he pushed back from the table and started to get up.

"Wait a moment, Wiggins," Mrs. Jeffries ordered. "Don't be in such a rush. I want to think about what this could mean."

"But Mrs. Jeffries, they might need me at Brook Green," Wiggins whined. He didn't want to be stuck here if something interesting was going to happen, and he had a strong suspicion that was where the excitement would be.

She thought for a moment. "That's true, they might, and it isn't as if you can walk up to the Kettering house and tell the constable what I suspect finding the stolen goods might mean."

Witherspoon hadn't a clue as to what he ought to be looking for, but he diligently tapped on the walls and examined the baseboards of the servants' dining hall. So far, he'd found nothing. Constable Barnes was across the hall in what had once been the butler's pantry but now served as a storage room.

The inspector pulled the least rickety of the chairs over to the shelves and climbed up. He pushed gingerly against the corner of a cabinet and then realized he was being silly. There was so much crockery in this cupboard the thing would rattle and shake like the very dickens if someone tried to used it as a doorway. Suddenly, he felt awfully foolish. Secret passages indeed! That was the sort of nonsense one saw at the theater or read about in novels.

"I've found something, sir."

Barnes' voice startled him and he jerked, rocking the chair. He jumped onto the floor and landed so hard he felt it in his knees.

"Are you alright, sir?" Barnes asked anxiously. "I didn't mean to scare you."

"I'm fine." Witherspoon straightened up. "And I was surprised, not scared. What have you found?"

"I'm not sure." Barnes nodded toward the butler's pantry. "I know your methods, sir, so I left the evidence right where it was. You'd better come have a look yourself."

Witherspoon followed him across the corridor. The pantry was a good-sized room where the good china and glassware were stored. Directly opposite the door were three glass-fronted cabinets filled with fine china and crystal. At the end of the row of cabinets, the room lengthened another five feet, ending in a wall filled with shelves holding brightly colored tablecloths, stacks of folded serviettes, fringed tabletop shawls, and lace runners.

"It's here, sir," Barnes said, moving toward the shelves. He turned and looked at the wall.

Witherspoon moved next to him and Barnes pointed

at a piece of cloth caught on a nail on the edge of the cabinets. "There, sir, that doesn't look like it belongs there, does it?"

"Indeed it doesn't. Get it and let's have a closer look."

The constable retrieved the fabric. "It looks like green lace," he said, handing it to Witherspoon. "But that's an odd place to find such a thing."

The inspector had no idea why he did what he did, but before he could stop himself, he leaned forward, lifted his arm so that it brushed against the nail, and then pressed hard against the wall. Nothing happened.

"Bring your arm down a bit, sir," Barnes suggested. "And try pressing on the center piece of the molding."

Witherspoon drew back and looked at the wood. The molding had once been painted but was now a dullish gray color. At first glance it appeared to be three rounded edges carved into a single piece of wood. But on closer examination, he realized there were cracks between the layers. He pressed hard against the center one and heard a faint click. "I heard something; let's push against the wall."

Both men pushed hard, but they needn't have exerted themselves, as the wall suddenly opened inward, revealing a narrow passage.

"Oh, my gracious, look at that, look at that. There is a secret passage." Witherspoon was as excited as a schoolboy.

Barnes knew what to say. "Why are you surprised, sir? You said there would be something here. Well, you didn't say it in so many words, but that was certainly what you implied." This was stretching the truth just a bit, but if Mrs. Jeffries' theory was correct, it was in a good cause. He'd planted the seeds of her idea as he and Witherspoon made their way here today, and he was relieved that, thus far, she appeared to be right. "Should I go get a lamp? It looks dark in there."

"Yes, yes, of course," the inspector murmured. He barely heard the constable; his entire attention was focused on the opening. A secret passage, gracious, he'd always wanted to find one. "I wonder how far it goes. Do you suppose it goes all the way to the upper floors? In which case, there'd need to be a secret staircase. My word, Constable, this is really something, isn't it?"

"Yes, sir, of course," Barnes muttered. "I'll just get us some light and then we'll have a proper look-see."

While the constable was gone, Witherspoon tried to bring his emotions under control. He wanted to think about this properly. First they'd found the stolen items from the house and now they'd stumbled across this secret passage. But what did it all mean? Would it help him catch the killer? What if it had nothing to do with the murder? What if it was simply an old servants' staircase that had been boarded up and forgotten?

"I've got a lamp, sir." Barnes returned, holding up an old-fashioned paraffin lamp. "And I've sent the maid to fetch the constables from upstairs. I thought you might want to post them at the outside doors."

It took the inspector a moment to understand. "Oh yes, that's a very good idea. The news of this discovery won't stay secret for very long, especially if we're walking about making noise; and if we find evidence in here, we don't want anyone leaving the house."

The sound of footsteps in the corridor signaled the arrival of the two police constables. Barnes stepped out into the hall and gave them their instructions.

"The lads will be at their posts in a couple of minutes, sir," he reported. He reached for the lamp.

Witherspoon nodded. He'd been thinking furiously. He wished Mrs. Jeffries were here. Talking with her always helped him clarify his thoughts.

"Shall we go, sir?" Barnes asked eagerly. Holding the lamp high, he stepped into the passageway. The inspector was right behind him.

The space was long and narrow. Barnes lowered the lamp and examined the floor. "There doesn't seem to be much dust, sir."

"Which could mean that someone has been using this passage quite regularly," Witherspoon commented. An idea was beginning to grow and take shape in his mind as his eyes adjusted to the darkness. "What's that straight ahead of us?"

Barnes blinked. He'd not seen anything, but then, the inspector's eyes were a bit younger. He held the light up. "It's a staircase, sir."

The staircase was enclosed between two walls, steep and with a low ceiling. Moving cautiously, they crossed the small space and Barnes put his foot on the first step. He pressed down hard, testing to make sure it would hold their weight. "This looks pretty old and it's cramped and narrow to boot. Let's hope the wood isn't rotten and that we don't fall through and break an ankle or a leg."

"It won't collapse, Constable," the inspector said with utter certainty. Keeping their heads low, they started up the stairs. The old wood creaked and moaned as they climbed.

"There's a landing of some sort here," Barnes said, lifting the light higher. Despite the coolness of the day, he was sweating. "And it looks like there's a cabinet or some kind of table as well." He reached the top and stopped. On the table sat what looked like a bundle of cloth and a small tin box. He put the lamp down on the corner.

"What's that, Constable?" Witherspoon stepped around him and gingerly poked at the bundle. "There's nothing alive in there." He picked up the heap and shook it out. "It's a cloak. What's it doing up here?"

"That's not all, sir." Barnes pointed to the spot the cloak had covered. "It looks like we've found the gun."

Witherspoon nodded in agreement. "That other thing, is it a tea tin?"

Barnes picked it up. "I think so, sir." He opened the lid and took a sniff. "No, I tell a lie, it's drinking chocolate."

"I expect that's the reason poor Mrs. McAllister was hearing footsteps in the night," Witherspoon murmured. He was a bit dazed as the ideas whirled about in his head and began to come together and point to a killer. But it could be either of two people. Drat. Which one was it?

"I don't understand, sir," Barnes said. "What's this drinking chocolate got to do with footsteps in the night?" According to Mrs. Jeffries' theory, the drinking chocolate should have been found in the late cook's room.

"The killer must have realized we were close and used this passageway to move about the house and try to hide the evidence." He was seeing the sequence of events in his mind's eye as he spoke and he was sure he was on the right path. "Don't you see, this cocoa was meant for Olive Kettering. The cook switched it and kept it for herself because she was angry at her mistress. The cook then died. I think that drinking chocolate contains poison, and the killer, thinking we'd be back for another look at the house, decided not to take any chances. He or she snatched the tin out of the cook's room and hid it up here until they could dispose of it."

"Why didn't they just chuck it in the river?" Barnes muttered.

"Perhaps the murderer didn't have the chance; there have been a fair number of people about the place." The inspector jerked his chin to his left, where the staircase wound back on itself to climb to the next floor. "Let's see if we can find where in the house this staircase leads."

It took them over an hour to find three entrances to the main house. One was in a bedroom on the third floor, one was in the hallway outside Olive Kettering's quarters on the second level, and one was all the way up on the fourth-floor landing.

"It looks like an old servants' staircase that's been built over," Barnes commented as they came out onto the landing. Mrs. McAllister, two of the maids who had been cleaning the bedrooms, and a constable stood in front of them, their eyes wide with surprise.

"Oh, my Lord, Inspector," Mrs. McAllister exclaimed. "You frightened us so badly I sent Susan to fetch a constable. You should have said what you were going to be doing. The entire household is in an uproar. We kept hearing footsteps and horrible noises. What on earth is going on?"

"I do apologize," Witherspoon said. "But we were just searching the house. I believe we've found the reason you've been hearing footsteps at night."

* * *

"What's taking them so long?" Mrs. Goodge complained. "I think those boys of ours are just larkin' about."

Betsy, Mrs. Jeffries, and the cook were at the kitchen table having a very late midday meal. They hadn't seen nor heard from anyone since Wiggins had reappeared with his startling news.

"Perhaps nothing is happening and they are just keeping watch," the housekeeper suggested.

"Can you pass me the stew, please?" Betsy asked.

"You're a hungry girl today, aren't you?" The cook pushed the platter across the table. "Do you want more bread?"

"Um, yes, please." She pushed her bread plate toward the cook with one hand while picking up the serving spoon and ladling out another helping of meat and vegetables with the other. "This is wonderful, Mrs. Goodge. You're the best cook in the world."

Mrs. Goodge chuckled. "Thank you kindly. You're in a good mood today." She glanced at the housekeeper, her expression inquiring.

"I feel wonderful," Betsy said. "But I think that if you're right and those boys of ours are larking about, then Mrs. Jeffries should tell us what she suspects."

"Agreed." Mrs. Goodge nodded and looked at the housekeeper. "Just tell us what you think. If you're wrong, we'll not hold it against you."

Mrs. Jeffries laughed. Her own spirits were high, so what harm could it do? After all, soon, if all went well, she'd be a grandmother . . . well, not officially a grandmother, but certainly one in spirit. "Alright, I'll tell you what I think *might* be happening but I'm not completely sure who the killer actually is. It could be one of two people. But I do know this: If my assumption is correct, Olive Kettering wasn't losing her mind. There was someone in the house many nights walking about. Furthermore, I suspect that person did it deliberately and over a long period of time for their own purposes. They wanted everyone to think that Olive Kettering was out of her mind."

"But why would someone do such an awful thing?" Betsy asked. "Just to be cruel?"

"I think the killer has been planning this murder for a long time and I think that person hated the victim, so, yes, cruelty was definitely part of the scheme. But I imagine the bigger part was laying the groundwork to challenge her will in court." Mrs. Jeffries pushed her empty plate to one side.

"Of course!" Mrs. Goodge helped herself to another slice of bread. "We should have thought of that all along—it's as obvious as the nose on your face. If the heirs don't like what she's done with the estate, whoever killed her can now produce half a dozen witnesses claimin' she wasn't of sound mind."

"So you're sure that whoever killed her is also the person who's been walking about and tormenting her?" Betsy asked. "And how did they get in the house?"

"Oh, that's easy." Mrs. Jeffries laughed. "They had a key, and, no, I'm not absolutely certain that the two things are connected. But I think it's more than likely."

"But even if they had a key to get in the house," Mrs. Goodge said, reaching for the butter pot, "why didn't any of the servants see or hear them? Miss Kettering was always waking people up in the night."

"If I'm right, they were never spotted because that house is riddled with secret passages."

"We need to go to the carriage house," Witherspoon said to Barnes as they came down the staircase to the main floor. Mrs. McAllister walked behind them. Once her initial shock at seeing the wall open had worn off, she and the other servants seemed to be more relieved than alarmed at this new turn of events. She'd identified the fabric they'd found snagged on the nail.

"Definitely, sir, a word with Mrs. Fox is in order," Barnes said. He carried the cloak and the tin of drinking chocolate. Witherspoon had the gun. Barnes was a bit nervous about the inspector keeping a loaded weapon in his coat pocket, but he'd assured the constable that he'd move carefully and that having it at hand might be useful in solving this murder.

"Mrs. Fox is in the drawing room," Mrs. McAllister said. "She wants the black crepe taken down today."

Witherspoon raised his eyebrows in surprise. "That's rather unusual. I thought mourning black was kept up for at least a year."

"Yes, I rather thought so as well." Mrs. McAllister sniffed disapprovingly. "But she informed me that it was a silly and old-fashioned custom. Now, if you gentlemen will excuse me, I've got to speak to the cook and then get back upstairs and supervise the new girls. We've some additional help from an agency and the whole place is to have a good clean. As I said, you'll find Mrs. Fox in the drawing room."

With that, she turned and disappeared down the corridor. The two policemen made their way to the drawing room. As Barnes' hands were full, Witherspoon opened the double doors and went inside first.

Mrs. Fox wasn't the only person present; Dorian Kettering was there as well. He was on a chair by the fireplace and she was across the room by the window, fussing with the curtains. A lamp identical to the one they'd used to search the passage was on a table next to her.

She whirled about and glared at them. "What do you want?"

"I'm glad you're both here," Witherspoon said. "We'd like to ask you a few questions."

As they'd agreed, Barnes stayed behind the inspector with the cloak tightly bundled against his chest. He sniffed, trying to place what that odd smell in the air might be. Paraffin. Yes, that was it. He must have gotten some of the oil on his hands from the lamp when they were searching the passageway.

"Were the locks on this house changed when Miss Kettering bought the place?" Witherspoon asked.

"Of course they were," Bernadine Fox replied. She turned back to the heavy curtains and began picking specks of lint off the fabric.

"No, they weren't." Dorian Kettering frowned at her. "You know that as well as I do. You told me yourself last spring that you'd gone down to your family home to get a spare key to the carriage house."

"The gardener also confirmed the locks weren't changed." Witherspoon looked at Mrs. Fox. "Your family had the keys to the house, didn't they?"

She shrugged and glanced at Dorian. "I suppose. What of it?"

"You lived here as a child, didn't you?"

She turned and gave him her full attention. "Yes. I did."

"And you played in the secret passages, didn't you? You knew about them and you knew how to move from room to room without being caught."

"This should have been my house, not hers." A subtle change had come over her face and she no longer looked angry. A strange, faraway look came into her eyes.

Dorian Kettering, his expression confused, got to his feet. "Bernadine, what on earth are you saying? You must be careful, my dear—"

"Shut up," she interrupted. "You weren't man enough to defend me when I was a girl and I certainly don't need your help now."

Stunned, his mouth gaped open and he stumbled backward into his seat.

Witherspoon took the gun out of his pocket and held it up for her to see. "Do you recognize this weapon?"

"Of course I do; it belonged to my late husband. He used it to shoot vermin." She cocked her head to one side and gave Witherspoon a coquettish smile. "And so did I. This should have been mine, you see." She gestured widely, indicating the whole house. "But Dorian didn't love me enough to marry me when I was young so I was stuck marrying poor old Henry. He was a decent enough husband and he did his best to make me happy. But of course he couldn't. The only thing I ever really wanted was this house. It was supposed to be mine, you see. Grandpapa promised it to me. We used to play together in passageways where no one could see us. He said I could have the house. It's all I ever wanted. But then they came and took him away and said I had to leave so I was sent to live with Cousin Jeremiah."

"Oh, my God," Dorian whispered. His eyes filled with tears.

"You always were a big crybaby," she taunted. "If you had married me when I asked you to, I wouldn't have been forced to leave. We would have had the house. But no, you weren't man enough to do your duty. You wanted to go off to Scotland."

"Bernadine," he pleaded softly, "we were only children. I was sixteen and you were fifteen. Even if I'd married you, you would have still lost this house. It had to be sold to pay the debts. Your family hadn't any money."

"But yours did," she charged. "And that toff-nosed cousin of yours would have given you anything you wanted if you'd been nicer to her. Now look what you've made me go and do."

"What have you done, Mrs. Fox?" Witherspoon asked softly. The expression on her face made his blood run cold. He wished he'd brought in half a dozen constables before he started asking questions. Bernadine Fox was insane.

She turned and smiled at him again. "Oh, Inspector, I think we both know the answer to that. Why doesn't your constable step out where I can see him? Is he hiding? Olive tried to hide that day, but I banged on the wall next to her bedroom and that sent her scrambling out."

Witherspoon signaled for Barnes to move and he stepped out into plain view.

"I see you've got the cloak." She laughed. "Olive left it in a pile of clothes she was going to give to the Society of the Humble. She enjoyed giving them her castoffs. I stole it. It was quite useful when I needed to come over late at night, and if anyone had seen me, they'd all think it was that cow Olga Richards who was tormenting poor Olive," she said conversationally. "She can walk, you know. I saw her skulking about one day when the good reverend and Olive were strolling on Brook Green having one of their interminable and boring chats about the hereafter. She was following them. I think she did that quite often." She sighed and reached into the pocket of her skirt.

Dorian got up and started toward her. "Bernadine, you're ill. Please let me help you."

Witherspoon and Barnes both moved at the same time, but her next words stopped them in their tracks.

"Don't be a fool, Dorian, they're going to hang me. I've killed two people. Well, three if you count Henry, but all I did to him was hold a pillow over his face when he complained he couldn't sleep." She chuckled. "He slept quite well after that and, even better, I didn't have to listen to any more of his incessant whining."

Dorian stared at her, a look of horrified disbelief on his face.

"Who else have you killed?" Witherspoon asked casually. He wanted to hear the rest of what she had to say before they took her to the station. If she decided not to repeat her story, at least by hearing her out now, they had witnesses to what she'd confessed.

She gave him a pitying look. "Don't be coy, Inspector. I think you know who I'm talking about. But I'm not sure that death is really my fault—it was Olive's doing. The cook would never have switched that lovely cocoa I got from Holland if Olive hadn't been so nasty to her. Poor Mrs. Grant, I guess it was just her bad luck that the chocolate she stole was poisoned. It's very easy to

get one's hands on arsenic," she said earnestly, her gaze
focused on Witherspoon. "The police ought to do something about that."

The inspector remained very calm. He'd dealt with
unbalanced people before. They were often women and
they were often from the same background and class
as Bernadine Fox. Goodness, he wondered, could one's
class cause one to become unhinged? But then he realized that most upper-class females didn't go insane and
certainly didn't go about murdering innocent people.
"So you've murdered your late husband, Mrs. Grant,
and Miss Kettering," he prodded. "Is that all?"

She looked amused. "I should think that is quite
enough, Inspector." Her expression darkened. "But
despite all my hard work, that stupid cow left this house
to those pathetic fools. But they're not going to have it."

Barnes noticed her hand was still in her pocket. He
started forward just as she pulled a box of matches out
of her pocket. Too late, he realized the scent of paraffin
wasn't on his hands, it was in the room.

In a second, the match was lighted. She gave them
a brilliant smile and tossed it at the curtains. "I'll see
it burned to the ground before I'll let them have my
home."

The curtains caught fire and Barnes, because he'd
realized what she'd done a heartbeat before the inspector,
rushed across the room.

Witherspoon was right on his heels. "Get the constable
out front to fetch the fire brigade," he ordered Dorian
Kettering, "and then raise the alarm and get everyone
out of the house." He saw Bernadine Fox run out the
door, but the fire was spreading quickly and he couldn't

give chase now. There were too many people in this house and he couldn't risk their lives.

The flames raced up the drapes. Witherspoon looked around quickly, trying to find something to use. He grabbed a heavy, fringed shawl off a sideboard just as Barnes yanked up the small rug from in front of a footstool. Together they beat at the flames. But it was no use. The room filled with smoke and the flames spread quickly.

"We've got to get everyone out of the house." Witherspoon dropped the shawl and Barnes tossed the rug away just as the settee caught fire, forcing them back toward the door. Coughing, they stumbled out of the drawing room, the inspector pushing Barnes out first.

Witherspoon pulled the doors shut behind him, hoping to contain the inferno. "Check downstairs and make certain everyone's outside," he ordered the constable as he ran for the stairs.

"Where are you going, sir?" Barnes yelled.

"To make sure there isn't anyone left upstairs," he called. "Don't worry about me, I'll get out before the flames reach the first floor." He'd remembered that Mrs. McAllister had said they had servants from a domestic agency cleaning the upstairs floors.

The inspector took the stairs two at a time. He ran down the corridor, opening the doors to the bedrooms and making certain there was no one inside. By the time he reached the last one, he was panting hard, sweat was running down his face, and he could barely breathe as the smoke had already gotten up here. He threw open the door and saw a young maid, her eyes wide as saucers, standing in the corner with a look of terror on her face.

Witherspoon could see she was immobilized by fright. He charged across the room, grabbed her hand, and pulled her toward the door. She was moaning and weeping, half out of her mind with fear as he pulled her down the hallway to the stairs. The sight that greeted him made his skin crawl.

Bernadine Fox was on the staircase just below, holding a lamp. A paraffin lamp. "This is all your fault," she snarled, her face contorted in rage. "I'm sick to death of people interfering with my plans. You're going to pay for this." She slammed the lamp on the staircase, lit another match, and tossed it onto the spilled oil.

The maid made a high-pitched keening cry and jumped backward as the carpeted staircase burst into flames. Ye gods, Witherspoon thought, has that demented woman doused the entire house? Why hasn't someone stopped her? Keeping a firm grip on the girl's hand, he turned and yanked her behind him as he hurried down the hallway, his attention on the molding along the ceiling. There was an entry to the secret staircase here, but he hadn't paid attention when they'd found it. Barnes had ducked his head out, not him.

"We're goin' to die!" the girl screamed. "We're goin' to die!"

"We most certainly are not," Witherspoon snapped. "If need be, we'll open a window, chuck some pillows out, and jump if we have to, but I don't think that will be necessary. Now, what's your name?" He'd spotted a break in the molding.

"Sally, Sally Hughley," she replied.

He stopped. "Stay right here, Sally," he ordered the girl. He spread his hands along the wall, pushing along the seams of the wallpaper, hoping it would open. He pushed and pushed, moving his hands up and down, but the walls stayed stubbornly firm.

"Try this." Sally dropped to her knees and pressed against the baseboard. A narrow strip of the wall swung inward and she scrambled to her feet.

"Clever girl." He beamed at her approvingly and she grinned back. "Come along, hang on to my hand; it's dark in there but you mustn't be frightened."

"I'm not scared of the dark, sir, only the fire." Sally clutched his hand tightly and followed him through the opening.

It took a few moments for his eyes to adjust, but soon he was leading her down the staircase. When they neared the bottom, they could see light. "Almost there," Witherspoon said.

Barnes must have heard him because he called out, "Hurry, sir, hurry. That cow has spread paraffin everywhere and the whole place is in flames. We've got to get out before it starts to collapse."

"Get out yourself, Constable," the inspector ordered as he quickened their pace. "We're almost there."

At the bottom, Sally stumbled and fell. Witherspoon yanked her to her feet and pushed her through the opening. Barnes, a wet cloth over his face, grabbed her hand as Witherspoon scrambled out behind her.

"This way, sir," the constable yelled. Smoke was everywhere. The fire roared in their ears, the building crackled, and they could hear glass and china exploding from the heat. "Keep low," he ordered.

Gasping for air, the three of them made it outside and staggered across the lawn. Firemen and police constables had formed a fire line to a pump on the side of the carriage house. Other constables held the curious back a safe distance as the fire climbed higher and higher up the floors of the house.

Mrs. McAllister rushed toward them and slipped a cloak around Sally. "Oh, thank goodness, I was so frightened you'd been trapped."

"I would have been if that nice feller hadn't come and saved me." She pointed to Witherspoon. "He's a right brave one, 'e is. I was so scared I couldn't move."

Luty Belle and Ruth returned to Upper Edmonton Gardens a few moments before the men came home. Wiggins raced in before the other two. "You'll never guess what happened," he cried. "There's been a bloomin' great fire and the Kettering house is burning. The flames are everywhere and even with two fire wagons, they can't get them out."

"When the fire started we wanted to help, but as we didn't wish to expose our activities to the inspector we were in a bit of a bind," Hatchet added. He slipped into the empty chair next to Luty.

"What happened?" Mrs. Jeffries demanded. "Did the inspector catch the killer?"

"We're not really sure," Smythe said. He sat down next to Betsy and grabbed for her hand. "But we did hear one of the constables say that the fire was started by Bernadine Fox."

"I knew it," Mrs. Jeffries stated. "I just knew it."

"We waited to come back until we knew the inspector was alright," Wiggins said. "I hid in the bushes along the side of the house until I saw him come outside. He saved a girl's life. I heard it with my own ears. She said if the inspector hadn't come and got her, she'd have burned to death."

"I don't understand any of this," Mrs. Goodge cried. "Now can someone please tell us exactly what happened?"

"But that's just it." Smythe shrugged apologetically. "We can't. We were in the carriage on a side street when the fire started and, after that, all we heard was bits and pieces."

"However, I do believe Inspector Witherspoon will be here momentarily," Hatchet advised. "If the inspector pulled a young woman out of a burning house, he might have inhaled a substantial amount of smoke. I imagine his superiors will insist he come home for a rest."

No one wanted to leave until they found out what had happened, so they were still sitting around the table when Witherspoon walked into the kitchen twenty minutes later. He stopped at the doorway when he saw everyone. There was soot on his cheeks, his tie was askew, his right hand was bandaged, and his clothes were covered in ash.

"My gracious, sir, are you alright?" Mrs. Jeffries got up. "What has happened and why is there a bandage on your hand?"

Witherspoon smiled uncertainly. He felt a bit awkward in front of Lady Cannonberry. "There was a fire at the Kettering house and I'm afraid Constable Barnes and I got caught up in it."

"Is the constable alright?" Mrs. Goodge asked quickly.

"He's fine. Er, may I have a cup of tea?"

"Of course, sir, uh, Luty Belle and Hatchet came by to have tea and Lady Cannonberry stopped by to uh . . ."

"To invite you to supper tomorrow night," Ruth

finished. "But of course, now that you've made such a dramatic appearance, I shan't move until you tell me everything that's happened. Gracious, Gerald, are you certain you're alright? You look a bit of a mess."

Witherspoon laughed and sat down at the end of the table next to her. "I'm fine, my dear. I look worse than I feel."

Mrs. Jeffries got another cup and poured his tea while Betsy got down another plate and put it down on the table.

"Let me," Ruth offered as she stacked a treacle tart, two slices of brown bread, and a slice of seedcake onto the small plate. "You look as if you could do with some sustenance."

"What happened, sir?" Mrs. Jeffries asked as she sat down. She felt just a bit awkward sitting at the head of the table while he was present, but it didn't seem to bother him.

"We found out who murdered Olive Kettering." He took a sip of tea. "It was Bernadine Fox. Apparently, she's conceived a very strange and rather demented passion about the Kettering house. She felt it was hers, and the reason it's now burned down is that, rather than see it go to the Society of the Humble, she doused most of the ground floor with paraffin and set it on fire. But, luckily, no one was injured or killed."

"Have you arrested her, sir?" Smythe asked.

Witherspoon swallowed the bite of tart he'd popped into his mouth. "No. Unfortunately, while we——and by that I mean the police—were trying to put the fire out and get everyone out of the house, she scarped off. But we've got men watching all the train stations, the coaching houses, and the docks. She'll not get away."

He was a bit sensitive about this particular subject, as the only criminal who'd ever gotten away from him was a woman. However, he had arrested her accomplice and partner.

"And you know for sure it was 'er?" Wiggins helped himself to a slice of cake.

"She confessed." Witherspoon shook his head in disbelief. "We confronted her with the evidence we'd found and she stood right there in the drawing room and told us how she'd murdered three people in cold blood."

"Three people?" Mrs. Jeffries exclaimed. By her reckoning, there should only have been two.

"Oh yes, she murdered her late husband by smothering him with a pillow—apparently she was tired of listening to him complain that he couldn't sleep; she murdered Elsa Grant, the Kettering cook, but doesn't think that one ought to count because it was an accident—she'd meant to poison Olive Kettering but the cook had switched the cocoa; and, of course, she shot Miss Kettering."

"How very clever you are, Gerald." Ruth patted his hand. "How did you figure it out?"

He smiled modestly. "Once I realized the house needed to be searched again, we discovered a secret staircase that goes all the way through the house."

"Goodness, that's amazing." Ruth murmured in approval. Everyone else at the table had the good sense to look suitably impressed as well.

"She'd left the gun and a tin of cocoa on a table there," he continued. "I imagine with all the people around, she'd felt it safe to leave everything there rather than move it to her flat over the carriage house. Once we had the evidence, well, as I said, she confessed. I think she's quite mad. But it's the sort of madness that one can hide if one is clever, and, despite it all, I think she's a very intelligent woman."

"If she doused the entire ground floor in paraffin and then she set it on fire, then why didn't you smell it?" Luty exclaimed. "Nell's bells, that stuff stinks."

"Really, madam," Hatchet hissed. "You mustn't use such coarse language."

The inspector laughed. "You're right, Luty. It does stink. But Constable Barnes and I had spent over an hour searching along the hidden passage and we'd used a paraffin lamp for light. Both of us thought we must have spilled the oil on our fingers."

"Or that you'd become used to the smell," Ruth said. "Oh dear, Gerald, now tell us, how did you injure your hand?"

"He hurt it saving a young girl's life," Constable Barnes said from the doorway.

CHAPTER 11

Barnes grinned broadly. "I'm sorry to barge in, but I did knock. When no one answered, I thought you must be down here."

"Come and have tea, Constable," Witherspoon ordered. "You look all done in."

"I'm just on my way home, sir. But I could do with something hot." He sat down next to Wiggins. "The superintendent asked me to give you a message. He said to remind you that you weren't to come into the station tomorrow if you're feeling poorly, sir. You got more smoke in your lungs than anyone."

"You said the inspector saved a young woman's life," Mrs. Goodge pressed. "Do tell us, Constable. You know the inspector is too modest to blow his own horn."

"Now, now, I did no more than any other police officer would do," Witherspoon began.

Barnes interrupted. "He brought a young housemaid

that was trapped on the second floor down a secret staircase to safety. Sally Hughley was so terrified she couldn't move. What's more, when the inspector tried to bring the girl down the main stairs, Bernadine Fox tried to murder him by smashing a lamp of paraffin oil onto the stairs and lighting it on fire. Oh, and he cut his hand on a piece of exploding glass as we ran for our lives."

Witherspoon blushed profusely. "You exaggerate, Constable. You did your fair share today. You correctly anticipated that once the main stairs were blocked, I'd use the other ones, and you waited for us at great risk to yourself. So I'm not the only one who went above and beyond the call of duty today."

"Thank you, sir." Barnes blushed as well.

Betsy, who'd gotten up to get the tea, slid a mug in front of him. "Have they caught her yet?"

"No." He shook his head. "But we will. She'll not get away."

"You told us that Mrs. Fox confessed, Inspector, but what made you confront her in the first place? How did you determine that she was the culprit?" Hatchet asked.

"Actually, we weren't positive. We found a bit of lace on a nail, which was what led us to discover the hidden staircase. When I showed the fabric to Mrs. McAllister, she was fairly certain the cloth hadn't come from any of Miss Kettering's garments. It didn't belong to any of the servants, either, as the material was of a very high quality which few people could afford. Then she remembered that Mrs. Fox had a green dress decorated with lace on the sleeves."

"But why did Mrs. Fox want Miss Kettering dead?"

Wiggins asked. "She's not really a relative, so she'd not be inheriting anything."

"I think her original idea was that she could murder Miss Kettering and then get Mr. Dorian Kettering to marry her so she could get the house," Witherspoon said slowly. "That's what she really wanted, you see. When she realized that the Society of the Humble and the Reverend Samuel Richards might be displacing Dorian Kettering and that he might not get anything, she decided to take action. Everyone seemed to believe that both Mr. Kettering and Mrs. Cameron might have been cut out of the estate. But what people forget is that Mrs. Fox and Miss Kettering were confidants. Mrs. Fox probably knew the truth, that the family hadn't been cut out completely. But as Samuel Richards gained more and more influence over Olive Kettering, she probably thought there was a real possibility that Miss Kettering would change her will and leave everything to the Society of the Humble. That was a risk she couldn't take." The inspector reached for his tea. "Mrs. Fox wasn't going to tolerate that situation. Even if she and Kettering didn't marry, as long as he was an heir and owned the house, she'd at least be allowed to stay in the carriage house."

"But you don't know that she knew the truth, that the family was still gettin' something. If she thought Mr. Kettering might have already been cut out of the will, what was the point of murdering Miss Kettering?" Smythe argued. "It's a bit like shutting the barn door after the 'orses have run off."

"Not if you laid the groundwork to challenge the will." Mrs. Jeffries clamped her mouth shut, thinking she'd said too much and might have given the game away.

"Good observation, Mrs. Jeffries." Witherspoon gave her an approving smile. "I can see my methods are rubbing off on you. The constable and I had come to that very conclusion; it was the only explanation for why Mrs. Fox had spent so many nights walking around the house. She was deliberately scaring Miss Kettering, hoping she would start speaking and behaving in such an odd manner that the relatives would have grounds to challenge the will. When she heard that Samuel Richards had inherited the house and a third of the estate, she told Dorian Kettering he ought to take them to court and that they deserved nothing."

"But that was the one thing she didn't admit to doing," Barnes said, his expression curious. "Mind you, she was in a bit of a hurry to burn the place down so perhaps she simply didn't have time."

Everyone laughed.

"I think you two have done a perfectly splendid job," Mrs. Jeffries declared.

"But it was lucky for us she confessed; otherwise we'd have had a devil of a time getting a conviction in court on the evidence we had." Barnes drained his mug and got up. "Should I be here at my normal time, sir?" he asked the inspector. "Or are you staying home?"

"I'm feeling fine, so I'll see you tomorrow, providing, of course, that you suffer no ill effects from the smoke."

"Let me walk you to the door," Mrs. Jeffries offered as she got up. As soon as the two of them were out of earshot, she said, "Is there anything you need to tell me?"

"No, you sussed it out right. Spotting that bit of

lace was fortunate; otherwise, finding that passageway wouldn't have been easy."

"I wasn't sure who was the killer; my idea was it could have been either Mrs. Fox or Dorian Kettering," she admitted in a low voice. They'd reached the back door. "Both of them were good candidates for the murderer. Both of them had been in the house as children and could have known how to move about without being seen. I must say, I had originally discounted Bernadine Fox as a suspect because I couldn't see what her motive might be. She was never in line to inherit anything."

"You thought the motive was money, didn't you?" he asked.

"I did."

"So did I." He laughed. "Instead, it was a crazy woman's obsession." He broke off and frowned. "Make sure you lock the place up good and tight tonight."

"You think the inspector is in danger?" Mrs. Jeffries asked.

"I doubt it. If Mrs. Fox has any brains at all, she'll not be hanging about London." He turned the knob and stepped outside. "But it's always good to be careful, at least until we catch her."

Mrs. Jeffries closed the door and turned to go back up the hallway. The inspector and Lady Cannonberry came out of the kitchen.

"I'm escorting Lady Cannonberry home," he told her. "I'll be dining with her tonight but I won't be late."

"That's an excellent idea, sir," she replied. "But wouldn't you like to change your clothes or have a wash?"

"His clothes are fine and he can wash his face and hands at my house," Ruth replied.

*   *   *

For the next hour, they discussed the case. Luty and Hatchet left and the household settled into their evening routine. They ate the evening meal, cleared the table, and then Betsy and Smythe left.

"You're in a better mood today," Smythe said to his wife as they crossed the garden. "Are you feelin' better?"

"I'm fine." She squeezed his hand. She started to tell him their wonderful news and then just as quickly decided to hold her tongue. The inspector hadn't made an arrest as yet and there might still be some work to be done before that happened. "I know I've been cranky lately, but I'm much better now."

"You've not been that bad, love." He chuckled. "It's 'ard for both of us to adjust to bein' married. We're both used to makin' decisions on our own and now we've got to think of each other."

"True," she replied. She knew darn good and well that once he knew about the baby, he'd be the one who wanted to decide whether or not she ought to be out chasing clues and asking questions. Just in case something interesting cropped up, she'd wait until that crazy woman was behind bars before she told him. It was bad enough that she was going to be forced to the sidelines for the next seven or eight months as it was, she wasn't going to give this one up until she absolutely must. "Can I borrow your key to the back door?"

"What for?" he asked curiously. "We always walk over together."

"I know, but I'd like to do something for everyone to make up for the way I've been acting. Everyone's been nice about it, but I know I've been horrid, especially to poor Phyllis."

"Betsy." He laughed. "You don't have to do anything. Everyone understands that making changes in life is 'ard."

"Yes, I do," she insisted. "My sister sent me that wonderful cookery book and I want to make a special treat for breakfast tomorrow morning."

"You want to cook breakfast?"

She looked at him sharply. "What's wrong with that? Don't you like my cooking?" She'd actually not made that many meals for him, as they usually ate at Upper Edmonton Gardens.

"I love yer cookin'." He fumbled in his pocket, found the back door key, and yanked it out. Since they'd married, he'd noticed she got her feelings hurt easily. She was happy now and he wanted to keep her that way. "Here," he said as he handed her the key. "What are you going to cook for us?"

Betsy tucked it into her pocket. "That's to be a surprise, but I know you'll all love it. I'm going to come over very early because it takes some time to make what I've got in mind."

Early the next morning, Betsy yawned as she slipped through the gate into the communal garden. She carried the cookery book her sister had sent her from Canada, a tin of cinnamon, and a cone of sugar tied together in a packet of brown paper. It was still very dark outside and she was sure that if Smythe had realized how early she meant to leave the flat, he'd have insisted on accompanying her. She chuckled as she stepped onto the main path, delighted that she'd slipped out while he was still sound asleep.

A heavy mist had rolled in from the river, blanketing the garden in fog, which drifted in patches among the trees and bushes. She sobered and picked up her pace. Getting into the garden required a key or the ability to climb a six-foot wall, so she knew she was perfectly safe.

She hurried toward the house, her footsteps smacking lightly against the solid earth. She stopped suddenly as she heard a loud thump. What on earth could that be? *Thump, thump* . . . there it was again. She realized the noise was coming from the far end of the garden, from the inspector's house.

Hanging on to her bundle, she ran down the path, coming to a halt when she was still two hundred feet away. A figure swathed in a long, black cape was standing at the small window in the rear of Upper Edmonton Gardens.

"What are you doing?" she shouted at the top of her lungs. Dropping her package, she raced toward the house, raising the alarm with her cries. "Help, help!" she called. "Someone's breaking into the house!" She heard the sound of glass breaking and she increased her speed, charging across the small terrace just as the intruder chucked something through the window and into the storage room. Betsy grabbed at the cloak, pulling the figure away from the window, all the while screaming at the top of her lungs. From inside, Fred barked wildly. The intruder twisted around and pushed at her, but Betsy had been raised in the tough neighborhoods of the East End so she kicked out, sweeping her assailant's legs out and sending them both sprawling onto the brick terrace. Betsy rolled onto the intruder's back, balled up her fists, and pounded at the covered head. "You'll not hurt my family, you'll not, you'll not!" Behind her, she was vaguely aware of the door opening, and then a pair of strong hands pulled her to her feet just as Fred leapt onto the spot she'd just vacated.

Inspector Witherspoon, Mrs. Jeffries, Wiggins, and Mrs. Goodge, all of them in their nightclothes, spilled out of the house.

She blinked in surprise as Smythe pulled her briefly into his arms and then thrust her behind him. She turned her head, seeing for the first time the flames leaping up at the window. "The house is on fire!" she cried.

"Go for the fire brigade." Witherspoon tossed his police whistle to Wiggins. "And use this to summon some constables." He rushed back into the house.

Smythe hesitated. He didn't want the attacker escaping, but he didn't want the inspector to fight the flames alone.

Betsy shoved Fred to one side and plopped down on the spot she'd just vacated. Fred, still snarling and barking, stood over them, standing guard. "Go help the inspector," she ordered. "We can make sure no one gets away this time."

Mrs. Jeffries and Mrs. Goodge, not to be outdone, rushed over and the housekeeper sat down on the figure's legs, eliciting a muffled squeal of pain from the depths of the hood. The cook, who'd grabbed a rolling pin on her way out of the house, held it up like a club over the intruder's head.

But the fire was out even before the fire brigade arrived.

Witherspoon hurried over to the women, motioning

for the constables Wiggins had brought to follow him. "Are you alright?" he asked anxiously as he helped Mrs. Jeffries to her feet.

Smythe pulled Betsy into his arms. He didn't trust himself to speak.

"Fred, it's alright, boy, you can stop now." Wiggins soothed the dog and pulled him away from the figure on the ground. Mrs. Goodge stepped back as well, but she kept a firm grip on her rolling pin.

"We're all fine," Mrs. Jeffries assured him. She glanced anxiously at Betsy. A strand of hair had tumbled down and dangled by her ear, several buttons on her jacket were gone, and there were dirt stains on her dress skirt, but she didn't appear to be harmed.

Relieved, Witherspoon turned his attention to the intruder splayed across the terrace. "You can get up now, Mrs. Fox."

The constables moved to the edges of the terrace and fanned out along the rim, cutting off an escape route.

As she rolled over, her hood fell back. "You are such a tiresome person, Inspector," she said calmly. "But you do seem to have the devil's own luck."

"Mrs. Fox, you're under arrest for the murders of Henry Fox, Elsa Grant, and Olive Kettering. Please get up and please do it slowly." Witherspoon watched her closely as she climbed to her feet, keeping his gaze locked on her hands. He had no idea what had happened to the gun after the fire had started at the Kettering house the previous day and he wanted to make sure she hadn't snatched it up when their attention had been diverted.

She saw how he watched her and she smiled coldly in amusement. "Worried that I've got more matches,

Inspector? I don't. What would be the point? You've ruined everything, absolutely everything, so I don't much care what happens to me now."

"You cared enough to come here and try and kill us all." Mrs. Goodge shook her rolling pin at the woman.

"You're a bad person," Wiggins added. He'd knelt down beside the dog, holding him back. Fred growled and showed his teeth. "I ought to let him go, let him sink his teeth into you. That'd teach you go around 'urtin' innocent people."

"No one is innocent," she replied, but she didn't look at the footman, she kept her gaze fixed on the inspector.

"You're wrong," Witherspoon said. "But I'm not going to waste my time debating philosophy with you. You obviously don't care what happens to anyone else, either," he charged. "You risked the lives of half a dozen innocent people just because you had a grudge against me. That's unconscionable."

"What's unconscionable is what you've done," she cried. "If you'd left it alone, it would have been fine. Olive was dead and Samuel Richards was going to die next. But no, you had to keep on asking questions, snooping around and ruining everything. Do you know how many years I'd waited to get my house? Do you have any idea what it was like for me, watching that stupid woman flounce about like she owned the place? God, why didn't you just mind your own business?"

He stared at her in disbelief. The expression on her face told him that she believed every word she was saying. She actually didn't think she'd done anything wrong. It was as if she didn't see the rest of the world as real people.

"Well, has the cat got your tongue?" she snapped. "What have you got to say for yourself?"

Her outburst stunned everyone into silence. It was as if they all understood they were in the presence of true madness.

"Catching criminals is my business," Witherspoon said. "And you, Mrs. Fox, are nothing more than a murderer."

He looked past her and nodded. Simultaneously, two constables moved toward her, one going on each side and taking her firmly by the arm. But she didn't appear to even notice they were there. She kept looking at the inspector with a cool, calculating expression on her face.

"I expect once we get you down to the station, there will be more charges filed against you," he told her. "Take her away. I'll be at the station as soon as I've dressed."

She started laughing as they led her off, the sound lingering eerily even as the small group disappeared down the path.

For a long moment, the household of Upper Edmonton Gardens stood on the terrace. Then Betsy giggled. "Oh, goodness, we are a funny-looking lot. I'm a mess and all of you are in your nightclothes."

Mrs. Goodge, who had flung a voluminous brown and orange striped shawl over her green flannel nightgown, glanced down at herself and began to laugh. Mrs. Jeffries, who had tossed her cloak on over her nightdress, chuckled. Wiggins, who wasn't wearing a dressing gown but had stuffed his nightshirt into a pair of trousers, grinned, and even the inspector smiled. "I suppose we do look a strange sight. Perhaps we ought to go inside."

"That's an excellent idea, sir." Mrs. Jeffries started across the terrace. "We can have a nice sit-down and discuss the morning's events."

Betsy turned in her husband's arms. "Why did you come after me? I'm glad you did, but you were sound asleep when I left."

"I just pretended to be asleep," he admitted. "I know how you love your independence, but I didn't want you walking even the short distance over here in the dark. So I followed you. When I 'eard you screaming, I just about died. Don't scare me like that again, love."

"You must have gotten dressed in two shakes of a lamb's tail," she muttered as she moved toward the back door.

Witherspoon led them into the house, pausing briefly by the door of the storage room to assess the damage. He sighed. It wasn't extensive, but it would need work.

As soon as they were in the kitchen, Mrs. Goodge grabbed the teakettle, filled it with water, and put it on the cooker. "You'll have a cup of tea before you leave, sir?" she inquired.

He hesitated. "Yes, I will. Mrs. Fox won't be going anywhere and I do have some questions." He glanced at Betsy. "Betsy, we're all terribly grateful to you. If you'd not raised the alarm, we might very well be dead. But why did you come here so early?"

"I wanted to make everyone a nice breakfast treat," Betsy said as she went toward the cupboard and opened the door. "I've been so moody lately and you've all been so very patient. I wanted to do something nice for everyone." She reached inside and began taking down the tea things.

"I'd say you've done that," Wiggins said as he pulled out his chair and slipped into the seat. "Thanks to you we weren't burned up in our beds."

"I can still make you the treat." Betsy put the cups on the table and started for the back door. "I'll be right back—I dropped my new cookery book. My sister sent it to me all the way from Canada."

"You don't have to do that, love," Smythe cried as she disappeared down the hallway. "You've saved everyone's life."

"But I want to make them a coffee cake," she yelled. "I need to practice my baking."

Witherspoon sighed and shook his head. He wasn't sure what to say. He was so proud of his household, he could burst, but on the other hand, he was deeply aware that he had almost gotten them killed. If he wasn't a policeman, they'd be safe.

"What happens next, sir?" Mrs. Jeffries asked. "Will she be charged with arson and attempted murder, too?"

"That will be up to the prosecution," he murmured.

"Will they 'ang 'er?" Wiggins asked. "I 'ope so. She's killed a lot of people and would 'ave killed a lot more if Betsy 'adn't come along when she did."

"On the other hand, she is quite insane," Mrs. Jeffries commented. She wasn't sure how she felt about the whole situation. Was it Bernadine Fox's fault that her mind had taken a terrible turn and led her down what had turned out to be a path of utter destruction? "And that is a kind of sickness, I suppose."

"Sick or not, she's no right to go about murdering people," the cook declared.

Smythe glanced toward the hallway. What was taking her so long? He started to get up but then he heard the back door open and close so he sat back down.

The kettle whistled just as Betsy came back into the kitchen. "I'll pour." She dropped her package onto the pine sideboard and ran for the kettle, snatching up a tea towel as she moved. A few minutes later, steaming mugs of hot tea were passed around the table.

At their morning meeting, Mrs. Jeffries and the others went over everything that had happened that morning.

"Dang, it ain't fair, we missed all the excitement," Luty complained.

"For once, madam, I agree with you." Hatchet looked at Mrs. Jeffries. "How did you know for certain it was Mrs. Fox?"

"I wasn't absolutely sure, not even after I suspected that the cook had been murdered. But I didn't know for certain until Wiggins told us that Susan Edwards had whined that Elsa Grant had kept the drinking chocolate for herself. She hadn't shared with the rest of the Kettering servants. That's when I understood that her death wasn't from natural causes, but from poison."

"The way people described her stomach problem does sound like arsenic poisoning," Ruth murmured. She smiled self-consciously. "I've been reading up on the subject; it's really most interesting."

"And if she'd been poisoned, then she wasn't the intended victim, Olive Kettering was," the cook exclaimed. "And you knew that it was Bernadine Fox who'd sent Olive the cocoa."

"What I didn't know was whether or not Dorian Kettering might have had access to the cocoa," she replied.

"He was often at his cousin's house. The cocoa was sent there directly from Holland. He could easily have tampered with it, and his alibi for the morning of the murder wasn't very good."

"I wonder where he went," Smythe mused.

"Where were any of 'em?" Wiggins said. "Both Mr. and Mrs. Richards and Angus Cameron were out that morning as well, and we don't know what any of 'em was up to."

"And now that the inspector has made an arrest, I don't expect we ever will." Mrs. Jeffries saw Betsy yawn. "You look dead on your feet. You and Smythe go on home and have a rest. You can come back this afternoon for tea."

"I'm fine," the maid protested. "Really I am. I want to have a word with Phyllis."

"We should take our leave as well, madam," Hatchet said to Luty.

"Yup, I guess we better. This case is solved." She started to get up. "But we'll be back in a day or two to get the rest of the details."

"I'd best be off as well." Ruth pushed back from the table. "I'm going to have a word with my butler and find out why he didn't wake me this morning. I know he must have heard all the commotion in the garden."

"Your butler's a snob," Luty teased. "You know he don't like lowerin' himself to find out what's goin' on with the common folk."

"Well, *I do* want to know what's going on, especially if it involves this house." Ruth laughed. "And you're right, he is a terrible snob."

"Betsy must have been ever so brave," Phyllis said admiringly. "Fancy tackling an intruder like that." She swept the last of the glass onto the dustpan, scooped it up, and dumped it into the old flour sack. She and the housekeeper were in the storage room, cleaning up as best they could.

"She was very brave indeed." Mrs. Jeffries surveyed the room. The fire hadn't really spread very far. All that was really needed was a coat of paint on the wall, a new window, and a bit of lino for the floor. "She saved all our lives."

"And she said she was going to make us a coffee cake," Phyllis continued. "She told me so on her way out. I'm not sure what that is, but it sounds lovely."

"I'm sure it will be delicious." Mrs. Jeffries smiled. It had taken the entire household to convince Betsy that the "treat" could wait until tomorrow. Finally, Mrs. Goodge had promised she'd supervise the baking if Betsy would go home and rest. "Phyllis, would you like to live in?"

Phyllis gasped. "Oh, that would be lovely, Mrs. Jeffries. But I don't want to upset . . ."

"Betsy will understand and, what's more, she's very embarrassed about how badly she's treated you. She's just been a bit under the weather, but she's feeling much better now. So, shall I speak to the inspector and see if he's amenable to adding you to the household?"

"Yes, yes, yes," Phyllis cried happily. "That would be wonderful. Thank you, Mrs. Jeffries, thank you. Working here is the best thing that's ever happened to me."

"I'll speak to the inspector this evening but I'm sure it will be alright. You can move into Betsy's old room on Monday."

Not more than a quarter mile away, Betsy smiled at Smythe. "I need to tell you something."

He sighed. "Blast a Spaniard, love, I don't know if my poor heart can take any more surprises today. When I saw you charging at that madwoman, I almost died. You could have been 'urt.'"

"Nonsense." She got up from her chair, crossed the parlor, and sat down next to him on the couch. "If you saw what happened, you'd have seen that I was more than holding my own. I was on top of her, not the other way around."

"But she might 'ave 'ad a gun," he protested.

Betsy looked at him. "She didn't have a gun and you forget where I was raised. You didn't survive in the neighborhood where I grew up unless you could take care of yourself."

He sighed. "I know. I was right proud of ya. I just can't bear the thought of you bein' 'urt or me losin' you."

"We won't lose each other," she said earnestly. "But you've got to stop trying to wrap me in cotton wool. Life is filled with risks. That's what makes it worth living. Now, I've got to tell you something, but I want your word of honor you'll respect my wishes and that, after I've said my piece, you'll try to look at our life from my point of view, no matter what."

"If you mean I should try to put myself in your shoes, I do that now, love." Puzzled, he stared at her. "When 'ave I ever not respected your wishes? Betsy, what is it? Is something wrong?"

"Nothing is wrong. I just want your word of honor that you'll respect my wishes and that you'll understand that I am as capable of taking care of myself as you are of taking care of yourself."

Smythe knew she was up to something, but for the life of him, he couldn't figure out what it might be. She had done him proud today, and though it went against his nature not to try and protect her from everything he possibly could, she was right, she could take care of herself. "Alright, you've got my word. Now, tell me what this is all about. Is something botherin' you? Are you still bothered by Phyllis?"

"Nothing is bothering me and I made my peace with Phyllis this morning. As a matter of fact, everything is wonderful." She took a deep breath. "But our life is going to change. We're going to have a baby."

Dumbstruck, he gaped at her.

"Did you hear me?" She poked him in the arm. "I said we're going to have a baby."

"Oh, my God in heaven." He pulled her close and enveloped her against his chest in a tight hug. "I'm going to be a father! I'm going to be a father!"

"Yes, you are." She laughed.

"Blast a Spaniard! You've made me the happiest man in the world." He suddenly released her and drew back, looking at her closely. "Are you alright? Should I call a doctor? Do you need to sit down?"

"I am sitting down," she said dryly. "And now we'd better have that discussion about respecting my wishes."

Witherspoon walked slowly down the stairs to the kitchen. He knew his household would be having their afternoon tea and he had something important he needed to share with them. He'd thought hard about his decision and, to some degree, it made him very sad, but on the other hand he knew it was the right thing to do.

"Why, Inspector, I didn't hear you come in," Mrs. Jeffries said as he entered the room. "Would you like some tea? There's plenty."

"Yes, I believe a cup would be nice," he replied. She started to get up but he waved her back into her chair. "I can sit anywhere, Mrs. Jeffries, you're fine where you are." He slipped into the spot next to Wiggins.

Betsy got up and grabbed another place setting. She put it on the table and sat down. She looked at the housekeeper and noted her easy smile had disappeared. Mrs. Goodge had sobered as well.

No one said a word as Mrs. Jeffries poured the tea and passed the cup down to the inspector. "There's plenty of food, sir," she said brightly.

"Perhaps later, Mrs. Jeffries," he replied. He cleared his throat. "I've something I want to say to all of you. This morning, you all came very close to having your lives taken by a madwoman. All of you acted with good sense and bravery. I was very proud."

There were murmurs of "thank you" all around the table.

"But despite how brave or clever any of you might be, you wouldn't have been in danger if it wasn't for me." They started to protest, but he held up his hand for silence. "It's the truth."

"Inspector, what are you trying to tell us?" Mrs. Jeffries had a terrible feeling about this.

"Before I tell you, I want you all to know something." He looked away for a moment and cleared his throat again. When he turned back to them, he said, "Most of my life, I lived in very modest circumstances, and after my mother passed away, the only person I had to consider was myself. I come from a very small family. My father died when I was two and, growing up, I had only my mother and my aunt, Euphemia. When I inherited this house from Euphemia, and the means to keep it up, I had no idea at that time that I'd be gaining another family, all of you."

"We feel the same, Inspector," Wiggins muttered.

"And I'm very glad you do," he replied. "Nonetheless, once one has feelings for others, once one has watched a young lad grow to manhood or walked a young woman down the aisle"—he smiled at Betsy, who was blinking back tears—"one can't turn away from one's true duty. I'm responsible for all of you and I almost cost you your lives." He took another deep breath. "I can't let that happen again. I won't let it happen again. That's why, tomorrow, I'm resigning from the Metropolitan Police Force."

There was a shocked silence.

Mrs. Jeffries pushed back from the table and stood up. "In that case, sir, you'll have no objection if I speak my mind."

"No, of course not," he replied. "But you shan't make me change my mind—"

"I won't try, sir," she interrupted. "I'll simply speak my mind and you can do as you will."

"Go ahead." He eyed her warily.

"To begin with, you certainly didn't do anything that would jeopardize our lives; Bernadine Fox did."

"But she wouldn't have come here if she hadn't wanted to kill me. You heard her, she told me I'd ruined all her plans," he stated flatly. "If not for me, none of you would have been in danger."

"You give yourself too much credit, sir," she said bluntly. His eyes widened in surprise, but she continued speaking. "Not that you aren't a brilliant detective,

sir—you are—but any of us could have come across a
demented soul like Mrs. Fox in the normal course of
our lives. Life is filled with risk. Each morning when
we get out of our beds, we're taking the chance this will
be the day we draw our last breath. But we do it anyway,
we get up and face the world. We don't lie there with
the covers over our heads, too scared to get out and live
our lives."

"No, of course we don't," he murmured.

"Inspector, none of us can really understand what
you face each and every time you step out the door and
go to work, but we've all felt that, in some small way,
we've helped to contribute to your success."

"Your contributions haven't been small." He smiled.
"I wouldn't have been successful without my household,
without all of you."

"Thank you, sir," she replied. "That is kind of you to
say, but, much as we all enjoy working for the famous
Inspector Witherspoon, I think I can safely speak for
everyone when I say that what we're most proud of is your
commitment to justice. You're not afraid of the truth;
you don't let politics, social status, or wealth influence
you when you're trying to catch a killer. That is a very
rare quality, sir. Because you believe in truth, you've
arrested the truly guilty and saved countless innocent
people from prison or, even worse, the gallows."

He blushed with pleasure. "Nonetheless, I don't want
to put anyone else I care about at risk, ever again."

"You ain't puttin' us at risk, sir, life is," Wiggins muttered. "People die all the time, sir, even without crazy
people chuckin' lamps through windows. Most of us in
this room don't have anyone but each other because all

the people we loved died a long time ago. None of them was murdered. They just died."

"Well put, Wiggins." Mrs. Goodge stared at Witherspoon. "I can honestly say that the fact that I can make you good meals and occasionally share a bit of gossip about one of your suspects has been the best thing that's ever happened to me. I know it's not much, but I like to think I play a tiny part in catchin' killers. That has made my life worthwhile. For the sake of an old woman, please don't leave your position."

"If you'll remember, sir," Betsy added, "Bernadine Fox might have tried to kill us, but when you all come running out of the house, I was pounding her, not the other way around. If Smythe hadn't pulled me off, I'd have beaten her good and proper. We can take care of ourselves and each other, sir."

Witherspoon looked around the faces at the table and they stared back at him with their features mirroring all manner of emotions, but the one thing he didn't see was fear. He smiled broadly. "I don't know what I've done to deserve such a household, but I am a very blessed man."

"Does that mean you ain't quittin'?" Wiggins wanted to be sure about this before he allowed himself to feel relief.

"Yes, that means I'm not quitting." Witherspoon laughed. "I guess the Metropolitan Police Force will be stuck with me for some time to come."

"Good, then," Betsy said. She cleared her throat. "Now that that's settled, Smythe and I have something we'd like to say."

"I hope you're not announcing you're going to Australia," the cook groused. "My nerves can't take any more bad news."

Mrs. Jeffries ducked her head to hide her smile. She didn't want to steal their thunder.

"It's good news, Mrs. Goodge," Betsy promised. She glanced at her husband. "Do you want to tell them or should I?"